UNBREAKABLE BONDS

ALIYAH BURKE and TAIGE CRENSHAW

Unbreakable Bonds
ISBN # 978-1-78430-565-9
©Copyright Taige Crenshaw and Aliyah Burke 2015
Cover Art by Posh Gosh ©Copyright April 2015
Interior text design by Claire Siemaszkiewicz
Totally Bound Publishing

UNBREAKABLE
BONDS

Dedication

To my mother, who has always been my number one fan. Because of you, I love to read and write. To my big sister and second mother who has always believed in me. To my co-writer, Aliyah as always it is a pleasure working with you and I thank you for doing this book with me. I loved working on it with you. □
—Taige

To my husband for your unending support. Thank you. To my readers, y'all rock! To Taige for another adventure, it's been a blast. And last and never least: To the men and women of the Armed Forces who sacrifice so much for all of us, God Bless!
—Aliyah

Chapter One

The shot had torn through flesh and bone, making each movement—from breathing to continuing his forward motion—a painful chore. The man stumbled occasionally, yet pressed on. Baying dogs gained on him as his steps slowed. Sticky blood ran down his bare arm and mingled with the rain that cascaded around him. Wet branches reached out and ripped at his exposed upper body. Any and all air was ingested desperately as he ran farther into the forest.

He couldn't be caught. He didn't want to die without knowing who had killed her. He had to find a way to survive.

His Calliope.

Her sweet brown face appeared before him—plump lips, a somewhat flat nose and eyes the color of a mug brimming full of rich hot chocolate.

Calliope.

Tears mixed with rain as he ran on. A gun barked seconds before he collapsed as a bullet ripped through the back of his thigh. His fingers dug into the fertile soil as he struggled to regain his footing.

"There is nowhere for you to run, Levi. We will find you." The deep, drawling voice rose above the storm, carrying through the trees.

Blood loss, combined with pure exhaustion brought on by his days of being held and beaten, overwhelmed him. Levi Jefferson Davis Madison sank ungraciously back to the forest floor, knowing he wouldn't be able to continue. "I'm so sorry, Calliope. I tried, my love. I tried." The tortured words were full of sorrow and pain.

Despite the cold his body had experienced for the past week, Levi felt a warmth flow over him like a feather blanket. A heat he hadn't felt since before the day he'd lost his love.

A whisper came through the dark to reach his ears. *Levi, you are a man whose love is pure. In a world divided by color, you never faltered. Despite everything put to you, you stayed true to your heart and never turned your back on your soul mate. For that, I tell you this... Rest now. Fear not, for you shall be returned to the arms of your love. Trust your heart, for it will not lead you astray.*

Levi couldn't explain it, but the words calmed his breaking heart. With a sigh that was more of a gurgle of blood, the man closed his eyes, ready to accept his death. He knew he would one day be reunited with the love who had died in his arms. The ones who had killed her were the same men who chased him.

One day couldn't come too soon.

Lightning lit the sky as he turned tired eyes up and watched the night shadows become men whose faces were full of hate. Two watched him, one with green and one with blue, as they told him they were the ones who'd killed the love of his life.

The thunder rolled.

* * * *

Ta-Mara LeBreaux sniffled and smiled to herself behind the counter of the used bookstore she worked in, Roberta's Reads. She closed the book and fondly ran her hand over the front cover.

What better way to pass the stormy afternoon than by reading about real men and real love? This was one of her favorite books. A story of the Old South, where despite the laws, one man had stood up for his beliefs and openly admitted his love for a freed slave. And although they hadn't been able to get married, he'd claimed he was married in the eyes of God to her.

Levi Jefferson Davis Madison, raised in the Deep South, had fallen in love with a woman known as Calliope Jones.

She sniffed again. How wonderful it would be to have a man like him — tall, handsome, dangerously alpha and yet totally in love with his woman, willing to stand up to the bigots and take whatever crap they dished out.

"The only thing that sucks about this is that I don't know if he dies or not."

Age had yellowed the pages and the final bit was missing. The only thing resembling a title was faded script on the front that read *Unbreakable Bonds*. She had asked her friend, Reginald 'Reggie' Carpenter — the store's owner — about the book and had even gone to the library and checked online to see if she could figure out more about this mysterious story. Nothing came up. And she couldn't find an author name anywhere on it either.

Reginald had given her the book for helping him out in the store. She carried it with her always and reread it when she had any free time like now, on this dark stormy afternoon in Louisiana. Not many people were out, so after cleaning a bit, she had hunkered down and begun to read.

The book wasn't very thick, but the words resonated with the passion Levi and Calliope had for one another. "I wish I knew the ending of this." Her imaginative mind had created lots of different endings for the story. Of course, she substituted herself in place of Calliope, but at least Levi found his love.

A loud rumble of thunder echoed through the small brick building but it wasn't until the lights flickered that she looked away from the object in her hands. The hum of the lights, which normally filled her with familiarity, seemed odd and unsettling. Almost like they were still trying to catch up from the power surge.

"What I need is to turn on some more music," she muttered to herself as she placed the book down on the now clean desk. "My imagination is beginning to make me think I'm crazy."

She headed down the middle of the store, her eyes traveling over the numerous shelves packed with books. This place made her feel at home. Rounding the final shelf, she turned toward the entrance of the back room.

Numerous boxes of books were stored there—extra copies, books for donating to literacy programs and more. Nimbly avoiding them, Ta-Mara finally reached the CD player. She dragged a finger over the stack of CDs before she made her selection and pulled a disc free from its case. "John Legend is always good to listen to."

Content all was set, she headed out of the stockroom to return to the front of the store. Ta-Mara frowned as the smell of dirt and rain hit her nose. *Okay, I get it. No more wild daydreams.* She shook her head to rid herself of the crazy trip her mind was taking.

Two steps then she stopped as the entire place went pitch black. Lightning flashed and in its eerie glow, Ta-Mara found herself face-to-face with a man—a man with blood and water streaking his face. A man who lurched toward her and reached out as if to grab her.

An inhuman scream left her before she crumpled to the floor.

* * * *

Ta-Mara stirred. She moaned as she rubbed her head. *Damn that hurts.* The lights were still out in the store, so she got up slowly.

"Hello?" she asked the dark.

Was someone there? She would swear she had seen a man, but on the off chance he remained, did she really want him to know where in the store she was?

Oh, get a grip, Ta-Mara. You imagined it. That's all.

There was a soft groan in the darkness. A whimper of fear slipped out as she realized she *wasn't* alone in the store.

"Hello? Is someone there?" She reached behind her to the shelf where they kept hardbacks and she grabbed a thick one. Ta-Mara gripped it before her and said with more bravado than she felt, "Answer me. I'm armed and...and I know karate."

Okay, I thought about taking karate. Now I wish I had.

No answer. Not even another groan.

Gritting her teeth, Ta-Mara positioned her body to head back to the storage area and the fuse box. "I can do this," she whispered to herself. The situation would have been laughable if not for the pounding of her heart and her sweaty palms.

Normally of solid character, panicking was so unlike her—and she didn't like it. Moving carefully, Ta-Mara made her way through the blackness to where she knew the box was.

Sliding her feet along the carpet to make sure she didn't trip, Ta-Mara hesitated as she brought up a mental image of the back room. What, if anything, sat on the floor between her and the wall supporting the fuse box?

Crack! Another lightning flash was followed immediately by more rumbling thunder.

She was ready to jump out of her skin, as tight as her body was wound. Ta-Mara felt the hum of electricity before the lights actually came back on. They flickered a bit but with a final surge, a sigh escaped her as the glow of florescent bulbs flooded the back room.

Closing her eyes in relief, Ta-Mara heard the sexy voice of John Legend fill the air and she turned around to see if anyone was behind her. Her hands remained curled around the heavy book and she was ready, just in case. She put the CD player on batteries so it wouldn't skip again with the inclement weather.

She checked each aisle and didn't find a single person. Wearily, she headed back to the spot where she had retrieved her hardback weapon and returned it. There was no one in the store aside from herself as she walked to the front desk.

Her book was gone.

Brow furrowed, she mentally retraced her steps. "I'm positive I left it here." She shook her head. "I'm losing it."

The clock chimed, telling her it was time to close up. Not like she'd had anyone pop in for a while. She locked the door and counted the money. Once the nightly deposit was prepared, Ta-Mara went to the back, intent on cleaning up and shelving some more books. She wasn't in any rush to go out in this weather.

The impressive vocals of John Legend stilled her wayward nerves as another rumble of thunder rolled overhead. Humming along, she entered the back room and headed to the far corner to work on some sci-fi books.

A gasp exploded from her throat. A body cloaked in black lay on the floor. Water pooled around him and he wasn't moving. He remained on his side.

"Oh my God!" Ta-Mara scrambled over before kneeling beside him. She felt for a pulse, disturbing his cloak and revealing tanned skin. It was there. Faint, but there. "Are you okay?" She pulled away from the tingling that moved up her skin at first contact with his body.

She reached for his shoulder, and shook him. Something warm met her skin despite the cold of his clothing. Her eyes narrowed as she drew back her hand and saw the red of his blood on her palm. Her stomach heaved. Blood was never a good thing with her.

Still, Ta-Mara loathed leaving him. There was no phone in the back and her cell was also in the front room. She reached out to touch his dripping wet, black hair—so long it fell past the collar on his coat. Her fingers slid easily into its thickness.

She brushed it away from his face as she took stock of the man lying silently beside her. His face was gaunt, but she would bet it was not a normal look for him. His size alone told her he was a man of immense strength. Not right now, however. Now, he appeared helpless.

His eyes were closed, his long lashes curved against a dirt-smeared cheek. Lips were dry and cracked but his Cupid's bow was attractive. There was a red line around his throat, as if someone had strangled him — or rather tried to hang him.

Ta-Mara cocked her head. "Hey, I'm going to call for help. Hang in there." One final stroke along his cheek then she pushed away and dashed up to the front desk. Yanking the receiver up, she swore as she got no dial tone. She dug through her purse until she grabbed her cell and flipped it open. "Damn it!" No service.

She ran back to where her mysterious man lay, her cell phone in hand. He hadn't moved, so Ta-Mara crouched back down beside him but refrained from touching him. "Hey, can you hear me?" She kept a partial eye on her cell, waiting for the moment it could be used.

"Come on, Tall, Dark and Handsome. Answer me," Ta-Mara commanded after a while.

Was he dead? He didn't think you could feel pain in death and he felt pain — burning pain that flowed through his body like nothing he'd felt before. He shifted slightly and clenched his jaw, trapping in the moan to ensure the men following didn't hear him.

His memory was fuzzy. *What just happened?* He had been running and fell, the voices had grown louder and he had felt hands on him. *Then what?*

A rope. They had put a rope around his neck and strung him up in a tree. *Fighting for his breath, the rope cutting into his skin...* He remembered the sweet, satisfying breaths he'd taken once the branch cracked beneath his weight and dropped him unceremoniously on the muddy ground. The thunder had clapped loudly and shook everything.

That was all he remembered. A gentle touch caressed his cheek.

Am I dead? What he lay on wasn't soft but it also wasn't the muddy mess he had been in before. He figured he must be dead—shot twice and hanged, not very good odds of survival.

Footsteps approached and he tensed. Did he have the strength to fight off whoever it was?

A thick, syrupy female voice called out to him, "Hey, can you hear me?"

That voice created a sense of calm in him and he couldn't explain it, but he knew wherever he was, he was safe. His panic eased and he moved cautiously, opening his eyes.

Slowly his vision came into focus and he swallowed at the view before him. It confused him.

A woman knelt beside him, yet didn't look at him. Her attention was on a small object in her hand. His eyes traveled over her clothing and he was struck by how odd they appeared.

She wore trousers as he did, but hers were white and hugged her like a second skin. And as she crouched there, he was able to see how nicely they outlined her. Her shirt exposed arms—defined arms, shoulders, and as she turned away from him he could see part of her back. Her skin was the color of roasted pecans with a hint of molasses.

A thick mass of black hair tumbled down the middle of her back. The ringlets called to his fingers to touch, stroke, and indulge in.

His body reacted and despite the pain from earlier, his cock began to swell inside his slacks. *When did women begin wearing things like that? And if I'm dead, why am I feeling lust?*

He didn't know anyone who dressed like that—white or black, free or slave.

He nearly shut his eyes as her head swung toward him, feigning death, watching her through slits. When she looked away, he watched her face as she continued to stare at and push things on whatever it was in her hand. The myriad of expressions crossing her face amazed him. He didn't sense fear from her, despite their color difference. The people who were acquainted with him knew where he stood on slavery, but he didn't recognize her.

"Come on, Tall, Dark and Handsome, answer me." Her sultry voice flowed over him.

Peeking at her from under his lashes, he moaned and waited for her reaction. Her head snapped around to his and he saw the first sign of fear before concern masked it. He moaned again.

She stretched for him and his heart increased in speed as she placed a hand upon his forehead. "Can you hear me?" she questioned softly. A brief pause. "Can you understand me?"

He nodded slightly as a sigh of relief escaped from between her full lips. Then he opened his eyes and met her gaze. Big, beautiful, dark brown eyes stared at him. Her face was oval-shaped and her skin as smooth as any he had ever seen.

His body trembled.

"We have to get you out of this wet coat. Can you sit up?" She reached for the shiny object beside her and opened it before snapping it shut with a mild curse.

She cursed? It was adorable—the way it rolled off her lips and her almost sheepish look. But not at all as though she believed herself of a lower status.

"Yes," he said. He pushed up gingerly and noticed the way she kept staring at him. "Who are you?"

She stood and helped him to do the same, but refused to answer. He allowed her to assist in removing the cloak. A scent he hadn't smelled before wafted from her body to his nose. It was subtle and feminine. Fresh and arousing. Simple and yet exotic on her.

She must be a free woman. He'd noticed the gold rings on her fingers as she had offered him a hand. Her hands were much softer than he'd expected. But then, nothing about her was anything he would have expected.

"Sit here," she commanded as she pushed him toward a chair. "I'll get something to clean up the blood on your head. Sorry... Thanks to this crazy storm I can't get any cell service to call an ambulance, but I'll keep trying." Easy strides took her away from him.

Her attitude reminded him of someone — a woman from his past. This was a bit much for him. All the light in the room came from the ceiling as opposed to a lamp or fire. He got up from the chair and looked at the thin black folder item on the desk. Telegraph keys were on it, but it was unlike any contraption he'd ever seen.

"Hey, don't drip on the computer." She spoke from behind him.

He looked at the thing again as he nodded and stepped back. *What the hell is a computer? Where am I? None of this is familiar to me, except books.*

"Sit," she ordered, pointing at the chair.

He did and accepted the towel she handed him. It was so soft and smelled like crushed lavender. "Thank you. I think I should leave. I don't want to get you into trouble."

She arched an eyebrow. "As long as you aren't planning on hurting me, I'm sure I'll be fine. Besides, I want to know how you got in here."

"Hurt you?"

"Look, man. You're the one who just showed up here—bleeding, I might add. Are you bleeding anywhere else?" She wiped his head.

"I don't think so," he responded. She didn't look so comfortable wiping his head, almost as if she were going to be sick. Funny how where he had been shot before just ached but he no longer believed he bled. He could move with just a little stiffness, his neck hurt the worst. "Are you sure you won't get into trouble by being here?"

"I work here. Where were you? By your clothing, I would say some kind of historical reenactment. Civil War perhaps?"

"Reenactment? Of the Civil War?" This woman—although beautiful—was daft. Why would anyone reenact that?

"Perhaps not, sorry. I need to get you to a hospital for a CT."

A CT? What is a CT? He didn't understand. "Why would anyone do such a thing?"

"It's part of history. Don't need to get all in your role as being a Confederate. I was just asking." She placed his hand over the cloth on his head. "Hold that there for a minute."

"My role?" He frowned. "I *am* a Confederate—" He paused. "But I mean you no harm. If you are running from your owner, I can help."

A short bark of laughter escaped from her as her eyes grew wide. "Running from my owner? Man, I think you *are* a little too into your role or else, I seriously need to get you to a hospital. I don't have an owner—never had, never will."

"So you are a free woman?"

She stepped farther back from him and opened that shiny thing in her hand again then closed it. Her brow furrowed as she watched him in the light and she chewed on her bottom lip. "Look, you're really starting to freak me out, so drop the act, okay? Remember, Lincoln freed the slaves, the Civil War ended and the South lost. End of story. Can we drop it, please? Remember, this *is* the twenty-first century."

Levi frowned. All that she said was confusing. A war hadn't happened yet. There was talk of an impending one if Lincoln freed the Negros, but nothing yet. And here she was talking about it as if such a thing had already occurred. Maybe she wasn't all there? *Twenty-first century?*

One thing was for sure, he didn't like the nervousness that filled her face as she watched him. Pushing away from the stool, he moved toward her. His steps were slow and as unthreatening as he could make them.

He watched her as he prowled closer. Her eyes widened slightly before she narrowed them and stared right back. He knew she was scared but he admired how she refused to give into it.

Her gaze swept over his body and he recognized the admiration. Ignoring that, he stopped before her and bowed slightly. "I apologize for 'freaking' you out. I guess I did get into the role more than I had thought. My name is Levi."

He noticed how her eyes grew larger as he said Levi, but he filed that information away for later. Would she pick up on his lie? Would she figure out that he had no idea how he'd got to where he was and recognized none of the things she had in her building, aside from the basics? Would she know how scared he was about his body's reaction to her?

Ta-Mara shoved back her sexual reaction to this man. He had moved like a predator across the room toward her. His eyes were equivalent to the Kanchanaburi Sapphire, in her opinion—a deep, endless blue. They swirled with many different emotions but the one she focused on was passion. This man desired her.

She trembled. When she licked her lips, she saw another flare in his eyes. The closer he got, the more impressive he became. Even dripping wet, there was this power about him. His pants only accentuated the strength in his legs, and the shirt plastered to his torso showed off his wide shoulders, flat belly and strong arms.

Her body reminded her in a not-so-subtle way that it had been missing the touch of a good man for far too long. And to top off the gorgeous package he was, he went and told her his name is none other than that of the man she had been fantasizing about from her book, Levi. Moisture pooled between her thighs.

This must be a dream. One night with him would be heaven, but would it be enough? The way he made her feel with a look was more intense than any touch from previous lovers.

"Levi, is it?"

He nodded.

"My name is Ta-Mara LeBreaux."

"Ta-Mara," he drawled it out, rolling the 'r' as if making love to it.

Her breathing became heavier. He moved closer to her, his eyes dropped to the pulse in her neck and he smiled as if he could tell how fast her heart was beating.

"You should get out of those clothes," she sputtered, desperate to say something.

Perhaps something different.

One jet-black eyebrow rose.

"I...I...I only meant that you could get sick if you stay in them." Ta-Mara knew she was blushing. Oh, she just wanted to fall below the floorboards.

Another step closer then there was nowhere for her to go. Her back was against part of the wall that didn't have any books on it. She could feel the light switch poking her but she didn't care. All her focus was on the man taking up most of her air.

Her knees were weak and her heart pounded so hard she was surprised it was still behind her ribs. Each inhalation swamped her already overloaded senses with the scent of raw masculinity. He smelled like the outdoors. There was a hint of sweat but it only added to the allure, and something else which Ta-Mara merely labeled Levi.

He reached out with one hand and stroked the side of her face.

The room was encased in darkness as the lights went out again. Ta-Mara remained still, his hand by the corner of her mouth, the sensual strands of John Legend still playing.

"What happens now?" he murmured in her ear. Water dripped from his hair to her skin and seemed to sizzle with the heat between them.

Ignoring all the logical voices in her head, Ta-Mara pushed her face into his touch. "I don't know. You tell me, Levi."

Chapter Two

He knew what he wanted to do. Kiss her. Taste her full lips and see what flavor came from them. Would she open like a flower for him, or would she take a bit more persuasion? He couldn't help himself, and leaned closer.

The lights came back on, startling him. He'd heard about electricity but to see it in a house... He wanted to take a closer look. *Later.* Right now, he returned his attention to the woman between him and the wall.

So lush, so trusting. So fearless it amazed him.

Levi stared deep into her eyes. She waited for his kiss but he hesitated. His heart belonged to Calliope. Still it was with great reluctance that he lowered his hand from the satiny skin of her cheek.

A beeping filled the room and her disappointed look vanished, only to be replaced by relief. She sidestepped and reached into her pocket, pulling out that shiny object once more.

"Awesome. Hang tight. I'll call you an ambulance."

He watched her put the device to her ear and speak rapidly. He had no clue if there was anyone at the other end. She, however, appeared satisfied when she closed it, before returning the item to her pocket.

"They're on their way. You should probably sit down until they get here." She gestured to the chair she'd put him in earlier.

"Who is coming?" Despite the pounding of his head, he couldn't ignore the desire to protect her.

She frowned at him. "The ambulance. I told you I would call it. You've got a nasty cut that they should look at. Not to mention you seem to have a lack of remembering, which you may want to go to a hospital and have it checked out."

"You are helping me?"

"Really, dude. I don't know where the hell you came from. All of a sudden you're just here. Bleeding, I might add, on the floor. You're lucky I don't call the cops."

She confused him. There was no fear in her gaze. In fact, she seemed more than defiant. He liked it.

"I told you I wouldn't hurt you."

"Uh huh. Humor me. Get the checkup, then if you don't want to go with them you don't have to, but I can't have you bleeding all over my store."

He gingerly touched the cut on his head. She'd cleaned it but it had begun to bleed again. Unsure what to do—and of where he was—he went to the chair and sat. Eyes on her, he ran over her again.

She was beautiful. Thunder cracked and the lights flickered again. A loud pounding came from the back door and they both jumped. She recovered quickly and moved to open it. When two large white men walked in, he half rose from his chair, thinking he would need to protect her.

"Where is he?"

"Right over here." She gestured in his direction and the men approached him.

Interesting. They didn't blink over her color or his. The larger of the two men crouched beside him and gazed at him, taking in his clothing before focusing on him again.

"Nasty cut you got there. What happened?"

Past him, Levi could see Ta-Mara watching them with a concerned expression. He wanted to reassure her somehow but didn't know why or how.

"Sir? Your cut?"

He shook his head. "I do not remember."

The man looked at Ta-Mara, who shrugged. "Not sure. I...found him like that. He seemed disoriented and so came in to sit out the storm until we got cell service again and could call out."

Cell service? What is that? And why is she lying about me coming in? This was where he'd awoken.

He sat still as the strangers checked and cleaned his wound. As the man asked questions, Levi's headache returned, worse than before, and he winced with the onslaught of pain.

"I think you need to get to a hospital."

Every instinct within him rebelled. He'd seen them, seen the horrors that went on in them. The screams and cries from those who were losing limbs to gangrene or having bullets dug out of their body.

He glanced again to Ta-Mara who just watched him. What he really needed was a bed and some sleep...then some answers about what was going on.

"How about I bring him in if his headache doesn't go away?" Ta-Mara's offer surprised him.

The other man—the smaller of the two—moved to her side and Levi fought off a growl. They talked in hushed tones and he couldn't make out what they were saying. It didn't help the one beside him continued asking questions.

"I am okay," he said, pushing the man's hand away from the cut.

The men shared a look and gathered their things. "You sure you won't go to the hospital?"

He shook his head and moments later, they were left alone. The pounding in his head increased yet he refused to look away from Ta-Mara. She didn't look so sure any more.

"You are frightened of me."

She shook her head immediately. "No. Not frightened. Unsure of what I'm going to do with you now."

His attention drifted from her toward the box that played music. Pushing to his feet, he started toward it. At the rectangular shape, he reached out and pressed a button. Immediately it jacked up the volume and the noise—loud and pounding—flew from it. He jumped back before scrambling to fix it to how it had been.

She slid a strong arm past him and touched another button. The music returned to the lower level it had been at.

"Not a rap fan, I take it?" she asked.

Rap? What's rap? He just shook his head, not trusting his voice.

"You sure seem like you've not seen anything like this before." She crossed her arms. "Are you sure you don't want me to take you to a hospital?"

Oh, he was sure. He licked his lips, uncertain of what to say now. This was all new and foreign to him. He wanted to explore it more and yet he wanted to be around Ta-Mara.

"No hospital," he said after swallowing a few times.

She frowned slightly, a furrow appearing on her brow. "You need me to take you somewhere? Hotel? Or wherever you're staying for the reenactment?"

A dilemma. He had no money, no place to stay, no anything, save the wet, sodden clothes on his back.

"I have nowhere to go."

Ta-Mara studied him intently and he almost shifted under her gaze. What she saw he wasn't sure, but she seemed to be weighing some things. Whether he wanted to admit it or not, his life was in her hands.

It didn't take too much for him to realize this was not his time. There were too many things he couldn't explain and hadn't ever seen before.

"I must be insane to even consider this," she muttered, shoving a hand through her hair.

He longed to touch the mass of black curls himself. There was something about her that reminded him so much of someone from his past—his precious Calliope.

"Consider what?"

She continued muttering to herself as if he'd not even spoken at all. Turning her back to him, she walked off and he found himself mesmerized by the gentle sway of her full hips clad in her white clothing.

He followed her, unwilling to leave her alone—or leave himself alone. Trailing behind her, he looked around the store they moved through. *Books everywhere*. The building was larger than some libraries he'd seen. It struck him as odd that she was here, for he didn't know many blacks who could read. However, the way she reached out and touched some of them as they passed, told him of a deep affection and familiarity with the tomes.

She checked the front door, ensuring it was locked securely then she swiped a few things off the desk and faced him. Even in the dim lighting, he couldn't help but notice the feminine appreciation in her gaze.

"Let's go then."

He raised an eyebrow. "Go?"

"Look, buddy. I'm not entirely sure who you are or where you came from, but I can't...hmm...*won't* leave you hear overnight. Since you won't go to a hospital and I'm not entirely sure that's a wise decision, I'll put you up for the night. Come morning, after the storm has passed, we can figure out what to do with you."

"I'm to go with you?"

"Taking that Confederate thing a bit far, don't you think?" She shrugged easily but he realized he'd insulted her. "You don't have to, if you have nowhere else to go, feel free to sleep outside in an alley and hopefully you'll make it through the night. Or, you can come with me and have a dry bed, et cetera. Your choice."

"You. I choose you."

Even to him, those words sounded an awful lot like a promise. She held his gaze before nodding.

"Let's get to it then. I'm hungry."

He could use some food himself. Following her back to where he first met her, he watched as she turned off the music and reached for a leather coat. Then she opened the back door and tilted her head at him.

"I'm the silver metallic Mariner." She waved him out of the door and into the rain.

He stepped out into the downpour and froze. Any doubt he wasn't in his time anymore, was eliminated. As far as he could see, tall buildings emitted bright light, cutting through the rain with disturbing ease. When he looked away from them, he focused on what was before him and saw strange contraptions—large, wheeled and totally new to him.

"Don't just stand there," she said over a loud rumble of thunder and streaks of lightning as it jagged across the sky. "Get in. I'll unlock it when you're closer."

His head spun and he wobbled a bit on his feet. This...was not anything like he'd expected. He was totally out of his element and had no idea what was going on. Not only that, but he had no idea what a silver metallic Mariner was. What would she do when she realized that?

Ta-Mara finished setting the alarm and locked the dead bolt. Spinning, she saw her stranger just standing there in the rain. She almost hollered to him again but the look on his face dried up her call. Lost, confused—those were the expressions she made out on his face.

I did say I would control my imagination, right? Perhaps because part of her wondered if he was even from this time. His costume looked extremely authentic and him… Well, she wondered.

Oh please, what are you thinking, that he traveled through time and ended up here? Right now, it didn't matter. She needed to get herself—and him—out of the rain. She rushed by him and headed for her SUV.

"Come on!" she called over her shoulder as she unlocked her vehicle. "Climb in the front."

He entered shortly after her and she tried hard—really hard—not to stare at the way his uniform molded to him. His cloak was in his lap and she tore her gaze away to start the engine. His jolt was so blatant she glanced at him again.

"Are you all right?"

"What is this?" His eyes were wide and he gripped the door handle as well as the armrest. His fingers were white.

Yep. It was official—she was losing her sanity. She truly believed from this unrehearsed reaction he'd never been in a vehicle before. Before she could talk herself out of it, she reached over and covered his hand with hers. There was no disguising the strength in him.

He focused those amazing eyes on her and she wanted only to reassure him.

"You'll be fine. Trust me." She buckled her belt and talked him through doing the same thing then she got them on the way to her house.

His already ghostly-pale face lost even more color as they got on the interstate. Cars coming at them, whizzing around them—she knew it must be hard for him to remain quiet. Soon they were on her street and the only one out on the road.

Pulling up the short, lined drive, Ta-Mara smiled. She loved her house. It was her dream home. Plantation style, two level and over four thousand square feet. Four bedrooms, three and a half bath. She parked beneath the *porte-cochère* and climbed out. Levi joined her near the hood.

Her breath caught as the outside lights shone on her guest. He truly was magnificent.

"This is your home?"

"Yes. Come on in. I suspect you'd like a shower and some dry clothing. I don't have that much which will fit you, but I should have something my brother wore last time he was here. I think you will be okay with those."

She led the way up the steps into the house, past her office where she paused for a moment. Mud and water covered nearly every inch of her guest, so she led him to the laundry room, which doubled as her mudroom. Thankfully, she had a pile of clean towels stacked on the dryer.

"Take off your clothes and wrap up in a towel. Then I'll take you up to your room so you can get cleaned up."

He didn't even blink, just dropped his cloak and went to work on tugging the shirt from the waist of his pants. She gulped and stepped back before ducking into the kitchen.

"Yell when you're done," she called over her shoulder.

Leaning against one of the counters, she waved a hand in front of her heated face, fanning herself. He had no shame and had begun stripping right in front of her. Turning to her left, she reached for a glass then went to the fridge to get some iced water. She'd just finished the drink when she got the feeling she was no longer alone.

She thought she'd be ready to see him again. She wasn't. He stood there wearing nothing but one of her towels tied around his lean hips. *Good Lord.* It was like staring at a romance book hero—all cuts and definitions, not an ounce of fat, and light smattering of hair that drew her gaze to where it disappeared below the towel.

Yep, she wanted to trace it with her fingers and see exactly where it would take her. Although she knew precisely where it would go. His eyes weren't on her at the moment. He was gazing about her kitchen, wonderment and suspicion on his face.

"I'll take you to your room."

Those amazing blue eyes found her and she gulped again. He looked hesitant, so she shoved her own lust for him to the side before approaching.

"Are you sure you're okay?" she asked, placing a hand on his arm.

"Will you be in trouble helping me?"

She blew out an exasperated breath. "Again, with that? I'm a grown woman and no one tells me what I can or cannot do. Come on."

Without another word, she left the kitchen, leading him through the living room, hall, foyer then up the stairs. At the top she veered to the left and led him to a bedroom. Opening the door, she stepped in then watched him enter.

Despite wearing nothing but a towel, he moved with fluid grace that made her want to take more than one look.

"The bathroom is over there, make yourself at home. I'll be back in a few minutes with some other clothing for you."

He nodded and she slipped out. She went to the room her brother used when he visited and dug through the closet. Her sibling wasn't as broad-shouldered as the man in her house but he tended to wear his clothes bigger. New stuff in hand, she made her way back to the room Levi occupied.

She knocked on the doorframe before entering. "Levi? I brought you some clothes."

A muttered shout filled the air. She dropped the clothes and bolted to the bathroom, fearful he'd fallen because of his head injury.

Stupid, stupid, stupid, Ta-Mara. Shoulda insisted he go to the hospital.

She skidded to a stop in the doorway and stared at his reflection. There was only one word she could think of for his expression—overwhelmed.

The towel he wore had loosened and dipped, allowing her to see a bit of his ass cheek. She cleared her throat and he spun toward her, gripping the sliding towel. Dampening her lips, she sighed. There were two ways to handle what she'd just realized. One would be to panic and call the cops to get this time traveler out of her house. Two, accept it and help him, as she'd planned on doing anyway.

For that reason, she didn't address the confusion on his face, just walked deeper into the bathroom and opened the glass shower door. Once the water was on, she looked over her shoulder. "I don't have it all that hot but you just adjust this to change the temperature."

He walked closer and leaned against her as he gazed past her. She stared at his tanned arm covered with a smattering of dark hair as he stretched it out into the streams of water.

"Is it okay?" she asked, trying to ignore how husky her voice sounded.

"I... Yes, fine."

She showed him how to shut if off once he had finished, then put a dry towel on the door for him to use. After mentioning the clothing she'd placed in the bedroom, she left him with the heat lamp running, along with the fan, not to mention instruction on how the toilet worked.

Ta-Mara headed directly downstairs and to her room, where she sat on the padded bench at the foot of her bed. Only for a moment, however, before she shot back to her feet and changed out of her work clothing into something much more comfortable—and not white, which had really shown off more than she wished, courtesy of the rain.

Clad in black shorts and a deep rose tank top, she made her way down to the laundry room to look at his soaked clothing. She frowned as she lifted the heavy woolen pants. Setting up a drying rack, she hung everything over it to air dry. She could take them to a dry cleaner for him.

What was she thinking? He could do what he wished with his own clothing. Shaking her head in amusement, she went back to the kitchen to start dinner. She had two days off, which would give her a bit of time to think more on what she now knew to be true.

Her guest wasn't an actor but an actual Confederate. How he got here, she had no clue but it didn't take her much to go from the book she'd been reading to the man who currently showered in her house. Both were named Levi. Both were from the Deep South. Hell, according to the description in the book, they were damn near identical.

Okay, so there was still a chance this was a dream and she would wake up feeling extremely embarrassed. On the other hand, if this *was* a dream, what the hell was she doing down here instead of being up in the shower with that man?

"Hell, can't even get some in a dream," she muttered as she slid the dinner she'd prepared before work into the oven.

"Cannot get some what?"

She jumped, not having expected him to be there, much less to overhear what she'd been complaining about to herself.

"Nothing," she said, rotating to face him.

It was a damn good thing she'd spoken before she got to see him completely or she wouldn't have even managed to get that word out. And she'd thought he looked good in the wool. That had nothing on him in jeans and a tee. The dark denim molded to his thighs like a second skin. The shirt as well. The charcoal gray cotton had never looked so good on her brother.

Levi's muscles rippled beneath the shirt. Her mouth went dry as she stared at him unabashedly. The ends of his hair were still wet and she swallowed hard as he walked toward her, those intense blue eyes focused on her.

"H…how are you feeling?"

Yes, inquire politely as if not thinking of ripping those clothes off him and impaling yourself on his cock, which is definitely large, given the bulge in the jeans.

"Much better, thank you."

Okay, this could prove to be a problem. Even his lashes were sexy—thick, long and curly. The stubble on his face tempted her to touch. Oh, what would it feel like abrading her inner thighs? Heat flashed through her and her pussy clenched with greedy need. *Get a grip, Ta-Mara.* Funny how she'd been telling herself that since she'd run into him.

Pasting a smile on her face—one she hoped didn't show how badly she was lusting after this virtual stranger—she nodded. "Good. Looks like your injury hasn't begun bleeding again. I'll have some supper ready in a bit. Feel free to look around." She walked to the fridge. "Or perhaps you would like something to drink. Tea? Beer? Coffee?"

No answer was forthcoming so she glanced over to see him investigating her Keurig coffeemaker and the carousel tree beside it, which was filled with different flavors of coffee and tea. Wiping her hand off on her shorts, she went to his side.

"It's a coffeemaker." She reached past him for a mug and placed it on the drip tray. With a light touch on his arm, she directed him to the tree of flavors. "I don't see you as a tea man, but more of a medium roast kind of guy. Grab that one there." She gestured.

He picked it up and turned it over in his hand, examining it with a cute furrow between his eyebrows. She directed him where to insert it, snapped the cover down and pointed at the button to push.

"This is making coffee?"

"Ready in about a minute," she answered, walking to the fridge for cream. Uncertain which he would prefer, she grabbed the four different flavors she had. She placed them beside the machine that continued to hold his attention as it began filling the mug. "Not sure what you like."

His eyes flashed up to hers and she felt it as if he'd touched her like he had in the store. Pressing her to the wall, sharing his heat with her.

She cleared her throat and tried to slow her breathing, which had suddenly kicked up. "Of cream. I have a few different ones you can choose from."

Heat filled his eyes and more moisture pooled between her legs. It wouldn't surprise her in the least if it ran down her inner thighs. The way he skimmed his gaze over her didn't help her state in the least. Oh yeah, she'd be having some delicious dreams tonight.

Chapter Three

Levi had never seen things like this. Sure, it smelled like coffee but the entire process was new to him. Then there was how she managed the lights. And that thing she pulled cold stuff from. They'd had a larder, this…this was so much more. It looked like a refrigerator, only better than the ones he'd seen.

He kept his eyes on the machine before him, determined to ignore everything else until this thing had been figured out. The aroma was divine. When the liquid no longer streamed down, he grasped the handle and took it out. Placing the large clear mug on the counter, he reached for the containers she'd set down. He opened each and sniffed them. Opting for Irish cream, he added a generous dollop then stirred it in.

"The way you keep looking at the mocha one, I'm surprised you didn't use it."

He glanced at her when she spoke. His heart hammered all that much harder. She was so beautiful. She stood there barefoot in her kitchen with a sparkling pink shine on her nails, those long, lean legs that weren't covered up but bare for all to see. Her upper body, amazing as it was, also didn't have much in the way of covering.

Not that I mind. And he didn't. The difficulty came in trying not to stare at her. Full breasts, flat stomach, hips that were made for a man — him — to hold as he drove into her. His shaft thickened and he turned deliberately away from her.

This is no way for a gentleman to behave. The question was, was he gentleman? He sure as hell wasn't feeling much like one. Far from it. Something about this woman made him want to behave as he had in her shop, press her against the wall and…

He shook his head. This wasn't the time for thoughts of such behavior.

"Are you hungry?"

He could do with some sustenance. "If it is not too much trouble."

"Not at all. I've put it in the oven so it should be ready soon." She rested her hip against the light brown countertop.

Her directness amused and pleased him. He didn't have much to say about quiet, shy women. The ability to look him in the eye and occasionally challenge him was part of what had deeply attracted him to Calliope.

He tracked her as she moved toward him, her hips swaying gently with each step. Beauty in motion. Her full lips were a distraction and one he wanted to taste. Part of him was full of reprimand over the fact he hadn't kissed her when the chance had been there.

"Excuse me," she murmured as she stepped around him.

He watched her as she swiftly put down another mug and made more coffee. While she set the table, he made his way around the kitchen, opening things and trying to figure out exactly how they worked. This stuff was incredible.

Levi peeked his head into her pantry and couldn't believe the amount of food in there. Did she live with others? Cook for others? Stepping back out, he spied a calendar on the wall. The date stopped him in his tracks.

"This…this date. Is it the truth?"

"Yes." She appeared by his side. "What year did you leave from?"

Her voice wobbled a bit and it helped him knowing this seemed to be stressful for her as well.

"Eighteen-sixty."

"Of course. Eighteen-sixty, why didn't I think of that," she muttered, heading back to the table and sitting down. She stood, went to get her drink then returned to the seat. "It makes perfect sense I find a man in my store who's come more than a century and a half into the future."

He moved to her side and sat in the chair next to her. Her face was stricken and he didn't much care for that look on her.

"Are you okay?" he questioned.

"Me? Oh, I'm fine. How about you?"

"A bit disconcerted by what has just been revealed to me. But, better than you, I fear."

She waved him off. "I'm good. I mean, it's a common thing for me to bring home men who by all accounts shouldn't even be alive in my time."

He remained beside her, not talking because he didn't believe she even addressed him. Levi had to dig his fingers into his palm to keep himself from reaching out to tuck her curls behind her ear. This close, she smelled divine. That same scent he'd gotten from her earlier surrounded him like ribbons and drew him closer.

Teasing him.

Tantalizing him.

Tempting him.

He waited her out. Until her confusing chatter stopped and she rubbed her temples with her fingers.

"Sorry. I'm good."

When a beep sounded, she got up and went to the stove. She took out a square container that had golden brown biscuits on the top. His stomach rumbled in anticipation.

"I hope this will do." She placed the dish on the trivet then removed the tray of biscuits. "Leftovers." With a spoon, she stirred the noodles and sauce then served him some. Once his plate was full, she put some on her own.

Ta-Mara sat only to bounce back up and hurry to the refrigerator—which he was used to, being in the brewery trade—and return with salad.

"Help yourself."

She sat for a few more minutes then went to get up again and he reached to grip her forearm. "Sit. Eat."

Fire burned his fingertips as he touched her. He couldn't recall anytime he'd wanted to kiss someone so much before—not even Calliope—and that bothered him. She had been the one for him. *Right?* Another woman shouldn't be affecting him this way. *Should she?*

Conflicted beyond belief, he released her arm and put his gaze on her. "You need to eat."

Ta-Mara nodded before lifting her fork and doing just that. They passed the meal in silence, each looking at one another only to look away and pretend it hadn't happened.

"This stuff," he began, wishing to converse with her. "What do you call it?"

"Technology?"

He frowned slightly. He knew the word, although his understanding didn't match what she referred to. "That thing you had in your hand at your shop. What was that?"

"My cell phone." She gave him a grin and got up from the table. When she returned, she set it before him.

He slid his plate to the side and stared at the item. "May I?"

She nodded and returned to her seat. Intrigued, he began pushing buttons and looking at the screen.

"Cell phone?"

"So I can call people, even if I'm not in the house and don't have access to my telephone."

Telephone, he knew that word. Used to signal from ship to ship—or musical notes.

"You talk to people on this?" *How is this possible?*

"Yes." She took it from him and pressed a few buttons. A ringing sound filled the room and he sat riveted in his chair.

"Hello?" a deep voice came through it.

"Richard, sorry to bother you. Just wanted to make sure you survived the power outages."

"No bother, sweets. I'm fine. How was work today?"

"Not bad. Look, I have to run, just wanted to check in."

"Talk to you later. Bye."

Ta-Mara pressed another button and the room fell silent.

Levi wasn't sure what to think. This was unlike anything he'd ever seen before. She gave a small laugh.

"What?"

"If you think this is odd, I can't wait to see what you do with the computer, television and more."

His head throbbed and he winced. Immediately her expression morphed into one of concern.

"Are you okay? Headache?"

"Yes. I am sorry. I think it has been a bit overwhelming."

She got to her feet. "Come on."

He stared at the dishes.

"Don't worry about it. I'll get them. I'd just prefer you not pass out down here."

Together they walked from the kitchen up the stairs to the room she'd taken him to before. He watched silently as she gave him a quick show of where things were if he needed more blankets or anything like that.

"I'll see you in the morning, then," she said.

He reached out to stop her and she paused, her large eyes waiting for him.

"Thank you."

She squeezed his arm. "We'll figure this out come morning. Sleep as late as you like. I'll be up early, but it's my day off so I have some things to attend around here. Good night, Levi. Sleep well." One final squeeze then she left.

With a deep breath, he looked around the room. Thick area rugs of silvered gold covered the floor. A large bed beckoned him, draped in an auburn comforter. Ta-Mara had drawn it back for him and he could see sheets and blankets beneath it—sea mist and champagne. Numerous pillows awaited his head and he yawned, exhaustion swarming him.

He stripped out of his borrowed clothing and slid beneath the sheets. Like silk along his skin, he groaned in pure pleasure. Reaching out, he touched the bedside lamp and the room sank into darkness.

It wasn't silent—he could hear some noises he couldn't identify—but his tired body gave in to the lure that beckoned him. Sleep claimed him swiftly.

* * * *

Sun upon his face woke him. He cautiously opened his eyes and found it hadn't been a dream. Shafts of golden light poured past the curtains with a warm, welcoming glow. He sat up and realized he felt much better—the headache had gone.

After swinging from the bed, he padded to the bathroom and turned on the light. Sitting on the sink was something that hadn't been there before. He frowned and picked it up, reading the container. Shaving cream.

He almost went to ask her then shook his head. *I can figure this out.* So he read the instructions and soon had the cream lathered up on his face. With care, he got to work. It didn't take him long to get the hang of it.

Cleaning up after, he stared at his reflection. Would she like him better this way? Shaking away that thought, he took care of his needs then went back to dress. More clothing had been set on a chair by the window. She must have come in while he was sleeping. But why?

After he dressed, he tidied up and hastened down the steps. He paused when he saw the clock. It was after ten in the morning. He *never* slept that long.

"Ta-Mara?" he called out.

There was no answer. He walked through the house and paused when he reached the living room. Staring out of one of the three doors leading both to the screened porch and the family room, he spied her in the backyard. He strolled closer and just watched her for a moment.

More of those scandalously short pants and a shirt with no sleeves graced her body as she knelt and worked in her garden. Her hair was piled up with some wisps around her face. He pushed out of the door and she looked up when it shut behind him.

"Morning," she said, getting to her feet.

Lust hit him hard. The shirt wasn't just sleeveless, it also left her belly bared to his hungry gaze. He was in trouble with this one. He moved down three of the steps.

"Hi."

"I didn't wake you, did I?" She wiped her hands off on the blue material covering part of her thighs.

"No."

"How are you feeling?"

Hot and aroused. Desperate to feel her lips on his, her curves under his hands, her taste mixing with his. "Fine, thank you."

"Let me get you some breakfast then we can decide what to do." She flashed him another grin and walked by.

Pivoting around, he stared at her ass as she made her way up the steps by him. *Yes, trouble.*

As she passed him, Ta-Mara could sense his gaze on her and need pooled in her belly, making her want to turn around, grab him and kiss him senseless. All that stopped her was that she didn't know if she was ready for what would happen should she take the initiative. Levi, from what he'd said and his lack of knowledge of things, seemed to be not from this time. Getting involved with him was a bad idea. Ta-Mara had no idea why he was even here, or for how long. The *how long* was what stopped her.

She reached the porch and Levi's sure steps came behind her. A slight moan made her turn and she watched, helpless, as Levi collapsed. Ta-Mara's heart leaped in her chest as she stepped to him before dropping to her knees.

"Levi!" She touched his neck, feeling for his pulse. Relief filled her as it beat steadily against her fingers.

She smoothed his hair away from his face, again taken with how handsome he was. Ta-Mara didn't know what had made him pass out but now she knew she definitely had to get him to the hospital. She rose and ran inside to get her cell before coming back and kneeling by his side.

Ta-Mara went to dial then lowered the phone. "Damn, I can't take him to the emergency room."

Levi had no identification and there would be lots of questions the doctor would ask that she didn't have any answers to. Even if Levi woke, she could only imagine his reaction being surrounded by the wonders of modern medicine. Her brow furrowed as she thought about how she could get him help. When it dawned on her, she sent a text and, moments later when the replies came, she blew out a relieved breath. Ta-Mara put her cell in her pocket then sat and watched Levi. His chest rose, slow and steady.

She looked up at the sound of a car pulling in then rose and went to stand overlooking the steps. She spotted another vehicle pulling in behind the first. The drivers exited their vehicles and came around them then stopped greeting each other before coming toward Ta-Mara.

"Thanks for coming, guys." Ta-Mara bit her lip and debated if she should say more.

"When you get a text from your friend saying 'I need help', you drop everything and come." Rachel came up the steps.

"What's wrong?" Heather followed with a frown on her face.

"I—"

"Damn, Ta-Mara, who did you kill?" Rachel stopped on the porch beside her and stared at Levi, still sprawled on the porch.

"Hush, Rachel." Heather glanced around anxiously. "We need to help her hide the body."

Ta-Mara stared at her in shock. Heather was the quieter of them and the most level-headed.

"Why are you standing there, Ta-Mara?" Heather went to step past her. "Grab his legs, Rachel."

"Okay." Rachel took a step.

Ta-Mara grabbed an arm for each of her friends to stop them. "He's alive."

"Oh…" Heather frowned then it cleared. "Oh, you need us to be an alibi because you knocked him out."

"I can give her one. She was at the bar with me helping me stock all day." Rachel offered.

"You were at home, so that's not plausible," Heather said. "Let's go with instead she was with us both at your place hanging out."

"Ladies." Ta-Mara stifled a laugh. "I didn't ask you here for this either."

"Then why are we here, if not to hide the body or give you an alibi." Rachel frowned.

"I wanted Heather to check him over because I can't take him to the hospital." Ta-Mara shrugged. "I know it's your day off, but can you—?"

"Sure." Heather went over and knelt beside Levi.

Heather was a doctor at the emergency room. Ta-Mara looked on, hoping he was okay.

"Who is he and why is he here?"

"Levi. He's—" Ta-Mara didn't know what to say or how to explain.

"Is sexy as hell." Rachel put her arm into the crook of Ta-Mara's elbow. "I noticed you evaded answering my question. Spill. You know you will."

Stalling for time to come up with something so she didn't sound crazy, Ta-Mara pushed against Rachel's shoulder.

"How could you all believe I would ask you to help me hide a body if I killed someone? Or, hell, give me an alibi for hitting him."

"You didn't ask." Heather replied from where she was by Levi. "And we'd do it because you're our girl. If you need help to hide a body, we're there for you."

"Or if you need an alibi for hitting him too. Hell, if you called from jail, I wouldn't even ask what you did. I'd just get bail money and come get you," Rachel said, firmly squeezing her hand.

"You do know you all are crazy, right?" Ta-Mara looked between the two women.

"Right back atcha. That's what makes us such good friends." Rachel laughed.

"We're all nutty as fruitcake," Heather said as she sat back. "He's a little dehydrated and thin—" She touched his throat. "Who tried to strangle him?"

"Why is he passed out and hasn't stirred?" Ta-Mara asked.

"He's not over his swoon." Heather rose. "He has the injury on his head but he doesn't have a concussion. If he did, no matter if you wanted him to go to the hospital or not, we'd have to take him." She came to Ta-Mara and stared at her. "Now, tell us what is going on."

"You're gonna think I *am* crazy."

"We already established we all are." Rachel pressed against her. "So tell us already.

Ta-Mara took a breath then told them what she suspected. Levi was the man she'd read about in her book and he had come to this time for some reason. Her friends knew of the story, since she read it so often and had told them about it. She also added what had happened in the bookstore when he'd appeared, and how he'd reacted to things. When she was finished speaking, Ta-Mara waited for her friends to respond. They just stared at her.

"Say something." Ta-Mara couldn't stand the silence.

"I'm just trying to figure out why you're so calm about this," Rachel said.

"Because I figure I hit my head and am lying unconscious in the store and no one's found me yet." Ta-Mara smiled wryly. "This is a really vivid dream and when I wake up, I'll share it with both of you and have a laugh."

Heather narrowed her eyes then, deliberately slowly, reached out then pinched her.

"Ow." Ta-Mara swatted at her hand. "Why'd you do that for?"

"Just so you can know you *are* awake," Heather replied solemnly then grinned. "You're not asleep, sweetie. We're all very awake."

"And you seem to believe me." Ta-Mara wondered why they would.

"I have no idea what to believe." Rachel shrugged. "Weird shit happens that folks can't explain all the time. I've never met anyone who had a time travel encounter, but hey, who am I to judge?"

"I trust you, and if that is what you believe, I'm going to go along with it for now." Heather patted her shoulder. "I won't even have you committed for being crazy."

Ta-Mara heard the teasing in her tone so she laughed and they joined her. She pulled Heather to her, and her friends on either side hugged her.

"We need to move him," Heather said after a few moments. "Get him someplace comfortable. Let him rest."

"Okay." Ta-Mara bit her lip. "I had planned to take him shopping to get some clothing, since he doesn't have anything."

"Well hold off on that for now. If he did travel through time, that would make anyone tired." Heather wiggled her eyebrows.

"We are so not going to tell anyone else about this" — Rachel shook her head — "or we will all be committed."

"No, we're telling no one else about this. We'll help you move him inside onto the couch. Then if he is still here when you officially introduce us to him, we'll act like we don't know him. Let's get this done." Heather clapped her hands together.

Ta-Mara nodded and they went to Levi. She grabbed him under the shoulder and her friends took a leg. They lifted him, puffing as they took him into the house.

"Christ, he's heavy," Rachel said.

"He's all muscle." Heather blew out a breath.

"Oh yes." Ta-Mara glanced down at his face. "He sure is."

They took him into the living room then placed him on the couch. Levi didn't stir, still breathing deeply.

"Are you sure he's okay?"

"With what I can see, he's fine." Heather slid her hands into her pockets. "If you want me to check further, then I'll need to take him to the hospital."

"No hospital," Ta-Mara said. "At least not yet. He has no ID so I can't explain him. I'll see how it goes and call you if I change my mind."

"Okay." Heather grabbed her hand. "Now, as for your crush on him...be careful, Ta-Mara."

"I don't have a crush on him," she protested.

"Yeah you do." Rachel held her other hand. "From that book you read all the time you did. Now this man is here in flesh supposedly being that perfect man you set up in your mind. And you're already looking at him like he's yours."

"Please, I'm not."

"You are," they said together.

"Okay I will admit I was...*am* a little taken with him from the book. But I know it's just a fantasy. He's a fantasy, and they aren't real." Ta-Mara glanced at him.

"We're gonna go," Rachel said.

She focused on her friends and went out to see them off. After they drove away, Ta-Mara returned to the living room. Levi was still passed out. She took the quilt off the back of the couch and draped it over him. Since it made no sense for her to watch over him, she did some chores. Five minutes later she checked on him then went to work again. She kept going back to his side. Knowing it was useless to do anything else, she grabbed her e-reader and sat in the chair closest to him. Ta-Mara studied him, taking in the long lashes on his cheeks, wanting to see his deep blue gaze. Warmth filled her and she put her hand on her chest.

He's not for you, Ta-Mara. Just help him find his way and don't get emotionally involved.

Staring at him, she realized she had to build some defenses against him, because the dynamic man could easily draw her in and make her wish for things that she couldn't possibly have.

Chapter Four

Levi jerked up, gasping, then turned his head, his eyes wide. Ta-Mara jumped at his sudden movement.

"Levi," she said cautiously, not sure if he was fully awake.

"Yes." He rubbed his hand over his face then lowered it. "What happened?"

"You passed out on the porch." Ta-Mara resisted the urge to go to him. She needed to keep him at a distance. "How are you feeling?"

"My head still aches but I am well." Levi said it slowly, as if he wasn't sure. "How long have I been sleeping?"

"About two hours." She decided not to push about how he was feeling. "You rest on the couch. I don't want you falling and possibly hitting your head. I'll get you something to drink."

"Wait, how did you get me to the couch?" Levi frowned.

"Lifted you under your shoulders to get you here." Ta-Mara rose. She told the partial truth as she headed out of the living room to retrieve his drink.

Levi was sitting, a frown on his face. She set the beverage on the table in front of the couch then stepped back.

"So no moving from the couch." Ta-Mara pointed in his direction. "Just in case I do need to take you to the hospital, I need to make some arrangements to get you some identification."

"No hospital," Levi replied. "I cannot sit here doing nothing."

"If you are not feeling better soon or if you pass out again, I will need to take you in to get checked out. Just to make sure you're okay. For now, we'll see how it goes." Ta-Mara crossed her arms over her chest. "And yes you *will* sit there and rest. You're dehydrated so I'll be giving you loads of liquid. You're also tired, and obviously from passing out, you need a little time to recover. Here, watch some TV." She picked up the remote and turned it on.

Levi stood eyes wide. "What—?"

She fought to breathe, having forgotten for a moment who he was and the time he came from. Ta-Mara quickly explained what the television was and how it worked. She gave him the remote. Levi sat heavily, staring in awe at the screen. She left him to it and went to make some calls. Pausing in the kitchen, she braced her hands on the counter.

What have I gotten myself into? There is no way I can deal with a man from the eighteen-sixties. Hell, I shouldn't even believe that he is some time traveler. Yet I do. Ta-Mara thought of his deep blue eyes and the intensity of them that stole her breath away. *And damn my luck, he's so fricking sexy.*

There was nothing she could do about any of it so she went to fix what she could—getting him some identification.

* * * *

Levi stared in the direction Ta-Mara had gone and he rubbed the bridge of his nose. He had no idea what had happened earlier. All he remembered was watching her ass then coldness. For a moment, he'd have sworn he was back in the forest, running, but that had to be impossible— *Doesn't it?*

"I'm in the here and now," Levi muttered. "Not my time, but I'm learning to adapt."

With that in mind, he glanced at the box thing she'd called a television. He frowned, seeing the moving people and color in it. He lifted the little black thing she gave him called a remote then pressed a button. Levi partially rose as a woman appeared. She was singing, but it was her clothing—or lack thereof—that made his eyes widen.

"Enjoying a little Beyoncé, I see," Ta-Mara said.

He glanced toward the doorway. She was peeking in at him with a small smile on her face. Levi returned it before gesturing toward the screen.

"Her clothing is much different than I am used to." He glanced at Ta-Mara's top and thought of her bottoms. Again, he hardened and he cleared his throat before speaking again. "Much different."

"Probably. Do you mind if I take a picture of you?" she asked, and when he nodded, she raised a small silver thing in her hands. "I also have a few questions. What is the month and day you were born, your height and eye color?"

He gave her the information then asked curiously, "What is that you used to take my picture? Why do you need to know these things?"

"Oh, this. It's a camera. And the reason why…it's a surprise." She smiled. "Don't know if I can get it for you, but I will try."

She left. He wondered what the surprise could be. Immediately he flashed to her wearing something more like the woman on the screen just for him. Levi shifted in his seat then turned his attention back to the television. His eyes widened as the woman Ta-Mara had called Beyoncé slithered across the floor, beckoning him.

"No thanks. Not what I prefer." He snorted. "Maybe if you were Ta-Mara, I'd be down on the floor with you."

Levi closed his eyes again, thinking of kissing Ta-Mara. *I wonder how she tastes.* He opened his eyes and pushed the thought away. Levi knew it was foolish to long for her when he had no idea why he was here and what would happen to him. He needed to learn what he could so he could blend in. He didn't want to cause Ta-Mara trouble. He changed the television to another show and leaned forward, staring at the images he was very familiar with—war. As the man spoke of the war, Levi wondered why, of all things, that hadn't changed or ceased to exist.

"The news." Ta-Mara came in again.

"I see people still have war. No matter the reasoning, it leads to senseless death on each side." Levi sat back.

"So you're against war." Ta-Mara perched in the chair she had occupied earlier.

Levi thought of what he had lost because of people waging war against an ideal that he would dare love someone of a different color. His Calliope hadn't done anything but love him, despite the obstacles and hate they'd faced. For a moment he wondered if they could have still been together had they been born later, during what seemed like a more enlightened time.

"I'm not against war. I'm against the pain it causes for people on both sides," Levi said softly.

"There is a lot of loss and it's sad. You've lost a lot, Levi." Ta-Mara's sympathetic gaze seemed more knowing than it should.

"Lost?" Levi frowned wondering how she would know what he lost.

Ta-Mara blinked then licked her lips. "I figured that coming from your time, there had to be people you cared about that you lost. If you need to talk, I'm here."

"You seem very accepting that I'm a Confederate."

"Accepting?" Ta-Mara laughed.

The melodious sound went straight to his cock. He clenched his fist on his knee, resisting the urge to fling himself out of the chair to grab her and kiss her, marking her as his.

"I wouldn't call it that." Ta-Mara shrugged. "I'm just going along with the flow. For all I know, I'm still in the store passed out and having a really good dream. I said something similar earlier."

He figured she's been talking to herself, as she had been when she'd found him in the store. He'd noticed that when she was in stressful situations, she tended to talk out loud.

"I'll go with the flow too." Levi smiled. "Not like I have a choice."

"We all have a choice." Ta-Mara leaned forward. "Your choice right now is to rest so we don't have you falling down again, or it will be the hospital for you."

He cringed just thinking of going to such a place. They were horrible, and he'd rather suffer than go there.

"When I mentioned the hospital the last time you had that same expression of distaste as you do now. Why?"

"Going to the hospital is not an option for me."

"They are nothing like that now," Ta-Mara said. "I'll find you some TV drama programs that show hospitals. It'll at least give you an idea it isn't so horrible. Ignore the sex that happens between people there. There are many that are sexualized."

Levi was curious about how comfortable she was talking about such things as sex but he didn't ask as he wanted to. He didn't want to be forward. He just nodded.

"So today you'll rest. I had planned to take you shopping for clothing and a few other things. But with your swoon earlier, it will be more prudent to stay home."

"Swoon." He scowled—that wasn't very masculine.

"From your expression, you don't like that word. I bet you think it isn't macho enough. It's just something I heard. We could say faint or pass out, if you prefer."

"Perhaps we don't mention it so much?" Levi leaned back on the couch.

"Okay." Ta-Mara returned to the chair then crossed her legs beneath her.

"We could go shopping. I'm feeling fine."

"Now. But what happens if you do what we shouldn't mention again in front of a whole lot of people? Then it will be off to the hospital for you—which could pose a problem, since you have no identification."

"Identification?"

"It's a little card that tells people who you are. There are a few pieces of things that you need that people ask for sometimes — driver's license, birth certificate, passport, social security card... Things like that."

"And I need this."

"Yes, because if you have to go to hospital or something like that, they'd want proof you are who you say you are. When they try to look you up and nothing comes up, it could be a problem." Ta-Mara picked up the thin item she had been holding earlier.

"I don't want to get you into trouble." Levi went to rise. "I should leave."

"Sit down." She waved her hand. "You're not going to cause me any problems. I'm working on some things. Now watch some TV and I'll just read."

"Read?"

"This is an e-reader." She held up the object. "You can get books digitally now."

"Digitally?"

"Oh, Levi, you have so much to learn." She smiled. "It'll be fun and some of it shocking, but I think you're going to find the information great."

"I like learning things." *Like how you taste.* He started at her lips.

"I bet you do." Ta-Mara swept her lips with her pink tongue and Levi wanted to follow with his.

He lifted his gaze and met hers. The desire in her eyes made him even harder. Ta-Mara averted her gaze.

"There are also many physical books I have. Feel free to check them out, as well as my e-reader."

"I will," he promised.

She glanced at him again then lowered her eyes to the screen. Levi observed her as she read before he went back to watching television. He had to get this need for her under control because it wasn't fair to either of them. Ta-Mara was helping him out without expecting anything in return. For him to take of advantage of that wasn't right.

I won't let my libido rule me.

* * * *

The next day Levi reminded himself of that as he followed Ta-Mara, staring at her bare shoulders and back in the pale yellow shirt she wore. The skin was oh so touchable and he wanted to taste before heading south to more succulent flesh. Levi let his gaze wander down to her butt, which was well displayed in her jeans. The hem stopped just below her knees and left her lower legs bare. Levi appreciated the open toes of her footwear, which showed her nails painted a lovely shade of red with a design. He'd never seen anything like it before. Before they'd left, he'd asked her what was on her toes, and he still didn't understand her explanation as to why she painted them. But it looked good on her—really good—and tempted him to have a closer look. Maybe even head north to get to the same destination that he wanted to taste. Either north or south, he didn't care where he started just that he got to taste Ta-Mara where he knew she was wet and lush.

What happened to keeping yourself under control? He'd been doing well all yesterday, keeping things light between them. By the time he'd gone to bed, he'd been convinced he could have Ta-Mara as just a friend. That was until she'd come down in the clothing she wore. He was convinced whoever made women's clothing during modern times did it to tempt a man into doing things they shouldn't. He glanced at a woman passing him and noticed she too had on clothing that showed off her skin, yet he felt nothing.

Levi returned his attention to Ta-Mara and instantly his breath caught. He tightened his grip on the handles of the cart he pushed.

"How about these?" Ta-Mara held up two packages. "Boxers or briefs?"

Levi stared at them then went around the cart and took them from her, looking at the image on the plastic then her. "Underwear," he said quietly then glanced around to make sure no one was listening before looking at her again. "Ta-Mara, you can't just be picking up things like this for me."

"Underwear." Ta-Mara frowned. "You need them."

"I do, but you just *can't*." He shook his head.

"Why?" Ta-Mara tilted her head to the side, studying him.

"Because it's just not done," Levi said firmly. "It's not proper."

"Oh...oh." Ta-Mara grinned widely then moved closer, whispering, "This is not during your time, Levi. You don't need to be uncomfortable with my picking up men's underwear. It is done during this time and no one will think it isn't proper."

"I can pick my own." He narrowed his gaze.

"Okay." Ta-Mara lifted her hands and stepped back. "Then pick some. Get a few of them. Maybe both boxers and briefs, so you can see which you like more."

She walked away. Levi watched her for a moment then started to pick his underwear. He was amazed at how many different kinds there were. He picked up a few types, noticing that there were different logos on it. He'd learned on television that there were many companies competing for your money, enticing you to pick them when making purchases. Levi frowned, wondering again about letting Ta-Mara pay for his things, but he had no money so he couldn't do it himself. He would make note of how much she spent, then find a way to pay her back.

"Do you need some help?" a woman asked, coming closer, her smile sultry.

Levi held back a sigh at seeing it. Since they had arrived at the place Ta-Mara called a department store, they'd had many offers of help. Ta-Mara had commented to him that she'd never had so many people wanting to help her before, then had looked at him pointedly. Levi knew he was somehow the cause. The women of this time were bold and he didn't want to be rude.

"No thanks, Miss." He made sure to look away.

"I'm over there if you change your mind," the woman said, then walked away.

Levi was relived. Some of the more aggressive ones hadn't known how to take a hint and Ta-Mara had had to step in. He didn't know what he would have done had she not been here. He glanced around the area looking for her. She was a little distance away at another table. Levi focused back on his choices. He did as she suggested, picking up a few mixes of boxers and briefs. Placing them in the cart, he then pushed it over to where Ta-Mara stood with her back to him.

"Ta-Mara, I'm ready."

"Take this." She turned and held out a bundled piece of cloth to him.

Levi accepted the item and opened it. The tri-color design on the boxer was nice and the fabric was soft to the touch. He liked how it felt, but still… "I told you not to pick my underwear."

Ta-Mara came to stand beside him then rose up slightly to his ear. "You'd look sexy in that."

Levi bit his lip to stifle a moan. "Ta-Mara."

"Fine. I won't pick any more of your underwear." Ta-Mara rolled her eyes.

"No." Levi touched her cheek. "If you like this, I want it."

"Okay." She blew out a breath.

"Is there any more you like?" Levi lowered his head to hers. "That you think I would look sexy in?"

"Yeah." Ta-Mara pushed her tongue in and out. The brief sight of pink made him want to follow it and taste her.

"Show me." He put the pair she had given him in the cart then held her hand.

Ta-Mara led him to the display and pointed out those she liked. He put them in the cart. Ta-Mara locked her gaze on the items in the cart then she lifted her head.

"Sexy is good."

"Yeah, yeah it is." Ta-Mara cleared her throat. "Now we need to get some clothing."

"Lead on," Levi said.

Ta-Mara did as he bade.

"Damn, me and my big mouth always gets me in trouble," she muttered.

Levi stifled a chuckle, not letting her know he had heard her. They went to the elevator and Levi pressed against the wall, still not used to the contraption. Ta-Mara came to him and touched his hand. He grabbed hers and she squeezed. When the door opened, they pushed the cart out, still holding hands. Soon they were in the men's clothing and Levi stared at the racks and racks of clothing.

"Let's get you outfitted." Ta-Mara pulled him along.

He went, noticing that women were watching them. Ta-Mara had explained that their nametags identified them as employees. The looks were ones he had been getting from the women since he had arrived. Ta-Mara pointed out some jeans and he picked them up. Levi smoothed his hand over the cloth.

Ta-Mara made a soft exhalation. Levi glanced up and her focus was on his hands.

"What do you think?" He smiled.

"They would fit you." She reached out but pulled back and coughed. "Very well."

It dawned on Levi then that whoever was making the different types of clothing now knew what they were doing. It could range from comfortable to not, but all in all, according to who was looking at it, it could be used to seduce someone you wanted. He filed that information away for future thought.

"I'll go try it on then."

"Take a few other things," Ta-Mara said.

"You want to help me pick stuff out."

"Ummm…give me a sec." Ta-Mara gestured behind her. "I need to go over there."

She pivoted then hurried away. Levi chuckled softly, knowing exactly why she had left. Ta-Mara was finding it hard to keep her hands off him and wanted some distance. Whistling softly, Levi went to get some more things. As he picked them up, he kept an eye on Ta-Mara across the room. Although he had tried to think of all the 'why not's when it came to getting involved with her, he already knew it was inevitable. Ta-Mara, after such a brief time, had already gotten under his skin. Now it was a matter how far he would be willing to let things go. Levi had no answer yet, but he would soon.

Ta-Mara bit the inside of her lower lip and shifted her feet as she tried to control the raw need coursing through her. Shopping for clothing hadn't ever been so difficult.

Never gone with Levi before, either.

It was an experience for sure. And she wasn't the only one watching. Many of the saleswomen continually dropped by to make sure they were doing okay, not that she blamed them.

He was hella hot. And seeing him trying on a mix of Wranglers and khakis kicked her body's libido into overdrive. There was no disguising his large package. Earlier she had thought it cute that he was so flustered about her helping him pick underwear. Their brief flirtation had only made her more aware of him. The power he exuded without any effort...that was intoxicating. The innate masculine strength and predatory grace drew women to him. They just didn't make men like Levi anymore. At least none that she recalled seeing.

Her breath hitched as he moved through the curtain and stood in front of her. His scent she knew was all him, since she hadn't given him any cologne to use. Tantalizing as hell, she clenched her fist so she wouldn't touch him. She blew out a deep breath and shoved her hands into her pockets, rocking back on her heels.

"What do you think?" he asked, his gaze lingering on her.

I think we should go in the curtained area, remove all clothing and see what happens from there. I'd really like to get a look at what you're boasting there.

She couldn't say that out loud, however. So she forced a smooth, non-telling smile on her face and nodded. "Looks good. Really good. I think you should get them, as well as some of the shirts you've tried on."

He nodded at her and slipped back behind the curtain. She shut her eyes and prayed for strength. Seconds later, she opened them again when he called her name.

"Ta-Mara, can you come here for a second?"

Her feet were moving even before the question registered completely. Pausing at the curtain, she glanced over to the right and saw three of the workers watching her with envious looks. Yes, she wanted to gloat. She didn't, but she wanted to.

She moved it aside and stepped in. All her breath whooshed from her lungs. Levi stood there shirtless, with the button on the jeans undone. *Ah shit. How the hell am I supposed to control myself with him looking so damn good?*

Chapter Five

Licking her lips, she gave him a smile.

"What's up?"

He held up two shirts and shrugged. "I don't know which color."

She stepped to him, took the dark blue one from his hand and pressed it against his chest. "This one. Magnifies the blue of your eyes. With the black jeans, you'll be fending off women in hordes."

His fingers curled around her wrist as he gripped her, tugging her nearer. "You like the blue?" he asked, his voice low and enticing.

"Yes. You have gorgeous eyes."

"And you're beautiful." He moved her closer still until her thin shirt brushed against his bare chest. "Absolutely beautiful."

His gaze drifted from her eyes to her lips and back again. Her heart thundered as she struggled to breathe. Another gentle caress from his amazing blue eyes then he kissed her.

He swooped in and took command. His mouth covered hers, and she whimpered at the immediate lust that swarmed her. Lord, he tasted good—a hint of mint and all man. Opening wider, she slipped her tongue into his mouth, instigating something that had been plaguing her since she'd met him. A kiss, a real kiss.

His arms banded around her, anchoring them together. Not that she had plans to go anywhere. He swept through her mouth, stroking and licking everywhere. Her legs trembled, nipples tightened in the shirt's built-in bra and her slit moistened. Lord, if he wanted to strip her and take her, she'd have zero complaints. They didn't even have to strip. She'd never been so horny before.

Heat exploded through her and she rubbed against him, loving the feel of his thickness pressing into her. He thrust his hips into her, and she moaned again. Wrapping her arms around him, she reveled in the feel of his taut skin beneath her fingertips. There was no excess fat on him, and she wanted to be able to explore him fully, take her time running her hands over his body.

She whimpered in disappointment when he stepped back. His eyes were smoky with desire and she reached up to touch his face.

"I am sorry about that."

Great. That was so not what she wanted to hear after the best kiss she'd ever received in her life.

Dropping her hands from him, she stepped back. "Right. I'll just…leave you alone then."

She turned around but didn't get anywhere. Levi grabbed her, spinning her back into his bronzed chest. Opening her mouth to ask him what was going on, she found herself embroiled in another kiss. This one was harder and more dominating. He was placing his stamp on her and she really didn't have any problem with that.

"I didn't mean it like that, Ta-Mara. I'm sorry because I did it here where I can't do anything about it. You deserve better."

She couldn't find the words. All she could do was stare at him like a fool. He cupped her jaw with callused hands.

"You've been nothing but wonderful to me and I took advantage of you. I don't understand this time at all, but you are still a woman and therefore someone who deserves to be treated better than what I did."

She moved her hands up to his shoulders. "For the record, Levi. I would have been just fine having it happen in here. Not sure how the store would feel about it, but me? I was more than ready, and I know for a fact there are some women out there who would have been just fine with it had you been with them. Now put some clothes on so we can get the rest of this shopping out of the way."

He still didn't let go. "I don't want them."

Okay, so that was *really* nice to hear. "I didn't say you did, I'm merely stating that there are some female employees here who wouldn't mind spending some quality time with you in here."

He shrugged as if he didn't give a damn. "Don't want them. I'm attracted to you."

Oh yeah, *so* damn nice to hear. Swallowing, she stepped back and made her way to the curtain. "I'll wait for you out here."

She pushed out, despite wanting to stay in there with him, and saw the changing room had been under surveillance. All three women shot her a look of pure envy before going back to their business. She wasn't about to tell them there wasn't any reason to be jealous, that nothing had happened in there.

Except that kiss. Oh yeah, that kiss that had turned her inside out and had her ready to beg for more. Just that. Throughout the rest of their shopping trip, Ta-Mara's thoughts kept going back to what happened in the dressing room with Levi. She rubbed her hand surreptitiously over her pebbled nipples and was glad her shirt wasn't fitted so didn't show how turned on she was. Levi glanced at her and she quickly lowered her hand and smiled. He went back to packing their bag as the cashier rang them out. The woman was moving slowly because she kept looking at Levi. Ta-Mara deliberately moved so she was in her line of sight and gave the woman a look that clearly told her Levi was hers.

She knew it wasn't the case but was tired after a day of women ogling and downright coming on to Levi. They acted like she was invisible or something. Ta-Mara wasn't used to feeling possessive of anyone. The cashier smiled sheepishly then focused on her job moving faster to get them out. When they were checked out, Levi pushed the full cart out to the parking lot.

"All that money." Levi met her gaze. "I'll pay you back, Ta-Mara."

"Don't worry about it." She shrugged. "You need help and that's what I am doing."

"I need to pay my own way."

"If you could, you would," Ta-Mara assured him.

Levi didn't say anything further about it. She opened the back of her SUV and he set the bags inside.

"Let's get some dinner. I know it's early but I'm hungry."

He nodded. Ta-Mara got behind the wheel of the vehicle then drove them to her favorite bar where she parked along the street. It was owned by her friend Rachel and she experienced a brief moment of panic as they crossed the parking lot until Ta-Mara remembered it was Rachel's usual day off. Although Rachel had helped her yesterday, Ta-Mara was relieved she wouldn't be in. She wanted some more time with Levi before she *officially* introduced him to her friends. Ta-Mara didn't want to get to deep into why she wanted him for now just for herself. She just did.

They went in and with it being the early dinner hour, it wasn't that busy so they were served quickly after they were seated.

As they sat there eating hamburgers, he looked at her and said, "Skin color doesn't matter anymore?"

She gazed around and saw the room from his point of view. "Not like it used to in your time but there are still instances where stuff gets ugly."

"I have much to learn."

"Well, I have a computer so you're free to read all you want on it. Or I could take you... Nope, never mind. It's probably best you read stuff online. Don't need you getting overwhelmed."

"Whatever you think best, Ta-Mara."

Shit, the way her name rolled off his tongue had her envisioning all kinds of things they could do to pass the day. Determined not to let it show on her face, she merely shrugged and ate some more fries. Even though they'd kissed, she didn't assume it would lead to anything further than that. He ate and observed. She watched him, amused by his constant look of amazement.

Not having his attention on her also helped her cool down. She ran over what they'd purchased and figured he had everything he'd need.

Look at me sitting here all calm with a man from the eighteen hundreds, as if our dining together is nothing out of the ordinary.

Huh, would you look at that. Thinking about it made her chest tighten and heart pound all that much faster. So, perhaps she wasn't as okay with it as she was trying to convince herself or her friends, as well as Levi.

And why should she be? One stormy night, Ta-Mara was reading a story about a man named Levi, a Confederate, who is willing to die for the woman he loves then the lights went out. When she got them back on, she found herself with a stranger in her building, soaking wet, who said his name is Levi and he's a Confederate.

Coincidence? Who knew? She obviously didn't. Perhaps it was time to make an appointment with a shrink. *Wonder how long they would allow me to be free before they decide to lock me up.* She shook off the thought.

She was fine as long as she didn't think of him as coming from a time before the Civil War had actually begun. So what if he shared a name with the book's hero? Who cared if he was from the same time? All that mattered was that he heal up and figure out whatever it was he needed to remember.

And in the meantime, the dude was fucking fine, so it was no hardship to be around him. She shook her head at herself and looked over to discover him avidly watching her.

"Everything okay?" she asked. "Still hungry? We can order dessert, if you like."

"I'd like that."

She handed him the menu and watched him as he skimmed the listings. When he lifted his gaze, she turned her attention to something else.

"What are you having?"

"The lemon cream cake. You?"

"This cheesecake sounds delicious. I've always enjoyed it."

"I heard theirs is good here."

"You've never had it?"

"Not a cheesecake fan." She pursed her lips. "Although if it's deep fried bites, I'll make an exception."

His grin set those butterflies a-fluttering in her belly again. It wasn't fair, really, for him to have such magnetism. Even in here, people looked at him. She understood — there was just something in the way Levi carried himself which demanded attention.

Levi stared at Ta-Mara as he ate his cheesecake. The more time he spent in her company, the more he found himself falling for her. It didn't make sense. He'd not even known her for a full two days yet in his heart, he *knew*.

Flashing back to the day he'd almost died, he recalled the voice of the woman in his ear and her exact words. *"Levi, you are a man whose love is pure. In a world divided by color, you never faltered. Despite everything put to you, you stayed true to your heart and never turned your back on your soul mate. For that, I tell you this… Rest now. Fear not, for you shall be returned to the arms of your love. Trust your heart, for it won't lead you astray."*

Which brought him back to his current dilemma. Returned to the arms of his love. Calliope. Not Ta-

Mara. But if he were to trust his heart, it was pointing him in the direction of his lovely host. He hadn't lied earlier about wishing he could go farther with the kissing.

He homed in on her mouth as she ate her cream cake. She had such plump lips. He was already addicted to them. Kissing her in the small room he'd changed in wasn't something he'd soon forget. She'd been so responsive. He'd nearly forgotten anything but the feel of her against him.

And now, how she ate was sending him to distraction. He shook his head to clear his thoughts. This wasn't like him at all. What he was experiencing was for young, untried men. Boys even.

He was well past the age when a pretty face turned his head. Wasn't he?

Not when that face belonged to Ta-Mara. He blew out a breath and finished his dessert.

"You ready?"

Snapped from his reverie, he glanced up to see her watching him.

"Yes, ma'am."

He watched, disgruntled, as she paid for their meal. After she signed a receipt—he'd already asked how she paid with a small card—they got up to leave. Levi noticed how other men stared at her and he moved up closer to her. With a smug grin, he settled his hand on the small of her back.

The bare skin that met his palm sent fire surging through his veins. He'd forgotten her shirt had an open back. Staring down at her, he loved the difference in their skin tones. He could make out the bumps of her spine and he had this urge to drag his tongue up her skin. Then back down and around until… He stopped that line of thought.

Holding the door for her, he followed her out into the muggy early evening sun. His gaze fixated on the simple bow that split the dark skin of her back as it kept her shirt on by connecting the top and sides. Not that he'd mind it falling off, of course, he wouldn't want any others to see her. Her pale yellow shirt beautifully contrasted her skin tone. All it would take to release would be grab a single strand and pull.

He moved his gaze down to rest along the top of her jeans, which rode low on her hips. Damn, she made him think things that one shouldn't be debating doing in public.

As they walked down the street to where she'd parked her car, he took in the sights and sounds of this city. Things had changed so much, it really was a bit of a shock. He'd spent a good deal of time playing with her electronics at her house. It amazed him, what people had been able to accomplish.

He hoped for a closer look at her car. *No, wait, she called it a sports utility vehicle.* A Mariner. He wanted to try driving it but she'd shaken her head and said something about rules. He wasn't a fan of riding in it with others racing around them and coming at them, their speeds high.

But he looked to her and she didn't seem the least bit fazed by any of it so he forced himself to copy that. Even now as they streaked by, she barely paid them any mind, just continued on.

At the lot, she unlocked the door and got in. He followed suit and she got them on the way. When she pulled into her drive, he sat up and smiled. He liked her house. It brought him great peace.

Gathering the bags, he then trailed her into the house and up the stairs to the room she'd allowed him to use.

"Why are you helping me?" he asked, as she set her items down.

"Would you rather I didn't?"

"No. I'm just curious as to why you would help a man who by all accounts came into your life dressed as a Confederate."

"You *were* dressed as a Confederate. I have the clothing downstairs to prove it." She crossed her arms and sat on the bed, beginning to empty out the nearest bag. "Still couldn't ignore you. You looked lost and like you could use some goodwill."

He couldn't argue that. "But you could have let me go to the hospital."

"You didn't seem too keen on that idea." She stacked his pants beside her and his shirts by them.

Levi moved to her side, the fading light of day sending in a faint golden hue through the windows. Reaching out, he cupped a hand around her cheek and tipped her face up to him. She gripped his shirt in her lap but didn't move, holding his gaze without blinking.

"You are a unique woman, Ta-Mara."

She attempted to shake her head, but his grip refused to allow her that. "Anyone would have helped."

"No. You are unlike anyone I've known." He put his second hand on her face. The smooth skin was such a temptation.

"I…I should let you put your things away. I'll set up my computer so you can look up whatever you wish to try and catch up on."

He dropped his hands and let her stand. However, he refused to move back so she had to press up along his body. When she did, he gripped her hips and lowered his mouth to hers. Despite the fire in his body, which demanded he claim her as his own, he kept the exchange gentle.

Nibbling along her lips, he waited for her to open and allow him entrance. She did and he sank his tongue into her heat. In and out he stroked, licking where he could reach, allowing her taste to embed itself onto him.

Gathering her tight, he wound his arms around her waist before deepening the kiss. He thought he had it all under control, thought he could keep it together and maintain some semblance of restraint. How wrong he'd been.

A small whimper slipped from her mouth into his and that was what snapped any remaining self-discipline he might have had. The urges that had been hounding him since he'd woken up on the floor of her shop now overflowed. He made short work of the single bow tie along her back. Going around to her front, he grabbed the bottom corner and tugged.

The pale yellow material fell away and he drew back to stare at her exposed body. Her breasts were perfect, full yet pert. Her nipples the color of dark chocolate, were pebbled and pointed. He cupped her breasts in his hands as he hefted their weight. As he teased the points, she trembled beneath his touch and he dipped his head.

She gasped aloud as he took nipple in his mouth. She pressed his head closer as her back arched. He sucked, tugged and rolled the nipple. Releasing it with a pop, he blew over the wetness before turning his attention to her other breast and applying the same treatment.

She gripped his shoulders, her short nails digging into his skin. Pushing her back onto the bed, he lowered his body over hers. She cradled him between her legs and moved her hands to his back, clenching the material of his new shirt. Back and forth, he moved between her breasts, unable to get enough. Her moans and mewls continually encouraged him.

When his shirt bunched up around his shoulders, he looked at her.

"Off," she demanded.

He didn't disappoint. Rising up enough to rip it off, he threw his shirt over his shoulder before he kissed her again. Her breasts, damp from his ministrations, pressed into his chest. She ran her hands over his back before grabbing his ass. He flexed his hips, driving his hard length against the seam of her jeans.

Levi stared at her. Her eyes swirled with desire, her lips were parted, emitting small, panting breaths. Her tongue snuck out, tracing a path and drawing his gaze back to her tempting mouth. He thrust again and she shook her head.

"Keep that up and I'm going to come, now."

"That is a problem." He ground into her, making another high-pitched moan slip free. "I want to feel you come. I want to taste your cream."

She shuddered and he nipped her chin before he moved down to make short work of removing her jeans. Her clothing soon joined his on the floor. Naked, he dropped to his knees, ignoring his demanding cock. It jerked as his gaze landed upon her pussy.

Very nearly hairless, she had a small strip above her dark lips which glistened with dampness. He leaned forward and dragged his tongue along her slit.

"Fuck!" she cried out, her hips bucking up against his mouth.

He slipped his hands under her thighs and hauled her closer, draping her legs over his shoulders. Using the flat of his tongue, he lapped at her—up and down. Circling her clit, he held her where he wanted her. Ta-Mara's taste flooded him. Rich, heady and oh-so addicting.

Her thighs clamped around his head, blocking her cries of pleasure. He moved one of his hands and dipped a finger inside her. She was so tight, and he took his time working his way in until his digit was buried completely in her. Her internal muscles rippled around him and he groaned. Back and forth, he moved his finger, until he slipped in a second one.

Thrusting with his fingers while his tongue worked on her clit, he fucked her. Her hips undulated faster and he knew she was close. Replacing his fingers with his tongue, he stabbed it deep inside her as he pressed his thumb against her clit. That did it.

Her release hit him. He continued to lick until there was no more for him to have. With care, he lowered her legs and kissed his way up her body until he reached her mouth. Hesitating right before their lips touched, he murmured, "Taste yourself on my kiss, Ta-Mara."

She drew hard on his tongue, her body writhing against his. He groaned as her slickness coated his shaft.

"Inside," she panted, releasing his back and reaching toward the side of her bed. "Just…protection."

It took him a moment for the word to sink in. He opened the drawer she'd gone for and pulled out a small, square package. When she took it from him and pushed on his chest, he got the idea and backed away.

She tore it open and licked her lips as she closed around his cock with one hand. It bobbed in her hand. "So big." Her voice had a dreamy quality to it. "So thick."

She swiped off the pearled drops on the top of his shaft then rolled on the condom. She sent him an encouraging smile as she lay back.

"I want to return the favor, but right now, I need you inside me."

He wasn't about to argue with her. Grabbing the base of his length, he moved nearer and slid home with one smooth push. Heaven engulfed him as her wet heat closed about him. He had to hold still in his struggle not to lose it.

She watched him through lowered lashes. "Move, Levi."

"Give me a minute, Ta-Mara, or I'm going to embarrass myself."

Her smile was intoxicating. "So we just start over then." She tightened the walls of her pussy around him, making them ripple along his cock.

He clenched his jaw and slowly withdrew until only the head of his cock remained in her. She watched him, eyes unwavering. He flexed his hips and drove fully into her again.

A sexy moan spilled from her lips. "More," she said.

So he gave her more, realizing he'd never felt like this before with anyone.

Chapter Six

Ta-Mara wanted to shatter into a million little pieces as Levi thrust his thickness deep inside her. Nothing had ever felt so good. He stretched her, filled her and had her writhing beneath him.

She placed the soles of her feet flat upon the mattress and arched up to allow him a better angle. Eyes locked on his, she moved with him. They found a rhythm they both liked and allowed it to take them away.

In and out. Back and forth.

Harder. Faster. Deeper.

His body was covered in sweat as he continued to pound away, catapulting her to her much desired release point even while withholding his own. Tendons stood out on his neck, his jaw was clenched tightly, and his gaze seemed to set her on fire whenever he placed it on her.

Levi dug his fingers into her hips and his strokes remained unrelenting. She reached out and clamped her hands around his forearms. Her eyes fluttered shut until he delivered two sharp thrusts.

"Eyes on me," he demanded.

She captured her lower lip in her teeth and managed to drag her lids up. Such primitive emotions washed over his face. Those amazing blue eyes singed her and she didn't quite understand the feelings that were set off inside her. This was more than just sex — granted really, *really* great sex — happening.

"Levi," she said.

He picked up his speed again and her words slipped from thought. When he bent down, she moved her hands to his shoulders and dug her nails into the tight skin over his muscles.

A growl, tinged with danger, rumbled up from his chest and she turned her lips into his torso. Finding a flat nipple, she flicked her tongue over it before grazing it with her teeth. He tensed and thrust faster. Encouraged, she did it again — and again.

He wrapped one of his hands into her hair and she gasped at the sting. She nipped at him in return before moaning as he stroked deeper.

"Oh...I... You... Need..." There was no way she could formulate any complete sentences. Nothing else existed aside from the pleasure she was experiencing. Her orgasm ran over her like a wave pounding the shoreline.

Her back bowed as she screamed her release into the sweaty skin of his chest. Moments later she felt his cock pulse within her and his roar echoed her cry. A few mini orgasms shook her and she gasped at the feeling. Before she could recover, the hand in her hair tugged her head back and he slammed his lips over hers.

Winding her arms around his neck, she wove her fingers through the damp strands of his hair and kissed him with all the passion she had. Their hearts both pounded out a fierce rhythm and she wrapped her legs around him, wanting…craving to be closer to him.

Levi rolled them over and held her as tight, as she did him. Ending the kiss, she closed her eyes, tucked her head beneath his chin and breathed deeply. The scents of sweat, sex and man not only filled her but soothed her.

"Are you okay?" His rasped question had her eyes opening again.

"Perfect. You?"

His grip on her tightened. She loved it, being held as if she was the most important thing. The last man she'd been with had hated to cuddle. He was more of a four-pump then finish man.

"Perfect."

She smiled and allowed her eyes to close again. She had no energy and definitely no desire to go anywhere at this present moment. Who knew when this would happen again? Why not allow herself to enjoy the moment?

* * * *

She woke to the intensity of the orgasm washing over her. She had her hands dug into the hair of the man between her legs who'd just brought her such pleasure.

"Levi!"

He moved up over her and sank back inside her. "Yes?"

Whatever she'd been about to say no longer mattered. That was how it went throughout the night—some rest and more exploring between the two of them.

When she woke in the morning, it was to find herself sprawled over a hard male body. It took her a few moments to convince herself it hadn't been a dream. She didn't want to move but unfortunately, she had to get up and go into work.

Slowly, she untangled herself from the blankets and climbed off the man whose bed she shared. He still slept, the stubble on his face only adding to his allure. Levi lay on his back, one arm out—which she'd been lying on—the other bent and partially covering his face. With her lower lip caught in her teeth, she stared at him.

What had she done to get a man like him in her bed? A perfect specimen who was like the men she read about in her romance novels. She shook her head and made her way downstairs to her room and subsequently to the bathroom where she showered and took care of everything else. Once dry, she stepped back into her bedroom and went to her closet to decide on today's outfit.

Deciding there was no point in waking him since he still slept up there, she planned to fix some breakfast first and let him sleep longer. Dressing in a dark gray handkerchief-hem skirt where the longer parts were in front and back while the shorter stopped right below the knee, she combined it with an off the shoulder purple and gold LSU Tigers shirt. She'd wear some slip-on shoes with it but they were by the door.

In the kitchen, she got to work and when the biscuits were in the oven cooking, she set the table, poured the juice then finally decided to wake him.

Yes, she was nervous about it. Most mornings after didn't go so well for her. *Didn't know you were such a pussy,* her subconscious sniped.

Apparently she was, for she really delayed going to his room. Breakfast would be done in two minutes and here she remained, in the kitchen like a baby — scared of her own damn shadow.

No, not quite, it wasn't a shadow that had her freaking out. It was the man sleeping in her guest room. Levi.

"Buck up, LeBreaux. Face your bed."

"Why are you needing to face your bed? Is that a new expression I should know the meaning of?"

She jumped at the unexpected sound of Levi's voice behind her. Whirling around, hand pressing to her chest covering her pounding heart, she gasped. Then gasped again for an entirely different reason.

It in no way could be fair to the rest of the world for someone to look so blasted good. A pair of his new jeans hung low on his lean hips and he'd covered his upper body in a dark blue T-shirt, which only amplified the hue of his amazing eyes. He also wore his brand new footwear, black rebar premium waterproof scuff proof Timberland boots.

Damnation!

She plastered a smile on her face, hoping it didn't look as pathetic as she believed it did. "Nothing, just talking to myself. How'd you sleep?"

The sapphires darkened as he stared at her. "I didn't think I could ever sleep so well." He stepped toward her. "But you weren't there when I woke."

She swallowed. "I got up a bit ago. Showered and fixed some breakfast, which should be ready just about now."

She prayed for the timer to go off on the oven so she could have something to do that didn't include her extremely overactive imagination having her jumping in his arms and asking him to take her right here in her kitchen. Closer and closer he came, until all his hardness was up in her personal space. She kind of liked it that way, if she were being honest with herself.

The way he studied her face, with intensity and focus, had her belly in knots and a wetness forming between her legs. God, he looked hungry and it seemed as though she was the only thing on the menu. The beeping from her oven jolted her and she backed away before withdrawing the sheet of biscuits.

"Ready to eat?"

He stood there in silence and watched her as she put the last bit of food on the table.

"I have to work today, so I'm not quite sure what you want to do. I could set you up with the computer and you could use that to look up things, or I could take you somewhere if you'd like to do that? Up to you."

He stood before her again. "Up to me?"

She could smell the faint lingering scent of aftershave and shaving cream on him. Goodness all she wanted to do was bury her face into his neck, hold him and let whatever happened, happen.

"Yes. You. It's a bit of a walk from here to town so I don't want you stranded out here if you'd rather be in there. There's food here in the house so you would be fine that way, or I could give you some money so you could eat in town." She forced herself away from him and backed up to her chair. "Think about it while we eat."

"I know where I want to be."

She sat, wiped her hands—with damn damp palms—on her skirt. "Where's that?"

He spun her in the chair and boxed her in with his body. Face lowered to hers, he said, "With you." Then he kissed her.

It sucked every remaining logical thought from her mind. The only thing she could grasp was how much she wanted him again. Fire lit up her blood and made it sing. Leaning into him, she pressed closer, needing more of what he offered. His deep rumble rippled through her and she whimpered in return.

Much to her frustration, he ended the kiss before she was ready. But to be fair, he was a man she could kiss forever. He ran the back of his hand down her cheek and she found herself nodding.

"With me."

"Exactly." Another short fast kiss then Levi took his seat across from her. Before she'd even recovered.

While they ate, she tried to find reasons he shouldn't go with her. Being a distraction was at the top of her list, but it wasn't his fault she had a hard time controlling her lust. As she finished off her eggs, she wondered why she even pretended to think on it. She wanted him with her. Bottom line.

* * * *

Levi sat at the small table, which was stacked high with books. Ta-Mara had him cleaning off the stickers on these ones that had been brought in by other people. It was a mundane task and monotonous. He didn't mind so much, since he was with Ta-Mara.

He got to see her interact with the people who entered the shop. They stayed busy. He was impressed at how many customers came in, how nice they were to her and more. To him, it was obvious how much she loved it here and it showed. She had this glow about her as she moved among the books, helping people find what they sought or putting up stock.

The door jangled and in walked a trio of women. Catlike smiles lifted their lips when they laid eyes upon him. He knew the look all too well and shifted in his seat as he gave them a nod.

"Well, well," the middle one said, sauntering toward him. "Ta-Mara didn't say she had any new help, much less anyone who looked like you. And who *are* you?"

His manners had been drilled into him and he couldn't stop himself even if he wanted to. He pushed to his feet and gave them a slight bow. "Levi Madison."

"Hello, Levi Madison. I'm Jasmine."

Her perfume reached him as he shook her hand and he had to fight a frown. It was highly unpleasant, burning his nose and eyes. "Ma'am."

She laughed. "No need to call me that. Jasmine works just fine."

Ta-Mara walked into view from the back room, more books in her hand. Levi watched her expression and wasn't sure what to think. He didn't see any jealousy in her face about him being there with those three. Instead, she smiled.

"Hey. What brings all y'all out here?"

Jasmine winked at him. "You didn't tell us you had such hot help."

Setting the books on the counter, Ta-Mara shook her head. "Behave. Have you met?"

"I have." Jasmine tucked some of her platinum blonde hair behind an ear.

"Levi, these are my friends, Jasmine, Rachel and Heather." She hugged them all with obvious affection. "Ladies, this is Levi."

He shook hands with them all. Jasmine was the thinnest and the biggest flirt. Rachel had dark brown skin and a brilliant smile, her hair in corkscrew curls.

Heather was the shy one, a bit heavy, and her skin was the palest.

"So," Ta-Mara said, stepping behind the counter, "what's up?"

"We wanted to see if you wanted to go out tonight. Louis' for some karaoke and drinks." Rachel was shoving her hands into her jeans as she asked the question. "You can bring Levi as well."

Jasmine winked at him. "That would be awesome. I'd love to see him up on stage, singing."

"I'm game." Ta-Mara faced him. "You up for it?"

He had no idea what karaoke was but he would go along to keep that excited look on her face. "Of course."

"Great. See you usual time. Come on, girls. I need to shop." Jasmine led them out, each of the women waving as they left.

He breathed easier once they were gone.

"Are you sure you want to go?"

He returned his attention to the woman near him. "I have no idea what this karaoke is, so I'm anxious to find out."

"Shit, I'm sorry, I forgot that. You wouldn't know that word." Stepping to his side where the computer was, she opened up what she called an Internet browser window and typed in a few words. "Here you go. All about karaoke."

He sat, trailing a hand along the curve of her spine. "Thank you."

She worked while he read, occasionally stopping to glance at her.

"You get up on stage and sing songs?"

"Yes. It's a lot of fun. Not everyone can sing well, but it's a very fun experience. Some nights they have contests for who does it the best." She glanced at him. "Do you sing?"

"I don't think so. There's not much time for it."

"Suppose not." A quick frown was wiped away. "Again, it's up to you if you wish to go. You may not want to sit in a smoky old tavern with all of us."

"I would love to accompany you. You have very colorful friends."

She laughed. "Jasmine is something else. Don't worry, her flirting is harmless with you."

He wasn't so sure but he had no wish to bring more attention to the fact her friend looked at him as if he was her last meal. Closing the window on the computer, he got back to work. After they ate lunch, work resumed and he was in one of the aisles when he heard the doorbell announce yet another person.

"Hey!"

Levi peeked around the corner at her enthusiastic greeting. His eyes narrowed dangerously as the man there pressed a kiss to her cheek as he held Ta-Mara with blatant intimacy. Stopping the growl from escaping, he returned to the books in his hands.

"I didn't think to see you today," she was saying. "How are you doing?"

"Good. They let me out early and I wanted to come by and see you. Everything going okay?"

"Fine, fine." She stepped back. "I have a friend in from…out of town who I brought in with me so he wouldn't have to be bored at the house. He's helping out. Levi," she called out.

Shelving the final book, he walked up to the front. "Yes, Ta-Mara?" He so wanted to haul her into his arms and kiss her. Place his claim over her before this other man.

"This is Reggie. Reggie, my friend Levi."

Reggie. That was his name? This man stood as tall as he did, muscular build with dark skin, a tightly clipped beard, large eyes and a possessive look on his face when he put his gaze on Ta-Mara. Something Levi really didn't like.

"Nice to meet you," Reggie said, holding out his hand.

Levi shook it. "And you."

"Where'd you meet Ta-Mara?"

Unsure how she wanted the question answered, he looked at her.

"We met on a rainy night, Reggie. Levi's just passing through. He's on his way back home."

"Where's home?"

There was no disguising the protectiveness in that question. Levi found himself bristling in return.

"Be nice, Reggie." Ta-Mara rolled her eyes and smacked him in the shoulder. "This is not needed.

Levi didn't have any plans to answer so he asked his own question instead after she went toward the back. "How do you know Ta-Mara?"

"We met in college." A shrug. "You know how that is, right? Long nights in a room with one another."

The implication had him fighting the desire to put his fist into Reggie's face. Levi knew he had no right to be upset. He had a past with Calliope. Wait, when had that just become a past? He was to be reunited with her again. Right?

He merely nodded, not trusting his voice. Or the words that would come out of his mouth. All he knew was he didn't want to make her work environment difficult. And he was extremely well versed in keeping his feelings for someone hidden.

"So I've known her for years. Funny, she's never mentioned you."

"She's never mentioned you to me, either," Levi replied.

"How long are you staying?"

"Not sure. I have to see how long I can."

"And where are you staying?"

He smiled arrogantly. "With Ta-Mara."

Reggie's expression closed up. "I see." The man walked toward the back and Levi sat back at the desk, picking up the next book and cleaning it.

Not too much later, Reggie left without so much as a good-bye and Ta-Mara came with yet another stack of books.

"What did you say to him?" she asked.

"About what? I just answered his questions. That was all."

"Nothing about how I found you? Or how you got here?"

"Nothing. He wanted to know how long I was staying and *where*."

"So you said?"

"With you."

"That explains his attitude." She shook her head and bent to pick something up off the floor.

"Attitude?"

"Yeah, attitude." She leaned over the counter and threw the paper away. "You know, all the bristling and posturing y'all were doing."

"He merely seemed a bit protective of you. I wouldn't say he was bristling and posturing."

She gave him a pointed look. "I was talking about *both* of you."

"I was a gentleman."

"Right, I saw that. Y'all both were so nice."

"Who is he to you?"

Her eyebrows shot up at his question and he realized he may have overstepped his bounds. Still, he didn't back down. He sat at the desk waiting for her answer.

"Reggie's my boss and a great friend."

"He said you went to college together." *Times have changed if they let blacks go to school. And I sure do not recall women and men at the same one.*

"We did. We were in the same dorm and began hanging out."

Not really anything he wanted to think about. That man shouldn't be touching his woman's body—at all. Swallowing back his rising jealousy, Levi cleared his throat.

"How did he come to own this shop?"

"It was his mother's and he took it over when she died."

"I'm sorry he lost his mother."

She had a sad smile on her face. "Yes, it was hard. She died in Katrina."

He shook his head.

"Sorry, Katrina was a huge hurricane that came ashore and...let's just say it was pretty damn catastrophic."

"You name hurricanes now?"

She nodded. "Yes."

His mind wasn't sure what to do about that bit of information. He knew about them but he'd never thought to give them names.

Someone else walked in and their conversation ceased again. Levi got back into the stack of books he had to finish cleaning before they could be recorded and shelved or put in the back.

* * * *

At the end of the workday, Levi was again glad when they pulled into the driveway of her house.

"We'll clean up and eat before going to meet my friends, but first..." Ta-Mara parked the car but didn't turn off the engine. "We give you your first driving lesson."

"You'll let me drive? What about the rules?"

"Well one of the rules is you need to know how to drive, so I'm going to teach you."

"Okay." He wiped his hand up and down his thighs. "What do I need to do first?"

"I'm going to show you by example and explain what I am doing. We'll keep it to just around my house. It has more than enough space for you to drive around without doing any damage."

"Damage?"

"Just in case." She patted his thigh. "You'll be fine."

Levi nodded. Ta-Mara started to drive again and explained what she was doing. He listened intently and asked questions. When it was finally time for him to get behind the wheel, Levi was nervous but determined to master learning to drive. He gripped the wheel then did as she said. Levi pressed down on the pedal and the car jumped forward.

"Not so heavy on the gas. Gently," Ta-Mara said from the passenger seat.

"Sorry." Levi eased up then continued moving slowly. "This is interesting."

"You'll get used to it," Ta-Mara replied.

Levi wasn't sure of that but he'd give it a chance. He drove for almost an hour then they returned home to make dinner. The teasing, which had begun during prep, continued as they ate—after which they parted ways to get ready to meet up with her friends.

Once he'd cleaned up, Levi descended the stairs. He stopped abruptly, watching as Ta-Mara spoke with a man in the doorway. When he said something too low for Levi to hear, Ta-Mara laughed and hugged him. Levi clenched his fist and fought a growl. She was entirely too friendly and seemed to always be hugging men. Ta-Mara closed the door and turned.

"Oh, shit you scared me. I didn't know you were there. You should have said something and I would have introduced you to my friend."

"Another friend." Levi was wondering how many men she was friends with as she hugged them so familiarly.

"Yes." She came to him and held out a folded item. "He brought by your wallet."

"I don't have a wallet." He knew what that was from the TV.

"You do now."

"What is it for? I don't have anything to put in it. No identification, money or those little cards you use to pay for stuff." He accepted the item and opened it.

"You have identification now." Ta-Mara was smug. "Also have a social security card, birth certificate and all sorts of other things you need so people won't know you're not from this time. You have a history so that if people look you up, they will be able to find out things about you, even a job history. I had him make it eclectic, since I wasn't sure what you like to do. I have it all here in this packet. The wallet has the basics for you, even a few bucks so you can have money. I didn't get any credit cards for you because that's something you have to decide, if you want to have credit. You have spectacular credit by the way, just so you have a credit history. I'll explain what taking credit cards means later."

Levi was awed at his likeness on the driver's license. It had his birthday but with the wrong year, which he figured was understandable since they couldn't put that year without raising flags. It had his height, eye color and the address was Ta-Mara's house. He took out some of the things from the wallet. There was a library card, medical card and other items.

"How did you do this?" He glanced at her. "This isn't legal, Ta-Mara." He'd seen enough on television to know that.

"Not exactly." She shrugged. "But you needed to have proof of who you are. Maybe later in your time, you won't need it. But we need something for the present or it'd cause problems if the need arose that you needed to give information or proof of who you are. So I had a buddy of mine set you up."

"You know criminals." He put back the items in the wallet.

"No, I don't. I just know people who can get things that are needed to help someone. It might skirt the law, but if it is necessary, we do it." Ta-Mara placed her hand on his. "Levi, you needed these things, at least on a temporary basis, so I got them for you."

"I did." He held up the wallet. "Thank you. Is this why you took my picture and asked that stuff about me?"

"Yes." Ta-Mara went to the table by the door. "I'll put the rest of the packet of information here. We'll go through it later and I'll explain what it is then."

"You keep saying it is temporary that I need this." Levi studied her. "I don't have any identification, Ta-Mara. It didn't time travel with me." He smiled.

"There is no such thing as time travel."

"Then how do you explain my being here?" Levi studied her.

"A blip, or maybe you just lost your memory and will regain it. Then, for all we know, you have a wife and a boat load of kids."

"I don't have any of those things." Levi reached for her. "I thought you believed me when I told you what time I was from?"

"I'm still struggling with it." She lifted her hands and rolled her eyes. "It doesn't fit my rational mind to believe such a thing. But the way you are so sure is convincing, and I just don't know, Levi." She rubbed her fingers through her hair. "How does it sound to someone that you came from the eighteen hundreds and time jumped somehow to be here?"

"Like my current circumstance." Levi slid the wallet into his pocket then his hands into them. "This isn't easy for me, either. I thought I was dead." He could still feel the ache from the noose on his neck.

Ta-Mara's gaze softened and she moved closer to him. She touched his neck. "It's fading but I'm sure the memories are still fresh."

They are. I lost my Calliope and now I'm here – with a woman who makes me want her when I vowed to love one woman.

"It'll be okay, Levi." Ta-Mara lowered her hand and gripped his palm. "Let's go meet my friends and relax a little. We won't worry about what time you're from or how you got here. It'll work itself out. At this time, there is nothing we can do and no way we can know why you ended up in the bookstore, and I found you."

"You're right." He decided to leave it for now. "Show me what this karaoke is."

"You're in for an adventure." Ta-Mara led him toward the door.

Levi was sure he was, but it had nothing to do with where they were going and had everything to do with the woman he was with. Ta-Mara was quickly becoming important to him and he was powerless to stop it. *Hell, he didn't want to.*

Chapter Seven

Ta-Mara watched Levi surreptitiously as they sat at their booth in the back of Louis'. His gaze constantly moved around the joint as if he was unsure what he truly saw. She suspected for him it was a bit shocking. There were a few times during the day she'd had to remind herself he wasn't from the here and now.

What she'd told him earlier was the truth. She didn't know what to believe moment to moment. On the one hand, she thought he was indeed from the past, then on the other, she thought he was from this time but had lost his memory. To Ta-Mara it didn't matter which year he was from in either scenario — if he time traveled back or regained his memory — he would go to whatever life he had, leaving her behind. She had to make sure to be aware that what they had was temporary and she couldn't get attached. Ta-Mara glanced at him and wondered if it was already too late.

He sat beside her on the outside of the booth. Jasmine, Heather and Rachel had all pouted when he wouldn't sit in the middle of them, however he'd been adamant on being where he was. She could feel his strong leg pressing against hers, feel the denim against her smooth skin.

Levi had worked hard all day with her and after their driving lesson, he'd helped with dinner. Then they'd come out here and he looked a bit uncomfortable. She leaned toward him, loving the scent of his body—it brought back memories of waking in his arms.

"You okay?" she asked in his ear.

"This is all"—he leaned closer, brushing her shoulder—"a lot to process."

She patted him on the thigh. Gods, he was strong. Nothing moved beneath her palm. She shook her head. "You'll be fine. Let me know if you want to leave."

"I'm looking forward to you doing this karaoke." His hand covered hers under the table and he squeezed gently before releasing it.

"Won't be long. I believe we're up after two more people." She needed to focus or she was going to sound like a dying whale while her thoughts were solely on the man beside her, and what his touch did to her.

He reached for his drink. "Is it always like this here?" This question was louder and more for the group.

"Pretty much," Rachel said, toasting him with her drink.

"And even though they can't sing, these people still get up there?"

"I'm still shocked you've never been to karaoke before, man," Jasmine said, finishing off her beer and waving for another.

Ta-Mara kept her counsel. It wasn't easy for her to imagine either, however, considering this man had just kind of *appeared* in the back of the shop—from another time—his not knowing karaoke didn't seem such a big thing to her. She stifled a chuckle at herself. In this instance, she believed he was from another time. Her mind was so scattered on what was true about him.

"Oh, oh, we're next." Rachel slid out first and the others followed.

Ta-Mara started to slide around as well, only to find Levi had stood up to allow her out that way. Sort of. He remained close so she had to brush by him to get out. His gaze burned as he looked down into her eyes. She was so tempted to touch him, she had to dig her nails into the palms of her hands. This wasn't the time or place for that.

"Be right back," she muttered, leaning back over the table for her drink. Another good-sized swallow then she was ready to go.

They stepped up on stage to a thunderous applause. Thoughts of Levi slipped into the back of her mind and she focused on the time with her friends. The familiarity of standing up with them and putting on a show for the crowd was front and center.

The music started and they began singing. It took her a moment before she realized they'd picked *Survivor* by Destiny's Child. That wasn't the song she'd been expecting. They did two songs then she hopped off and headed back while her friends were going to do a few more. She detoured to the ladies, then came out to head to her table.

Rachel and Heather flanked her, stopping then taking her close to the wall. Ta-Mara figured it had been coming from the looks they had been giving her all night. She leaned on the wall, sliding her hands into her pockets. From where she stood, she couldn't see Levi since there were people blocking her.

"He looks better than when we saw him," Heather said.

Ta-Mara focused on her friends. "I let him rest as you stated. After his swoon—thanks for putting that word in my head, by the way—he was fine."

"He *is* fine." Rachel wiggled her eyebrows.

"He is that." Ta-Mara clicked her tongue. "When we went shopping yesterday, women were all over him."

"And you wanted to punch them or snatch them bald." Heather laughed. "I would be the same way with a man like that."

"Me too." Rachel bared her teeth. "I'd tell them to back off, he's mine."

"Levi isn't mine."

"You look at him like he is." Heather moved closer, pressing her shoulder against hers. "What about him being a time traveler? Do you still believe that?"

"I have no idea what I believe." Ta-Mara slid an arm around each of them and hugged them. "Thanks for earlier in the store when you acted like you didn't know him."

"No problem. We said we'd act like that." Rachel put her arm behind Ta-Mara's back.

Heather did the same. "He really is gorgeous. Jasmine about swallowed her tongue when she saw him earlier."

"Yeah. I saw how she was looking at him." Ta-Mara frowned, thinking of her friend who would have no qualms about making a play for Levi. Heather and Rachel she didn't have to think that about. "She needs to cool it."

"I'm thinking she's not the only one you should be concerned about." Rachel gestured her head sideways.

Ta-Mara glanced over. With the people next to them moving away, she had a clear view of their table where Levi waited. She frowned at the sight of the women lingering around Levi. *I understand it, for sure, but damn if I like it.*

"Yep. In no way you think he's yours," Heather said dryly.

Rachel snickered. "She's having visions of bald heads."

"I hate you both." Ta-Mara released them before she poked them each in their side.

They laughed then said simultaneously, "You love us."

"I have no idea why." She shook her head then started forward. "I'm going back to our table."

Smoothing out her expression, she walked up as if not a care in the world — or that she didn't care that he had other women practically serving their breasts to him with a smile. *Nope, not a problem.* Granted, in her mind, she'd not only killed but disemboweled the lot of them a few times over.

He stood and reached out a hand when she approached. Pasting a smile on her face, she took it and allowed him to seat her. The women glared at her but walked off.

"Offers for the evening?"

"Are all women so…forward now?"

He hadn't released her hand and his thumb stroked tantalizingly along the back of hers. It was hard to remember that there had been other women near him when he touched her. Looked at her. Hell, when she thought about him. Yes, she had it bad. Her libido had been kick-started and it felt as if the switch to turn it off had been broken.

"Some are. So" — she lifted the numerous napkins with numbers on them — "calling any of them?"

"No." He voiced his refusal so fast it surprised her a bit.

"You may hit it off with one of them."

He turned from the stage and his gaze bore into hers. Intense. Arousing. Determined. "Is there a reason you are trying to push me toward another woman? Do you want me gone?"

"No." *Oh God, no.* "I just don't want you to think because we..." She gestured with her hand and searched for the words.

"Fucked long into the night?" His words slid along her skin, decadent and tempting.

Her slit grew damp and she struggled not to writhe on the seat. "Did what we did, you have to worry about my feelings. If one of them interests you, go for it." See, she could do the whole not being jealous thing. Thankfully, no one could see inside her for it would tell a completely different story.

"As I told you in the clothing store, none of them excite me as you do, Ta-Mara. Not a single one of them does this to me."

He moved her hand to settle upon his crotch and she felt his hard cock. Heat surged through her. She squeezed his length, loving how his gaze darkened.

"That's because of you, Ta-Mara. You. I want nothing more than to bend you over this table, flip that skirt up and fuck you until you lose your voice. Until your legs can no longer hold you. Then I want to flip you on your back and begin again."

"Damn, honey, if you don't want to take him home, I will."

The intruder was a woman who stood there in next to nothing, fanning her flushed face with her hand. Normally, Ta-Mara would be embarrassed by this but right now, she was too damn turned on. So she smiled, her hand still upon Levi, who never looked from her.

"Oh, I'm taking him home. Make no mistake about that."

"Want one more?" the woman asked.

"No thanks."

She shrugged. "Can't blame a woman for trying." Then she slipped away, but Ta-Mara had already focused back on Levi.

He slid closer to her, resting his arm along the back of the seat. Lowering his head, he nuzzled the curve of her neck where it met her shoulder. Each touch of his lips made her tremble. It wouldn't take much for him to push her over the edge. Not here, not like this, especially with his words reverberating in her head.

Through barely open eyes, she saw her friends returning and moved her hand. He didn't retreat. He lowered his arm so it boxed her in more, not that she had plans on going anywhere.

"Isn't that looking cozy?" Rachel winked as she slipped in the booth right up to her. "So, Levi. Are we going to get to hear you sing?"

Jasmine and Heather nodded while they slid into the booth across from them.

"Maybe some other time."

"Ta-Mara, get him up there to sing—or go sing with him." Jasmine had a big smile.

"Come on, you two. We're here to have fun." Heather smirked at her from across the table.

Ta-Mara glanced to her right and caught Levi's gaze. She didn't want to push it. He wasn't familiar with the music they played. Although he had been listening avidly to the radio—country music—and was good with some of those songs. "What do you think?"

"You want to sing with me?"

She shrugged. "I'm game. Your call though. I won't push it."

"We will," her friends all said in unison. "We want to hear him sing."

"Come on. He's a guest."

Heather shook her head. "Nope, he's part of the group, so we have the right to heckle until we get what we want. No *visitor* takes liberties with you like that, so he's something more."

He kissed her cheek and got up from the seat, holding out his hand. When she placed hers in his, he drew her up. "You heard them. I'm part of the group. Let's go."

"You don't have to do this, you know," she said as he led her through the tables to the stage.

"What's wrong?" he asked facing her. "Don't want to sing with me?"

"That's not it. Not at all. I don't want you feel pressured into doing something you may not want to."

His wink sent her insides to fluttering all over again. "I'm good. Trust me."

She reached up and pressed a kiss to his lips. "I already know how good you are. I hope you sing as well as you, well…you know."

He grinned and faced the stage again. Fingers firmly interlocked with his, she allowed him to pull her up on the rostrum when their turn came. When the familiar opening strands of Tim McGraw and Faith Hill's duet *Like We Never Loved At All* played, she fought her blush. This would prove interesting.

"I know this one." Levi smiled, partially lowering his lids.

The look in his eyes made her gulp. She knew the song. Ta-Mara sang her part. Levi stared at her not even looking at the words either. When his part came, he opened his mouth and Ta-Mara stared at his lips. The deepness of his baritone wrapped around her. Her gaze widened as she heard the perfect pitch of his voice. The emotions he poured into the song made her up her game. She turned to him and stared into his eyes, singing to him. Ta-Mara imagined what it would be like when he was gone and how she would feel when he did. Levi's eyes narrowed and he grabbed her, pulling her to him and rocking her, singing to her. Her voice broke on the lyric but she powered through and poured out what she would feel.

Shit, I'm already in too deep. Stupid, stupid, Ta-Mara. She closed her eyes, fighting back tears and finished the song.

The thunderous applause rose from the audience.

"Look at me," Levi whispered.

Ta-Mara blinked and drew in a breath at the intensity of his gaze.

"I won't ever forget you, Ta-Mara, no matter what happens."

His promise was in his words and expression. Ta-Mara knew he wouldn't, and neither would she. Levi would be etched in her memories long after they parted ways. Another song started, which Ta-Mara thought apt for this situation. Levi, if he was indeed from the time he said, could be taken from her at any moment—to a place where he belonged to another woman—Calliope—who knew she had his heart, body and soul. Ta-Mara led him to the stool on stage and encouraged him to sit as she sang the opening lyrics of Sugarland's *Stay*.

Ta-Mara turned away from him as she again let all her emotions out in song. She couldn't look at him when she sang or she'd cry, so she performed for the audience while meaning each word for him. She could have some great memories—or regrets about not enjoying each moment with him. For Ta-Mara, there was no decision. She would take each moment with Levi. As the song went on, she held out her hand to the people watching then pulled it into her chest. She rocked from side to side as she let them feel the loss she knew was coming. Finally, she turned to him and sang the last words to him.

Levi rose and Ta-Mara smiled shakily then put the mic back, getting down before he could reach her. She headed into the crowd who was on its feet cheering and congratulating her. Ta-Mara, blinded by what she was feeling, didn't really register it. Suddenly she was pulled and she glanced up, seeing Heather and Rachel who walked her rapidly across to the ladies room. Rachel checked and, seeing it was empty, locked the door. Heather released Ta-Mara and both women stared at her.

Rachel touched her shoulder. "Oh, Ta-Mara..."

"I'm fine." She turned away, hugging herself.

"You're already half in l—"

"Don't say it." Ta-Mara cut Heather off.

"T—"

"I'm fine," she said adamantly. "I have to go out there and face him. Act like it was just a song. So I don't need you making it worse."

They didn't say anything, just came to stand either side of her then rubbed their hands up and down her back. Ta-Mara appreciated their comfort and breathed in and out, then when she felt calm, she rolled her shoulders.

"I'm ready."

"Just one more thing." Heather hugged her. "If you need us, we are here."

"Come to us. Promise." Rachel hugged her too.

"I will if I need it." Ta-Mara shrugged. "It's gonna be fine. He's passing through and I know that. You don't get wrapped up in someone like that."

"Are you trying to convince yourself or us?" Rachel asked.

Ta-Mara didn't reply. She instead went to the door and opened it. A step outside and she stopped, her gaze locked on blue eyes. Levi leaned against the wall waiting for her. He held out his hand and, without hesitation, Ta-Mara took it. He led her down the hall then through the crowd and outside. Both were silent as Ta-Mara got in the vehicle and started it. On the drive home there were no words exchanged. The short ride felt like an eternity but once they arrived, she quickly got out and went to the house. The sound of his steps behind her made her move faster. Her hands shook as she opened the door and went in. He grabbed her and spun her into him.

"Levi." Ta-Mara gasped. "W—"

He kissed her and Ta-Mara melted. It was claiming and she was powerless to resist it. Levi kicked the door closed behind him, turned her then swept her into his arms. She wrapped her legs around him, moaning as she returned his kiss. She was on fire and the only thing she wanted…no…*needed*, more than her next breath, was him inside her. Levi quickly carried her to her bedroom and each step made his erection rub against her. She rocked then gyrated on him, wanting him now. He set her on her feet then took off her clothing. Ta-Mara helped him remove his then pressed herself against him. She whimpered at the sensation of his warm flesh against hers.

Levi picked her up again then stepped to the bed before placing her on the surface gently. He retrieved the condom from the bedside table and put it on. Levi stroked his erection and her mouth watered while her pussy clenched as she remembered how he felt inside her. She was already addicted to his touch. He lay on her then lifted her leg before he thrust deep into her. Ta-Mara came apart, flooded with need. She put her other leg around him, moving with him, countering each deep thrust.

"Yes." She hissed at each glide of him. "Take me, Levi."

He continued to move, his body bowing tight as he pleasured her. Ta-Mara's heart raced and she didn't know if she would ever be the same. Hell, she didn't want to be— each touch of his would be in her mind forever. She closed her eyes, not wanting to cry.

"Ta-Mara." At Levi's urgent tone, she stared into his fierce gaze. "Mine. I'm staying."

"You can't promise that, Levi," Ta-Mara roared.

"I—"

"Don't promise things that you can't." Ta-Mara gripped his face. "Let's just enjoy now."

Levi's reluctance was clear on his face. Ta-Mara tightened her inner walls and his eyes glazed. He kissed her and thrust harder. She held him, letting the passion overcome her.

Levi was lost in her and he didn't want to go anywhere. Yet Ta-Mara was right. He had no way of knowing what was to come. He couldn't make promises to her and it angered him that he didn't have that control over his own life.

Why am I here with this woman with the possibility of it being taken away hanging over us? Levi had no answers but he cursed whatever fate currently ruled his life. He stared at her and determination filled him. Even if time decided to draw him away from her, Levi would leave her something—he didn't know how yet—so she knew, no matter if centuries separated them, he would be thinking if her. He pushed in and she accepted him into her wetness. Heat pooled in his belly and he increased his motions. He braced his elbows on either side of her head, staring into her eyes.

Her gaze darkened then went slumberous as she arched under him—coming. As she broke apart in his arms, Levi's sac tightened and he joined her in pleasure. Levi shook under the power of his climax. He slumped on her and gathered her close. Levi pulled out, disposing of the condom, then cuddled her against him. He held Ta-Mara to his chest, kissing the side of her face. Ta-Mara relaxed into his arms and her breathing deepened as she went to sleep. It felt so right for her to be there.

Levi thought of the song she'd sung to him. He hadn't heard it before but then again since he was new to this century that wasn't such an uncommon thing. But the words and the way she had delivered the song to him had made his throat tight. He didn't want her to feel like she had to beg him to stay, share him with anyone else. Levi frowned wondering how she even knew about Calliope. He studied the side of her face, trying to recall if he had told her about Calliope. He couldn't remember. Come to think of it, he hadn't shared much with her beyond his being from another time. Ta-Mara hadn't asked but she seemed to know he had faced pain and lost.

How would she know that?

Chapter Eight

Levi stared at the woman making him dinner. She had such graceful movements—like a dancer. So light on her feet, and with elegance that emanated from her. He'd gone to work with her a few more times but most often he stayed at her house and learned more about this time he'd been sent to. He didn't want to mess up and cause any questions to arise about him that could affect Ta-Mara.

They'd not gone out with her friends since the karaoke two weeks ago, but the women had come over here. It had amazed them that he had his own room. He didn't want his own room but respected Ta-Mara enough he wouldn't push it. After the night they had sung together, then her singing to him, things had changed with Ta-Mara. Although he still wondered about her knowing details from his old life, the next morning he'd realized he'd made an assumption of things she said with no basis of fact. Ta-Mara, since that night, had been more open with him and demonstrative—touching him at random times. There was no denying the attraction between them, but he knew Ta-Mara was trying to avoid getting attached to him. She'd told him with the song she sang as well as many times since then…He would be leaving soon. He couldn't fault her for wanting some space between them, yet he longed for her to let down the wall she kept between them.

"Can you grab something for me from my room, Levi?"

He stood instantly. "Of course."

"On my dresser there is a card. Can you bring that out here? My neighbor will be stopping by and it's for her."

"I'll be right back."

He pushed up from the stool and walked from the kitchen through the living room and hall to her bedroom, which was done in caramels and burgundy. It was warm and sensual, much like the woman herself. Once in her room, he paused by the dresser and stared out of the open door, which led to the screened porch with fireplace. Her house was amazing, that was for sure. Shaking his head, he fought to keep his mind from what he'd like to do to her before that fireplace out there—or the one in here, as well as the one in the living room.

She was like a drug that'd gotten under his skin, and though some were bad, with Ta-Mara he had no desire to rid himself of the craving. On her dresser sat an envelope with the name Jessie Mae on it. He'd not met this person, so figured it was the one he needed.

He paused before leaving and turned a complete circle as he glanced around. These past few weeks, he'd been studying all he could about this time he'd landed in. He loved her computer and while she worked, he tended to spend hours in her office catching up on what had happened since his time. It hadn't hit him until now what was so different about her room. Heck, her entire house.

Heading back to the kitchen, this time opting to go from her room through the screened porch then living room to the final destination, he sat once again on the padded stool, placing the letter beside her.

"Why don't you have lots of little knickknacks around your room?" he asked, reaching for the glass of wine she'd poured him earlier.

"Knickknacks?"

He sipped and nodded. "On the television most times, the women have umpteen of them lying around, especially in their bedrooms, making it frilly and girly."

She burst out laughing. "Umpteen? Girly? Someone's been watching a lot of television."

He smiled at her gaiety. "I'm learning." In truth, it had mesmerized him. He'd no idea people lived like that. Yes, women in his time had a lot of things as well but compared to now? Well, it was a whole other type of thing.

"I don't have a lot of use for things like that. I prefer a clean house and all that requires a lot of dusting, plus it wasn't anything I had growing up. I have the large stuffed bear in the chair in my room. That's about as frilly and girly as I am. I have my umpteen out in my garden with my flowers—or as you've seen, in the den with my books."

That was true. He'd spent quite a bit of time in her den, reading book after book. She had a wonderful collection—fiction, nonfiction, biographies and more. Although he did tend to leave the romances alone, he really enjoyed the military fiction. He'd even tried out the e-reader she had, but he much preferred holding an actual, physical book in his hands.

Ta-Mara tucked some hair behind her ear before lifting the pot from the stovetop and draining the water from the spaghetti noodles. The doorbell rang and she placed the stockpot back on the stove. Wiping her hands on the towel hanging over one shoulder, she swiped the card from beside him, touched his shoulder then went to the door, carrying a covered pan of something.

He wanted to follow her. Wanted to meet her neighbor, but she'd not told him to come so he forced himself to stay right where he was. She wasn't gone that long and when she came back, she was shaking her head.

"Everything okay?"

"A bit. That was Jessie Mae's daughter. She came over to get some things so they'd have some food. I have to do some cooking tomorrow. Jessie Mae was in an accident and can't do any cooking right now. I didn't think she was getting out until tomorrow and when Susie—that's her daughter—called to say she was on her way home, I told her to come get something so they didn't have to cook, which is why we are no longer having casserole, but spaghetti."

"They don't have a housekeeper to do it for them?"

She burst out laughing. "More of that television. Most people around here don't have the money for that. It's not common anymore. There are a few who do, but Jessie Mae isn't one of them. We'll stop by tomorrow and see if there's anything we can do. I'm sure she's just going to want to sleep tonight."

He drank some more wine, appreciative of how she included him in her plans. They ate dinner right there at the counter. They sat on the stools with the wine between them. He helped her clean up and after with an all-too-brief goodnight kiss, he went to his room.

Unless Ta-Mara showed that she was interested in being with him, he wouldn't push. There were boundaries she'd set, and Levi did his best to respect them. Lying back on his bed, he yawned as the cool night breeze blew over him. The day hadn't been as muggy as previous ones, yet he still wore nothing but boxers.

Closing his eyes, he conjured up the image of Ta-Mara. He tried to bring up Calliope but couldn't quite manage to. He didn't feel as bad anymore. He'd loved Calliope when they'd been together, but she was gone. He couldn't hold on hope of having her back. Ta-Mara was real, alive and right here with him. What he felt for her shocked him and worried him a bit—such powerful feelings for a woman he'd not known very long.

It didn't matter. She was something special. His cock stiffened as he allowed himself to fully envision Ta-Mara. Hell, even tonight while she'd worn an old, tatty T-shirt and jean cut-offs, she'd taken his breath away.

Reaching down to free his shaft, he stroked it, fixated on the mental image of Ta-Mara. Up and down he moved his fist, slowly at first, only growing tighter around the length in his hand as he increased his speed. Feeling his release approaching swiftly, he slowed, pinching the head of his cock to stave off his ejaculation. A bit more in control, he began again.

Up and down, easy strokes. His hand was warm but nothing like the woman. Hell, a touch on his shoulder nearly burned him. To have her before him on her knees with his cock sliding in and out of her full lips... He groaned as he moved his hand faster still. He imagined her before him, eyes on him, hunger in her gaze as she swallowed all he had to give her. Her name slipped free as he bucked beneath his touch and came on his belly and chest with thick strands of his release.

Once he'd cleaned up, he crawled back in bed. Levi ignored the urge to go to her room and take her, then finally drifted off to sleep. He woke the same way he'd fallen asleep—his hard cock demanding attention as visions of Ta-Mara teased him.

They had a quick breakfast then he sat in the office reading while she cooked. He assisted her in loading her Mariner with all the things she'd made.

"Let's go," she said, tossing him the keys.

He caught them purely out of reflex. "You want me to drive?"

"You've been practicing around the property and now it's time for the next step. We're not going that far. If you want to get better, you need to practice on the road too." She closed the hatch and walked away from him.

Pivoting, he tracked her movements. Graceful. Alluring. Today she wore a pair of white pants, which stopped around mid-calf. Capris, she called them. A striped red and black shirt hugged her upper body. Although he'd never been a man to notice such minute details before, he was hyperaware of everything about Ta-Mara. He'd watched her slip on some red shoes as she'd gone out of the door.

Blowing out a breath, he climbed behind the wheel and fastened his belt. He'd been driving often since she'd first started teaching him. Yes, he practiced on her driveway, but that was hugely different than actually going out onto the road. She didn't look at all concerned—quite the opposite, in fact—as if she had full confidence in his ability.

He started them down her drive and stopped at the end, waiting for her to direct him on where to go.

"Left."

He made the turn and soon they were heading down the road. As he did, Levi was feeling better about driving outside his comfort zone.

"Not very far. You'll take the next left actually, just around this bend coming up."

He slowed and soon they bounced as they traveled over the rutted road. A smaller house sat at the end and he parked beside a rusty sedan. It looked as though both house and car were falling apart.

He got out as Ta-Mara did. She went up and disappeared inside the screen door only to return shortly with a younger woman following her. Blonde hair cascaded down her shoulders and she wore very little tight shorts and a shirt, no shoes.

"Levi," Ta-Mara said. "This is Jessie Mae's daughter, Susie. Susie, my friend Levi."

"Nice to meet you."

She smiled at him, returned the greeting and tucked some hair behind her ears.

"Come help us unload some things."

They worked well, carrying stuff inside the house and placing it on the kitchen table. While the outside might not be all that much to look at, the inside was spotless. As he placed the last bit from his arms to the table, a woman wheeled herself in the room.

"Jessie Mae," Ta-Mara said, hurrying to her side and brushing a kiss along her cheek. "You should have called me. I would have gotten you."

"Didn't want to be a hassle. You know you didn't have to do all this."

"You know I did. We're neighbors and friends. It's the least I could do. And I've told Susie to call me if you need anything, *anything* else."

He helped Susie put food away after being introduced to her mother. Jessie Mae had bandages around her face as well as left arm and leg. Still, it didn't detract from her smile, which was infectious. She was bubbly and very outgoing. Both her and her daughter had the same look.

When he and Ta-Mara went back outside, he stopped her by the steps. "What happened to her?"

"She was T-boned by a truck. Driver had been drinking and blew the stop sign. She's lucky to be alive. I honestly think if she didn't have Susie to live for and take care of, she would have given up."

"Where's her husband?"

She gave a sharp bark of laughter. "That no good, philandering bastard is far from here. She married a first-class asshole. He bailed on them a long time ago when Susie was a baby. They struggle to get by and I help when I can. She's a proud woman and doesn't like to accept charity."

"She needs a ramp built. How is she supposed to make it in and out of the house?"

She grabbed his arm. "You're so right. Why didn't I think of that? I'll see what—"

"I can do it."

She blinked at him. "What?"

"I can build it." He glanced back to the house before guiding her to the SUV. "So long as you think they'll be all right with me here. I'm a strange man."

"You're not strange. You came with me. You're fine. Are you sure you want to do that?"

"Yes. I've been spending a lot of time on your computer. It would do me good to get out and do something physical while you're working."

"Okay, then we'll go get some supplies for it and I'll drop you off tomorrow before I go to work. You'll have to walk home when you're done. There's a path through the woods" — she pointed past the shed — "that will take you right to the backyard and you can just go in the house."

He loved how she said home, like he belonged there with her. He guided her to the driver's side and caressed the swell of her ass. "I think you should drive. I don't know where the store is."

She took the keys from his pocket, ensuring to brush up against his groin. It got even harder when she cupped him through his jeans. "You're probably right. Let's go."

He gripped her wrist and held her flush to him before she could slip into the seat. There was only so much a man could take. "Keep that up, Ta-Mara, and there will be a whole other kind of pounding going on."

The tip of her tongue flashed out, dampening her lips. "I'll remember that." She jumped in with a wink.

Levi walked the long way around, readjusting himself to a more comfortable position before he entered the vehicle. She backed out the moment he buckled his belt. Music blared from the speakers as she raced off down the road. Yet all he could think of was how nice it would be to bend her over the back or front of the car, and slam his cock home in one smooth stroke. Take her hard and fast against the side of the Mariner until she screamed his name and couldn't stand on her own any longer.

* * * *

"Screw it." She pivoted then stared at him before grabbing his hand and pulling him along with her. All day, through getting the supplies and dropping them off at Jessie Mae's, she'd been trying to keep control and not jump Levi. She'd given up trying.

"Ta-Mara." Levi chuckled, a sensuous sound. "I recognize that look on your face."

"Good. Then you know what I need." She hurried them along to her bedroom.

"Yes. I'm yours any time, Ta-Mara." Levi cupped her ass and squeezed.

She pushed back into his touch and yanked him into her bedroom. In quick movements, she stripped him and while he did the same to her, she kissed him. Levi slid his hand down her now naked stomach and she widened her legs. He stroked along her pussy lips then pushed into her. Ta-Mara arched into his touch.

This man know all my buttons to push. How does he know me so well?

She gripped his shoulder and lost herself his embrace.

* * * *

"Are you sure you'll be okay?" Ta-Mara shifted from foot to foot.

Levi smiled patiently. "I'll be fine. No need to worry about me. Go to work before you are late."

It wasn't until this morning that Ta-Mara thought of what his working on Jessie Mae's ramp would mean. Levi would be alone with someone else without her near. In the weeks he'd been with her, she'd always been there when he was around other people or at least in the vicinity, yet today she was leaving him here alone. She was worried something would happen. She didn't think he would slip up and say something that would make Jessie Mae or her daughter suspicious. Ta-Mara was more concerned he would disappear like he'd appeared, and that she would never see him again. She knew it was stupid. There'd been all those times she'd left him at her house when she went to work or to run other errands—but she couldn't get over the irrational feeling. She'd started to think of her house as even more of a haven with him being there.

"Okay." She gestured to his waist. "Call me if you need to."

She'd got him a cell phone just in case he needed one.

"I will." Levi kissed her briefly. "Have a great day at work."

She nodded but didn't reply since she already figured she would be too focused on him to care about her own day. Ta-Mara took her leave. She didn't even register the ride to work and when she went inside, she did the opening procedures on auto-pilot. Throughout work, she glanced at the clock, willing time to pass quicker. That was how it was every minute and when she locked up for the night, she jumped in her car and headed home. When she pulled into her driveway, she sat there a moment.

Please let him still be here. She got out and went up the steps. Ta-Mara placed her hand on the knob and took a breath before she pushed it open. The scent of cooking made her relax. Ta-Mara hurried to the kitchen and stopped in the doorway. Levi was at the stove turning something in a frying pan. He glanced at her.

"Thought I heard you pull up." He smiled. "How was your day?"

"A day." She returned the smile and went to him. Ta-Mara kissed him then put her hand on his waist. "How about yours?"

"Good. Jessie Mae is a great lady—and her daughter too." Levi turned back to the stove. "The ramp is going…"

Ta-Mara leaned against the counter and listened to the rumble of his voice. Calm seeped into her and she really hoped she would get over this fear of leaving him alone, or she'd be a raving mess soon.

* * * *

Ta-Mara rubbed the back of her neck. Another day of worrying what Levi was up to while wondering if leaving him alone was a mistake. Yet when she got home, all was well. She glanced at Levi and noted he was frowning at the stovetop grill. That reminded her of what she had planned for this evening.

"Levi, I'm gonna to teach you to cook."

"I know how to cook." Levi glanced at her. "I've been helping you prepare meals."

"You've been doing what I said and not learning to cook a meal by yourself. I know that what we use is well…not what you might be used to." Ta-Mara smiled gently. "Think of it as another lesson similar to driving. It's a useful tool."

Levi studied her then he nodded before coming over to her. "Thank you, Ta-Mara. You always seem to know what I need to know without me asking."

"Anytime, Levi. But you do know if you need anything, you only need to ask. Okay. Let's start with preparing the meat for the grill. I use a simple rub to make it taste great. I already put it on from yesterday so it could soak in. I'll show you how to make it next time. So here's the meat." She held out the container.

Levi accepted it and they went to the stovetop grill. Ta-Mara gave him instructions for the whole meal and by the time they were finished, she smiled at Levi.

"Great first lesson." Ta-Mara lifted the plate and headed to the table. "There are videos and such online we can get you to look at too. Oh…the Food Network is a station that can show you about cooking."

"There is everything online or on TV these days." Levi shook his head. "I find it so weird yet fascinating it is."

"Sometimes it is a great tool but others times it can be dangerous." Ta-Mara shrugged. "In my opinion, we are so used to being connected we forget sometimes about times when we were not."

"Why would that be dangerous?" Levi set his plate down then went for the drinks.

"Because imagine if there is a time we don't have technology, or we use the technology for things that hurt others." Ta-Mara placed her dish on the table before sitting then placing her hand under her chin. "Like, for instance, there are videos on how to make bombs online."

"Why would that be there?"

"Because someone put it there."

"Isn't there monitoring and so on?" Levi put the pitcher of sweet tea on the table then sat.

"There is, but the Internet is a vast thing and not everything there should be there. There are places that people can find things if they want to." Ta-Mara picked up her fork.

"Hmmm…it makes you wonder if simpler times are better." Levi took a bite of his food. "A time when this technology you speak of didn't make things as accessible."

"It's a matter of what you think of as simple." Ta-Mara set her fork down. "I'm not saying having technology isn't valuable. What I'm saying is sometimes it's nice to disconnect from it. Like for example, when I was growing up, any sort of phones at the dinner table was a no-no."

"I noticed you always leave your cell off during dinner. I didn't know why."

"That's why. I guess it stuck with me and I kept it." Ta-Mara smiled. "Another thing that stuck is when you are spending time with someone, you shouldn't be texting, looking at your cell and email or so on. That's rude and distracts you from really being in the present."

"So there are both positives and negatives to this modern time and to the simpler times." Levi looked thoughtful. "Yeah, I can agree with that. Life, no matter what time you are in, has its own ups and downs. It is up to each person to make their decisions on what they do. Just like you decide to turn off your cell while having dinner."

"Exactly." Ta-Mara resumed eating.

"Thanks for starting to teach me to cook"—Levi touched her hand—"and your insight into this conversation. I am finding it interesting learning about all these new things."

"Good." She ate and they chatted about his day then hers.

* * * *

Ta-Mara stood beneath the shower and rinsed her hair. It had been a long day and she couldn't remember a time when she'd been so glad to leave the bookstore. Such a thing wasn't common. She loved it there. But today had just been draining all the way around.

Levi had been over at Jessie Mae's for the past few days, building the ramp as well as fixing odds and ends that needed to be done. Each day leaving him had become easier but still, by the day's end, she was eager to get home to see him. The lessons to cook had continued and Levi was picking it up well. As the days progressed, Levi had changed a bit as he worked at Jessie Mae's. From his happiness and the way he spoke, it was clear he loved working and doing something productive. Their nights had also differed a bit more. While she might normally sleep alone, there were nights where they spent the time together on the floor before a fireplace, in the living room or even on the screened porch. This morning she'd woken in his arms outside on the upstairs screened porch where they'd gone from watching the moonrise over the trees to making love while the rich scents from the numerous flowers and surrounding plants filled the air.

Shutting off the shower, she wrung all excess water from her hair before stepping from the stall. She tied her towel on and stood before the sink, staring at her foggy reflection. It didn't take her long to put the oil in her hair and brush it out.

She stopped by her walk-in closet, grabbed a loose-fitting outfit then continued to her bedroom. Draping the items over her bed, she sat on the bench positioned at the end of the four-poster frame.

Stifling a yawn, she bent down to put lotion on her legs and paused. Lying on the carpet beneath the seat sat a book. The temperature in the room dropped considerably and she fought off a shudder.

"How did you get in here?" she asked, even as she moved to sit in a different chair.

Moving swiftly, she applied her remaining lotion then dressed. She rubbed her arms, wondering if she should change into something with sleeves.

"Just get out of the room," she uttered.

The entire thing didn't feel right and she made her way to the door, the chill increasing. She found she couldn't leave, however and turned back to the bench. Shaking her head at herself, she marched back over.

"This is insane. I've never been scared of a book before, much less one that doesn't have a legible cover or even an *end*. It's not even a full book."

Her pep talk didn't help and she hesitated before crouching down. Reaching out, she touched the faded paper. The sensation of being sucked in, like into a vacuum, hit her with the force of a typhoon.

The woman was tall and willowy with smooth brown skin. Her loose natural curls blew in the wind that whipped around. Thick trees as far as the eye could see added an element of eeriness to the otherwise peaceful scene. The woman wore a shabby blue dress but none of it detracted from her beauty. She stood there, head high, a proud and almost haughty expression on her face — although the features weren't clear — as she stared straight ahead at something only she could see.

Her cheek and neck held the evidence of recent bruising and there were more, which unfortunately were evident beneath the hem of the threadbare dress along her legs. It didn't matter how poorly she was dressed. This woman carried herself like royalty.

A single shot barked and birds exploded from the trees, taking to the sky in a flock of black. Like lasers they rose, seeking the sky, their deafening and haunting cries filling the air. The blue-clad woman fell to the ground, a stain of red spreading with a bloom over her chest and blending with the material of her dress, creating an entirely different color. After she hit the unforgiving ground, the woman turned her head and her brown eyes shone with tears as her mouth moved, whispering a single word, "Levi", then her eyes closed.

Chapter Nine

"Ta-Mara?"

She jerked, releasing a small scream of terror and looked over her shoulder from where she lay on her floor. Levi stood there, a confused and worried expression on his face.

"Are you okay?"

Shit! Hell no, she wasn't okay. Her insides shook and she felt more than a bit nauseated as she realized what she'd just witnessed. That had been Calliope. She'd just seen the woman he professed to love die. Levi crouched beside her, his hand warm and comforting as it banished away the chills that had taken over her.

"Let's get you up," he said, lifting her in his arms with ease and settling her on the bed. His concerned gaze focused on her face as he touched her cheek and forehead. "Have you been feeling okay? Are you sick?"

She shook her head capturing his hand in hers. "I'm all right."

He frowned with disbelief. It was okay, she didn't believe herself either. *What am I going to say? I believe I just saw the woman you loved die?* Her head was spinning as she digested and processed all of this information. He was the same man from the story. There could be no more calling this entire incident a coincidence. He was the man — Levi Madison — the one she'd basically fallen in love with through the pages because of his endless and undeniable devotion to Calliope Jones.

Levi went to her bathroom and returned with a washcloth, which he wiped off her face with. She allowed him to because she didn't have to talk that way. Right now, she wasn't quite sure what she would say to him anyway. When he was not near her, the chill returned and it took a lot for her not to burrow tight against him just to feel warm.

Will I ever feel warm again?

She closed her eyes and found herself reliving that scene. She could smell the dew on the grass, that early morning fragrance, a rich, rejuvenating smell to which nothing else can compare. Unfortunately, it was soon overpowered. The powerful and unforgettable biting and pungent aroma of gunpowder leeched in, overtaking the gentle morning as it brought with it the cold, metallic scent of blood.

Never had her house made her feel this way before — it had always been comforting. She swallowed and took several deep breaths.

"You don't look like you're feeling well at all, Ta-Mara. Do I need to call that ambulance for you?"

If he did that, she had a feeling she'd be put in a room with lovely white walls, perhaps some padding to go with it. "No, I just got a little dizzy. I'll be fine. I bent over to get the book under the bench, it must have hit me harder than I thought."

He ducked and retrieved it for her. "Where do you want it?"

"Dresser, please."

"Let's get some food in you." He reached for her hand.

"I didn't cook yet." Ta-Mara shook her head, lacing her fingers with his. "Give me a sec and I'll come down to do it."

"I made our meal."

"What?"

"It was a surprise. I wanted to take the lessons you gave me and make you a meal." He shrugged. "I'll get you a plate and bring it to you." He went to rise.

She touched his arm to stop him and he lifted an eyebrow. Those dark blue eyes of his watched her with more concern.

"Hold me?" The question slipped free before she could even try to contain it.

She'd never know if he thought her request odd, for he moved instantly.

"Of course."

Within seconds, he had crawled onto her bed and drawn her into his embrace. Keeping her arms between them, she breathed easier as his heat poured over her.

"You're freezing," he muttered.

His hold on her tightened as if he believed the harder he held her, the warmer she'd be. A speculative theory, she was willing to see if it worked or not.

Closing her eyes, she allowed herself to settle against him, resting and fending off the unease that had been with her since he'd called her back from…whatever it was she'd experienced touching the book.

I don't get it. I've read that book so many times, nothing like that has ever happened to me before. Why now? Why that scene? It wasn't one in the book—she knew that—at least not the part she had read.

Fighting off another shiver, she burrowed closer to the hard, warm body in bed with her. In her ear, he continually murmured. She couldn't make out the words but the sound of his voice soothed her.

* * * *

When she woke, strong arms were banded about her, anchoring her to the man in her bed. His lips rested along her temple and when she moved, he spoke.

"Are you sure you're okay, Ta-Mara?"

"How long have I been sleeping?"

"About two hours. Not a restful sleep either, you've been tossing and turning. Do you want to talk about it?"

Most definitely not. "No. Let's go have this dinner you made."

He acted as if he wanted to say something else but let her go. She cast a glance to the dresser where the book lay, taunting her, as they left her room. The meal was a bit quieter than usual but she couldn't find it in her to make small talk. Her short, spaced-out dream had set her on edge. Thankfully, Levi didn't push any type of conversation.

Once they'd finished and cleaned up, she went out to her garden. The thick humid air warmed her more than she'd been ever since she touched the book and had the vision. Sinking to her knees, she ducked her head and fought the sobs that threatened.

She felt as if her life were spinning out of control. The rollercoaster had veered off its track and the new destination was unknown to her. She didn't much care for this feeling. *No, Ma'am, not in the least.*

"Want to tell me what's going on?"

The deep voice that curved out of the dark and wrapped around her from behind delivered a shiver that she had no hope of ever controlling, not with this man.

She shook her head, unable to find any words. The soft amber glow from her backyard's solar powered lights with their inlaid multicolor mosaic pattern allowed her to make out the dark footwear moving up beside her. She kept her gaze down on the ground, just needing a few moments to regain...well, whatever she had lost up in her bedroom.

"Ta-Mara?"

Damn it all, his voice was just so enticing, so decadent, that she didn't know how to deal with how it made her feel. Especially right now with the vulnerability hovering around her.

"I'm fine," she lied.

She wasn't sure what she expected from him but for him to sink to his knees beside her and reach for her hand, wasn't it. That much she could say for sure. His hand, so large and strong, made hers look tiny and petite. Much like he made her feel—as though he would protect her and keep her safe.

"No," he said in a firm voice. "You are not. Something has happened. If you don't wish to speak of it to me, can I call one of your friends for you? Perhaps telling them would be easier for you?"

Tell Heather, Jasmine, or Rachel easier? Not hardly. Heather and Rachel knew about Levi, or at least didn't think she was crazy, but there was no way she could tell them this. They would definitely have her committed. Hell, she was wondering if she was losing it. No, she wouldn't dare tell them anything. But how to tell this man?

"Is it me? Something I've done, not done? Please tell me, Ta-Mara."

"No, it's not you. I just think I need to sleep. Maybe I've been pushing myself a bit too much and it's caught up with me."

The words had barely faded from the air when he stood and helped her to her feet. She found herself swept up in his arms but didn't even bother to dispute him lifting her, merely allowed herself to burrow closer to him and let his scent and warmth to wrap her securely in a cocoon.

* * * *

Levi wiped the sweat from his brow and stood to stretch his back from the position he'd been in for the past while. The newly hung screen door slammed and he looked up to see Susie walking out with a glass in her hand.

"Figured you'd be thirsty out here working in the hot sun."

She walked down the steps and paused beside him, offering the drink. He took it, the condensation on the glass immediately cooling his palm. "Thank you." He took a large swallow of the lemonade. Perfect blend of sweet and tart.

"Thank you for helping."

He smiled at her. Susie was a great child. She went to school and worked before coming home to take care of her mother. She looked like the ditzy blonde on many shows on the television he'd seen with her perfect figure and wide eyes. He knew better. She had a heart of gold and currently wanted to become an attorney.

"Glad I could help." He gestured at the railing he was about to put up on either side of the ramp. "I'll be done within an hour, cleaned up and out of your way."

"You're not in the way, Mr. Madison. If you need anything, please just go in and help yourself. Mama is sleeping but I have to get to work."

He nodded and gave a wave as she hurried to the older model car, started it up after a fashion and drove off. True to his word, it didn't take him that long to finish. He knocked on the door before entering and putting the glass in the sink. Jessie Mae didn't make an appearance and he left the house before trekking along the trail between the homes, his tools over his shoulder.

Once the things he'd carried back and forth between the houses had been returned to their rightful place, Levi went in through the door off the *porte-cochère*. He caught the door so it didn't slam behind him as he stared at the woman at one of the kitchen counters.

White shorts that didn't seem to travel much past her firm ass highlighted the beauty of her darker skin. She wore no shoes and currently balanced herself on one foot, the other resting against her opposite leg. She had a light peach shirt on, which left a good amount of her skin exposed. At least of her back. Her hair tumbled freely down between her shoulder blades.

Music surrounded her and she nodded her head as she worked on whatever it was before her. His cock stiffened in his pants and he readjusted himself. She seemed better today. Whatever it was that had affected her a few days ago didn't appear to be bothering her anymore, either that or she'd discovered a better way to keep it hidden. He'd asked her again but she still hadn't told her what had happened to cause her passing out.

When she began belting along with the music, he just crossed his arms and listened. At the end of the song when the commercial began, he clapped.

"Oh shit!" she cried out, jumping and turning, one hand plastered against her chest. "You scared me."

"Sorry."

"How long have you been there?"

Long enough to think many dirty things about what I'd like to do to you. "Not long." His shaft pulsed as he took in the bared stomach she showcased.

"How'd it go with Jessie Mae?"

"She was sleeping when I left, Susie headed off to work and I'm done with things around there. I wish I could fix her car but I don't have any knowledge of these automobiles."

"That's okay, I'm sure she's grateful for what you've done. Besides, I have someone going to look at it tomorrow."

He frowned slightly. "Who?"

"Rachel's brother is a mechanic. He said to drop it by and he'd take a look at it. So Susie will do that on her way to school. I'll take her the rest of the way and we'll go from there."

Her smile hit him square in the gut. Walking to her, he leaned in and kissed her on the lips. "You do so much for others. When do you stop and take time for you?" He glanced over her shoulder and saw the casserole dishes she currently worked on filling.

"It's how we do things here. You help those in need. Besides, it's not like it's a lot of work taking her to school. I just have to go a bit earlier, but I'd rather do that than have the car breakdown on her, leaving her stranded somewhere."

"Could she not just call someone with one of those cell phones?" He still hadn't gotten used to those.

"No, they don't have any. Maybe I should get her a disposable one, you know, just for emergencies."

Another kiss, this time on the cheek. "I'm going to shower and get this sweat off me. Then I'll be back to help you."

He left before she could say anything else. It was necessary or he'd be carting her off with him. Each passing day he fell for her more and more. What would happen if he were yanked back in time, never to see her again? He ripped his shirt off his head at that thought, tossing it with frustration to the side. No, he couldn't let that happen. His future was entwined with this woman's—he knew it. Wasn't sure how he knew, but he did.

Kicking off his shoes, he toed off his socks then shoved his jeans and boxer briefs down his legs. Naked, he padded into the bathroom and adjusted the shower to the temperature he preferred then stepped beneath the spray. This modern plumbing was definitely something he approved of.

Calliope. Recently, her image had been popping up in his mind. She'd invaded his dreams last night. He couldn't entirely see what had happened but he'd heard her cries, her whimpers, and even her pleas. The night had been rough. He believed she'd been trying to tell him something, but what?

As he washed his hair, his thoughts turned to the woman whose house he was in currently. Ta-Mara. With her lush curves, tantalizing smile and amazing attitude, he couldn't forget her. Never would. The times he spent with her had been off the charts, and he didn't just mean sexually. He had a lot of fun with her, period.

He was worried about her. She did seem more tired lately. Even the nights when he held her throughout, she didn't rest easy. She tossed and turned quite often. Still whenever he broached the subject, she would tell him nothing was wrong. This world was vastly different from the one he'd been in but he wouldn't push, even if he didn't believe what she said to be true. Women had the right to their privacy.

Finished with his shower, he dried and had just pulled on a pair of jeans when he heard masculine laughter wafting up the stairs. An immediate spike of jealousy hit him hard and he scowled. The amount of control it took him to keep from running down there shocked him. Making his way to the window, he rested against the glass and took several deep breaths. He hadn't any right to be like that to her.

While standing there, he watched Ta-Mara walk into view, her snug shorts and cut-off T-shirt tempting him all over again. Unfortunately, following her was a man—one he didn't know, but who appeared to be in great shape. The man wore a suit and continued to follow her out toward a luxury car which was parked in the drive. Levi knew exactly why he walked behind her instead of beside her.

They stopped near the driver's door and turned sideways so he could see their profiles. The smile on Ta-Mara's face drove a knife to his gut. She obviously held this man in high esteem. They stood close, her hand resting on his arm.

The man watched her intently, nodding a lot. When he laughed, he showed off a wide, perfect smile and had a deep booming laugh. Levi fisted one hand beside his leg and continued to watch the interaction. A low growl slid free from his chest when the man tucked some of her hair back behind her ear, his touch lingering on her face. Their farewell consisted of her hugging him tightly and sharing a kiss. Levi didn't move from his spot until the car had backed up and left the driveway.

Unable to ignore the jealousy coursing through him, he made his way downstairs. Ta-Mara was back in the kitchen at the counter working. She looked up when he walked in and gave him a smile, which evaporated much of the ugliness rolling through him. Not all—he was a male who wanted to protect what he considered his—but most of it.

"You look like you feel better," she said lowering her gaze back to what she worked on.

"I do. Who was that?"

She looked over her shoulder. "That? You mean Mike? The guy who just left?"

Mike. Bastard's name was Mike.

"Yes." He couldn't hide the grumble from his voice and didn't care to. The proprietary feeling that enclosed about him wasn't going anywhere.

"Mike is a friend from college."

Not much information there. "I see."

If she picked up on his discontent, she didn't show it or didn't care. She added another layer of noodles to the lasagna she was making.

"He stopped by to ask about the party for Jasmine. Mike's her brother. He wanted to make sure we were still on for it and if I needed anything else to help with the preparations."

Nope, it didn't make him feel any better to know that man was Jasmine's brother, not when he knew how flirtatiously she acted. Most likely it was a family trait.

"When's her birthday?" he asked, moving to stand beside her.

"Two weeks from now. She's turning thirty—just don't tell her that, she's acting like it's the end of the world for her—but we're determined to give her one hell of a party anyway." Ta-Mara shook her head. "Have to lie to the bitch. She is fighting the party so we told her it would just be the four of us girls, but we were going to meet here for drinks before we went out. That way she doesn't have to drive being the birthday girl and all. She'll crash here."

"Will I be in the way?"

"Oh heavens, no. This place will be crawling with people. You're more than welcome to participate. We'll have a live band, drinks, food, dancing and more. Of course if you don't want to be in it, you may want to hide in your room." She grinned. "The attending women will definitely want to dance with you—and *more*."

He pressed against her and nipped her shoulder blade. "What about you?"

"I'd love to have a dance but I have a feeling you'll be spoken for by the rest of the female population."

"All you have to do is say you want to dance and I'm all yours."

She turned so they were chest to chest, her hands out to the sides so she didn't get food on him. "I'll keep that in mind." Her voice had become breathy, how he liked it.

He leaned in close. "Do that."

Their gazes locked onto one another until he finally stepped back, knowing full well if he kissed her there would be no stopping him from taking her. And she'd already stated how she wanted to get this stuff done.

"What can I do?"

Such a loaded question. Ta-Mara swallowed and took a deep breath. It just wasn't fair, not even a little bit. Levi wore nothing but a pair of jeans that may have been new but looked like they were a favorite pair, hanging just so on his hips. *Those lean hips.* His bare chest was bronzed and sculpted in a way she was hard-pressed to find on men who didn't spend their life in a gym.

She gave him instructions and went back to finishing up her lasagna. The fact he knew she wasn't telling him everything that was ripping through her mind faster than a hurricane and yet didn't press had her admiration for him increasing. She was still trying to come to terms with it herself.

They worked side-by-side, Led Zeppelin pumping through the docking station she had her MP3 player sitting in. He made a fruit salad and she took the opportunity to watch him. Fluid. Predatory. Masculine. Hell, she could go on and on about him.

As if sensing her gaze upon him, he turned his head and winked. "Yes?"

"Nothing," she said, putting her attention back upon what she was supposed to be working on. The flush raced up her cheeks and she rolled her eyes at herself. Acting like a schoolgirl with her first boyfriend.

"Is this for Jessie Mae?"

"Yes, except for the pie on the other counter. She doesn't eat that kind. Still too difficult for her to stand out of the chair longer than a few moments and Susie is so tired when she gets back from work and school. It's much easier for them to just slip something in and eat. Jessie Mae can even do that from the chair."

"You really care about them."

"Jessie Mae is a wonderful woman who's gotten the short end of the stick more than once. I just want to do my part in making it easier for her to speed along to her recovery."

A piece of watermelon appeared at her mouth. She accepted it and fought a groan as its rich juice ran down the back of her throat.

"I happen to think you're doing wonderfully." Whispered words in her ear.

Butterflies took off again and she had to lock her knees to keep from sinking to the floor. "Thank you. She'd do the same for me if the situations were reversed." Tipping her head to the side she asked, "Didn't they do that where you came from?"

A rough chuckle left him. "Well, the slaves would cook it and carry it, but sure… We can call it that if you want."

Washing her hands, she then covered the pan and set it to the side along with the other things she'd fixed. She propped her hip against the counter. *Why not address it now?* "Do you miss it?"

He looked up from where he'd returned to cutting up fruit, working on some peaches now. "Miss what? Living when people were allowed to own others? No. Living when some weren't even considered a real person? No. Do I miss the quiet we had instead of all the horns and cars? Yes. The air was cleaner then, and your cities tend to give me a headache if we're there long. Your house is perfect. I love the surrounding area as well—quiet, and I can sit out and hear myself think. I miss my horses though, riding them." He scraped the cubes into the bowl. "Did that answer your question?"

She thought about the story, *Unbreakable Bonds*, and couldn't recall it saying he had horses. Licking her lips, she weighed her words. "I have a friend who has a stable if you'd like to go riding?"

He tipped his head to the side and stared at her. "Do you ride?"

Images of her being on top of him as she rode him until pleasure overtook them both filled her mind. She swiped her tongue along her lower lip. Somehow, she didn't think he was talking about that kind of riding.

"Not really, no."

He lifted an eyebrow. "What were you thinking about?"

A sly smile teased her lips. "Probably not the type of riding you were talking about."

His grin matched hers. "I know you're good at that kind of riding. I meant on a horse. Although it could be fun on a horse as well."

That statement created a whole other swarm of visuals to her mind. She shifted a bit and tried to calm the throbbing of her clit. Didn't work, but she could say at least she'd tried.

"You've done it on a horse before?"

"Nope, but I'm up for it. What about you?"

"I'm not that good of a rider."

His grin did wicked things to her insides. "I'm sure you'll be fine." He moved closer. "Why don't you call your friend and set up a ride? I'd love to spend the day with you and some horses."

Heat flushed her and she struggled to get moisture into her mouth. "I'll call him about it. Probably won't be until after the party for Jasmine though. I got a shitload of books into the store which will keep me there longer."

"Take me in with you. I'm done with Jessie Mae's, so I can help."

"Are you sure you want to spend your days at the bookstore?" She didn't want him to feel obligated to help her.

"I'm sure I want to spend time with you, Ta-Mara. If working at the store helps you, that's another bonus." He touched her cheek. "Unless you'd rather I not be there."

"Oh no, you always tend to draw in more people, especially if I have you putting out the outside display or working on the one in the window. Women tend to flock in to get a glimpse of you."

His smile rocked her to the soles of her bare feet. "Glad to help."

"What do you want for dinner?" she asked. Lord he smelled good, like a perfect blend of his own scent and the fruit he'd chopped.

He ran his gaze over her and her body temperature skyrocketed as heat swarmed her. This man was dangerous and potent. All he had to do was crook his finger and she'd follow him anywhere.

"Leftovers?"

She smiled. He had come to like nights where they had leftovers. They tended to eat them out on the porch in a swing, cuddled up. When she cooked, they normally sat at the kitchen table.

"How about a salad and sandwiches?"

"I'll start on the salad."

He walked to the refrigerator as she stared at his retreating form. *Hot. Sexy. Amazing.* She didn't know what she'd done to have him in her life, but she liked having him there. They worked together. He gathered the evening meal while she finished up the stuff she was putting together for Jessie Mae.

They ate on the swing. Salad and grilled cheese, light and perfect. He cleaned up the meal while she packed the dishes to be delivered. She loaded them into her wagon, then together, she and Levi walked the path from her house to her neighbor's.

She jogged up the steps and knocked while Levi pulled the wagon up his newly installed ramp. "Jessie Mae? I'm coming in, honey. Levi's with me."

"I'll be right out!" The yelled response traveled down the hall and out of the screen door.

"Just bring the wagon in," she directed Levi.

They'd just gotten it all in when Jessie Mae rolled into the room. Her hair was done and she had a smile on her face. Ta-Mara pressed a kiss to her cheek.

"How are you doing?"

"Good. Thanks for the ramp, Levi. It's so helpful."

"My pleasure, ma'am."

Jessie Mae looked at her and grinned. "So polite. Call me Jessie Mae."

Levi nodded his agreement while Ta-Mara covered her mouth to hide her laughter.

"I'm going to put this food in the freezer and fridge, Jessie Mae."

"You really need to stop cooking for us. I'm not going to fit in my wheelchair if I keep eating like this."

"You need to eat," Ta-Mara said. "Stop arguing because you'll lose."

"Of course I will," Jessie Mae griped playfully. "Need to keep an eye on this one, Levi."

"I plan on it," he said, moving up behind her and handing her another dish.

"Good. She gets into trouble."

"Whatever," Ta-Mara defended herself. "You do. I'm the good one."

"Such shit. You know you're the bad one."

Ta-Mara winked at Levi. "That's probably true. Don't tell anyone though, or it will ruin my reputation."

The women looked at each other, burst into laughter and said at the same time, "What reputation?"

They visited for a while before leaving. Levi pulled the wagon and they walked side by side on the path.

"You two are a lot alike," he commented.

"You think so?"

"Yes. You feed off one another. I can imagine how much trouble you encounter out with one another."

She grinned. "I plead the fifth on that."

He stopped and pulled her tight to him. "Can I make you talk?"

Her chuckle escaped before she could keep it contained. "You can try."

His breath fanned her lips. "I think I may just do that."

She heard the handle of the wagon drop seconds before his other hand landed upon her body. Closing her eyes at the pure pleasure of having his touch on her, she went willingly along with his plans of attempting to make her talk.

Chapter Ten

The pile of books on the display taunted him in ways he'd never known books were able to do. Levi stared at them and shifted his weight from leg to leg. Standing outside the store, he began setting them as Ta-Mara had asked him to do.

They were all romance books, the covers depicting a man embracing a woman who seemed about to pop free from her dress—passionate images. And for each one he touched and set, all he envisioned was himself and Ta-Mara in place of the couple on them. Standing, lying, it didn't matter.

Great. He was getting aroused thinking about a woman in the store just through the glass and he had to finish his job before he could go in and see her. She'd been right, however, about him attracting women. They stayed busy and he knew a lot of them entered to see him. They browsed very little but stared at him for the majority of the time in the store. At least they bought. It might only be one book, but they purchased.

Masculine voices grabbed his attention and he looked away from the display only to tense from head to toe, his head held rigid. The men slowed as they passed the first display he'd put out this morning. Books on military fiction and the like.

Everything about them was familiar—height, weight, looks. John Marley and Matthew Kline—two of the men who'd shot him, chased him through the woods then strung him up for daring to love a black woman. Fear filled him as the sight of them transported him back to that helpless feeling he'd experienced. The only thing he could think of was how he had to protect Ta-Mara and not let them kill again.

"Levi?"

Ta-Mara's scent wafted around him and he blinked. What was she doing here? She should be hiding. Didn't she realize the danger? Grabbing her arm, he searched frantically for a place to stash her until the danger had passed.

"What are you doing out here?" he bit off, positioning himself between her and the men, hoping they wouldn't see her. "You need to hide."

A cute little furrow appeared on her brow. "What are you talking about?"

"I don't want them to hurt you. Please, Calliope." How could she not sense the menace surrounding them, growing thicker by each passing second?

Her expression shuttered before it transformed to one of concern then she nodded. "I know a place." She led him away, they ducked into the bookstore and thankfully the few patrons there didn't take any notice of them. It seemed to be a back room and he searched for somewhere to put her. *There, to the left.* He guided her there and blocked her in.

"You need to stay out of sight. Keep your voice down. I'll come for you when it's safe."

She reversed their positions pushed him against the wall and shook him. "Levi. Levi!"

His head pounded and he squinted. "What?"

"Are you okay?" Damn, she sounded concerned. Why did she sound so worried for him?

His head cleared and he shook it a few times to get the fuzzy feeling out. "I think so." He rubbed his eyes, removing the last bit of lingering cloudiness which had surrounded him, and looked around. "What are we doing in the back room?"

"How are you feeling?"

"Like I have a headache."

"I think I should call the hospital and get you checked out."

"Why? People have them all the times."

"Levi, don't you remember any of what just happened?"

Her tone was frightening him. "No. Did I do something embarrassing?"

"You should sit back here, you know, until you feel better. If it doesn't happen soon, I'm taking you to the hospital."

She wasn't telling him something and he didn't like it. "What aren't you telling me, Ta-Mara?" He reached out and captured her wrists in his hands, spoiling the hasty retreat he knew was coming.

If he didn't know any better, he would have sworn there were tears in her eyes. "You called me Calliope."

Well, shit. His hands fell away from her.

Ta-Mara left him there after getting a bottle of water for him and placing it at his side. He rocked back in the chair and rested his head against the smooth coolness of the wall. Calliope. He'd called her

Calliope. What an asshole. Ta-Mara didn't know who that was, but calling her by another woman's name was inexcusable.

Why would he do that? It rushed back and he remembered — the men, their expressions and looks. He shot up from the chair and strode through the back room doorway toward the front.

Ta-Mara's gentle laughter reached him and he slowed. If she were laughing, she couldn't possibly be in trouble. He shook his head again. He had to stop thinking that every man near her could be looking to rape and kill her. Times weren't the same as he was used to.

All this time he'd spent with her, he'd seen many couples together regardless of race. Still, it wasn't easy for him to forget the faces of the men who'd killed his woman and attempted to do the same thing to him. There was no way they were the same men though. How could they have gotten here?

How could he?

Rounding the final shelf, he stopped at the sight of Ta-Mara talking to the two lookalikes of his murderers. She didn't appear at all distressed — quite the opposite, in fact. Her hands rested comfortably in the back pockets of her pants and they spoke in animated tones and gestures.

She turned her head and gave him a smile, which didn't quite reach her eyes, but it was a start. "I'll also keep my eye out for it and if such book shows up, I'll give you a call," she said to the men.

"Thank you, ma'am." The one who looked like Matthew gave her a smile and nod before they both walked back out.

Ta-Mara helped two others before they were again alone in the shop. She whirled on him with a ferociousness he'd not expected.

"What the hell was that about?" she demanded.

"I don't know. I remember taking that last cart outside to set up, saw those two men and then I was with you in the back room."

His answer didn't appease her, a blind man could have picked up on that. Her full lips pursed in a way that had him thinking how much he wanted to kiss her over and over. He didn't like that strained expression on her face, but preferred the soft, well-pleasured one.

"It was like you were somewhere else." She shook her head. "I don't know how to explain it, other than while you looked at me, it felt like you looked *through* me, seeing someone else. Then of course when you called me Calliope, I realized you did see someone else."

There it was again. Calliope's name falling from Ta-Mara's lips. A chill skated across his skin and he fought the shiver. How did he begin to explain who she was to him? Or rather, who she had been.

"Ta-Mara, Calliope was—"

"Someone important to you. Someone you wanted to keep safe."

Her voice wobbled and he didn't understand it at all. Was she sad that he'd had a woman in his past?

"Yes, but—"

She cut him off again, "I have work to do. Excuse me."

Stepping behind the counter, she settled at her computer and stared at the screen while her fingers flew over the keyboard. He could take a hint. He'd been dismissed. Now wasn't the time to push the issue. Pivoting on his heels, he made his way to the back room and got to work on the books there. She'd seemed as though she would prefer a bit more time to herself. He could give her that. A little bit, anyway.

Ta-Mara surreptitiously watched him retreat as he strode away, her gaze locked on to the way his denim curled around his ass, advertising how nice it was. She blew out a breath and strove to stop her hands from shaking.

She knew he'd probably made the assumption she hated him calling her Calliope because she was jealous of being referred to by another woman's name. That wasn't it. Okay, so she wasn't a huge fan of that, but it wasn't the real reason for her reaction.

It had been strange enough for her to meet him under the circumstances she had, to hear his name and try to convince herself she wasn't going insane. However this was the first time he'd mentioned Calliope and that had driven home the point that he wasn't just from the past, but also from a book.

"I need psychiatric help," she bemoaned, actually sitting on her hands to keep them from shaking.

She'd had the scare of her life when she'd seen him standing there in front of the shop, staring at something only he could see with murder in his eyes. Then he'd grabbed her and talked about needing to hide. It had taken a lot for her not to fight him on it and slap his hand away. When he looked through her, she understood he wasn't right and the best thing would be to go along with him.

The phone rang and she jumped. Reaching for it, grateful for the interruption, she said, "Good afternoon. Roberta's Reads. This is Ta-Mara. May I help you?" Nothing. "Hello? Hello, is anyone there?"

Shaking her head, she replaced it on the charging base and stood before swiping up a stack of books to replace on the shelf. Levi gave her a wide berth for the rest of the day and as she closed out the register, he sat on a chair waiting.

His strong arms were crossed over his chest and she watched his expression. Tired. Drawn. Missing something. Whatever had happened to him today hadn't been fun for her but from the looks of things it had taken a lot out of Levi. Her heart ached for him and she had no idea what to do to make it better. And she desperately wanted to make him the happy man he'd been such a short time ago.

"Ready?" she asked.

He tipped his head up and looked at her. She trailed her gaze all over him. No excess fat, strong, powerful, capable and more. Levi reached out and tugged her closer until she straddled him and the chair he sat in. He didn't speak, just wrapped his arms around her and buried his head against her chest. It wasn't a sexual move. This was all about comfort.

Tossing the moneybag onto the counter, she returned the embrace, holding him tightly. Time ceased to matter as she offered what support she could. In the back of her mind, she thought about mentioning to him how she'd had an incident with Calliope as well. But she couldn't force the words past her mouth.

She shook her head slightly as she threaded her fingers through the silken strands at the nape of his neck. What a pair they made—a man who basically came from the pages of a book, who was in love with a woman from those pages, possibly still did love her. And Ta-Mara who was feeling something—she didn't know what to call it—for him. It might be a book to her but to him, it wouldn't be fiction. It was his life. She didn't even know the words to comfort him or let him know she'd read about him. Hell, this wouldn't be the time anyway. Not when he was looking so lost. He needed her to just be there, and that she could do.

"Let's go home," she whispered.

His fingers tightened on her shirt before he released her and she sat back in order to see his forlorn expression. She attempted a smile but knew it fell short. Levi may not have been with her for that long but she couldn't ignore how he'd managed to worm his way into her heart. Ta-Mara pressed her hand against his side and wanted to take him outside his mind. Yet she knew nothing could take away the memories of what he'd lost.

"Home?"

So much could be read into that one word and yet all she did was nod. His tone was filled with longing she didn't know what to say. There was nothing for something like this. No platitudes would make it better and she hated being powerless to help. Those sapphires he called eyes watched her intently as she climbed off his lap—not that she had a problem being there—and grabbed the bag she'd tossed on the counter earlier.

Locked up and closed for the night, they left from the back and made it through the muggy night to her vehicle. After a brief stop to deposit the day's money, she stopped to pick up her curbside order then drove home.

She changed then opened the containers while waiting for Levi to come back to the kitchen. One minute she was alone and the next he was there.

Smiling, she gestured to the food on the countertop. "Dig in. I'll have the rest of this set out, so grab whatever you want."

He moved toward her, not stopping until she was trapped between him and the counter's edge. Not a bad place to be actually, so she wouldn't complain.

"This," he rumbled against the skin of her neck. "This is what I want."

His hands slipped over her hips, drawing her back into the hard ridge in his jeans. Dropping the lid she'd just removed, she groaned as she rubbed against him. He lifted her skirt and she felt warm air hit her heated skin. Easy access — one delicious thing about skirts.

He ripped off her panties and covered her mound with his hand. He played with her clit, strummed it until she could hardly keep her legs up under her. Lower and lower, he dragged his touch, teasing her but never actually entering her.

"You're wet," he said, nipping her skin.

"You're hard. We can help each other out." Was that her voice sounding like she was begging? Yes it was, and she wasn't so proud not to beg even more.

Another two flicks over her clit had her whimpering. *Damn man and his touch.*

Widening her legs even more, she arched back into him, grinding along the definite erection he sported.

"Levi!" she gasped as he pressed two thick fingers deep inside her.

He didn't speak, just pistoned them within her. She gripped the edge of the counter purely so she didn't fall. Passion and need washed over her with the fury of a firestorm, blending and twisting so she couldn't differentiate between the two.

His fingers disappeared then, before she could summon up a protest, he was sliding home inside her.

His cock sank in with a single stroke, his weight nudging her further against the support. The counter was the perfect height for this.

Ta-Mara came hard and she cried out, turning her face so her cheek rested along the smooth coolness of her kitchen counter. Her nostrils filled with their scent, along with the food she'd been working with.

"Fuck me," she begged.

"I am." In and out he stroked. Nice and slow. A full thrust in followed by a withdrawal. Even paced.

"Hard. Please, Levi."

He pulsed within her, and she tightened her internal muscles before pushing back against him. His growl echoed in her ear and she smiled, content she was about to get what she so desired.

Hard and fast, he drove into her, his fingers clenching the bare flesh of her hips beneath her skirt. It wasn't romantic in the sense of there were no flowers, soft music or anything like that, but to Ta-Mara it was perfect. This was what she'd needed, craved. The raw primal joining where she felt *taken*. Claimed.

He lifted her and she hooked her feet around the backs of his knees, using more of the counter to hold her up. Thrust after thrust, he continued unrelentingly. Eyes closed, she lost herself to the feeling of being taken by him. She loved it.

"Come on my cock," he growled, punctuating his words with strokes.

It was almost like her body had waited for the permission that came to her on a rasped voice. Toes curling, she gripped the granite edges so hard she briefly wondered if she'd leave finger marks behind. Stars exploded behind her lids as she jumped fully off the ledge she'd been toying with. Seconds later, after a few more thrusts, his release coated her and his roar echoed in the kitchen.

Spent, sweaty and boneless, Ta-Mara sagged against the coolness beneath her, heart pounding as if she'd just completed a marathon. Levi remained buried inside her and when he locked his arms around her waist, she realized he had every intention of staying that way. Luckily, it wasn't that far from the kitchen to her bedroom. Not that she had doubts he could carry her, but she wanted more. A lot more.

He placed her on the mattress, his heavy weight pressing her deep. She liked him on her. He rotated her slowly and as she settled on her back, she could feel him stiffening within her. Reaching for him without any hesitation, she pulled him down for a kiss. Nothing else mattered right now. Life would wait and she would focus on what was important—just him. Her. And the passion between them.

* * * *

Levi sat on the edge of Ta-Mara's bed, watching her in the early pre-dawn light as she continued to sleep. He'd been doing this ever since he'd flashed back after seeing those men who looked like the ones who'd tried to kill him. Even if he didn't spend the night in Ta-Mara's arms, he came downstairs early and watched her sleep. It had been three days since the incident, yet the residual of it still sat with him. The faces of his past had shaken what he had started to build here and he hated it—hated seeing the look of helplessness in Ta-Mara's gaze. He could see her longing to help. That was innate to Ta-Mara—helping. Yet in this, there was nothing she could actually help with. Hell, Levi wasn't sure himself what could be done to reestablish his calm of three days ago. Ta-Mara shifted on the bed and the sheet lowered, showing off her breasts. Levi licked his lips, recalling what had happened when they'd gotten home after he'd seen those men. Immediately he silently cursed himself for even thinking of it.

Three days since he'd taken her like some wild animal in the kitchen as she'd dished up their food. She hadn't seemed to mind much, and the way her had pussy clamped on his cock as she'd screamed his name, *his* name, to the heavens only reinforced that knowledge.

Didn't stop his guilt, however. *How could I have called her Calliope?* While Ta-Mara had never said it had bothered her, he wasn't a fool. What woman wanted to be called by another's name? Another *woman's* name to be more specific. None he knew of. He felt bad and couldn't think of anything that would make that right.

She shifted on the bed again beside him. The sheet, which had pooled at the small of her back while she slept on her belly, slid sideways, offering him an all too tempting view of her firm ass.

Jerking his gaze from her flesh, he stared across the room to where he knew that book sat on her dresser. The book that had burned him when he'd picked it up for Ta-Mara. He'd almost dropped it back the second he'd touched it but the expression on her face had said she didn't wish to hold it. So he'd dealt with the fiery pain that had flared up his arm as he put it where she'd said.

Something about the book drew him and yet something else had him wanting to stay very far away from the item. He was going to have to look at it soon.

He knew that as well as he knew the beating of his heart.

"Mmm, Levi."

Arching his eyebrow, he glanced back down to the woman beside him. She still slept, however her hand had traveled between her legs and she slowly humped the mattress.

His cock, which had been mostly erect since he'd walked in and smelled her intoxicating scent, went completely hard. He shucked his clothing and fisted himself while watching her. She spread her legs and he could see her fingers working her pussy.

Nudging her legs wider, he crawled up between them, lowered his head and lapped at the nub waiting for him. A rumble of pleasure escaped him as she pushed into him. He continued working her clit while he speared his tongue in and out of her slit, her wetness coating him as he worked.

After she came with a muffled cry, he exchanged his mouth for his throbbing shaft. She bucked against him, rising up on her knees to take even more of him. Christ, he was ready to explode now. She had no idea what her tight, wet sheath did to him.

"Harder," she moaned, rotating her hips against him.

He couldn't do anything other than comply with her request. Soon they both cried out in release and he slumped over, landing on his side, bringing her with him.

"If that was a dream, I don't want to wake up. If it wasn't, then I want to be woken that way from now on."

He smirked at the breathless quality to her voice. "I think that can be arranged."

"Good."

She wriggled her ass against him and he realized he would need to focus on something else before he was oblivious to all but the raw need she created in him.

"Morning," she mumbled seconds later.

"Good morning," he said kissing her bare shoulder.

It didn't make any sense to him how she could have such soft skin. He'd asked and she just smiled at him. He used her soap but his never felt as hers did.

"Can we sleep the day away?"

She moaned. "I wish. But I know it's way too damn early to get up so close your eyes and get some more sleep."

"Are you sure you want to sleep?" he asked, rubbing his hardening cock against the crack of her ass.

She rolled in his arms so they were face-to-face. "Nope. Not at all."

He grinned, finishing the roll she'd started so she ended up on top of him. "Good to hear."

She dipped her head and planted little kisses all over his chest.

"You're going to kill me, woman," he uttered seconds before she slipped farther down and took him into his mouth. "Fuck!" Yep. He was going to die but he didn't care. Not right this minute.

* * * *

They didn't leave her bedroom for another few hours. The entire day was a lazy one. They sat on the porch, cuddled up to one another on the swing, took a lovely walk down her road and just enjoyed being in each other's company.

Once they'd ingested the meal they made and cleaned up after, they sat in the screened porch as the night storm dumped upon them. Burning logs filled the fireplace and she lay on her stomach, head resting on his leg. He trailed his hand up and down her bared back. Her skin was such a lovely thing to touch. He could spend all day doing so and never grow bored with the dips and swells combined with the smoothness and silken feel beneath his fingertips.

"Are you sure you're okay?"

He'd not been expecting her voice and startled a bit. Titling his head so he could see her better, he grabbed a section of her hair in his fingers and twirled it.

"I'm fine. Why?"

She didn't readjust to look him in the eyes, and he couldn't tell if her eyes were closed or focused on the flames.

"You were off the other day after that...that, well whatever it was that happened."

He blew out a frustrated breath. "I'm sorry."

She shook her head, the movement gentle against his thigh. "I didn't ask how you were to get an apology out of you, Levi. I asked because I am concerned."

"Regardless, I owe you one. It was wrong and thoughtless for me to call you by another's name." He gripped her hair tighter as if it would keep him from having to think much other than how soft it was in his fingers.

"No you don't."

He knew she'd never admit that he needed to apologize to her. So he changed the subject. "How are you doing? You've been putting in a lot of hours at work and I'm not sure you're sleeping right now." He frowned. "At least not enough."

"I believe my lack of sleep last night was because I had this man in my bed and he kept me up doing all sorts of things."

He grinned despite the fact she couldn't see it. "Did he now? Would you like me to hunt him down and beat him up for daring to keep you from your rest?"

"No, I think perhaps I'd like for him to stop by again. I do sleep well...you know, after he wears me out."

He bent down and nipped the shell of her ear. Thunder boomed in the distance while lightning flashed with a ferocity that would have worried him had he not been inside the screened porch.

"He's glad about that." Another rumble and he could see her almost melt into the sofa. "You aren't afraid of storms."

It wasn't a question. She shook her head and readjusted. Her hand settled on the inside of his thigh by her head.

"I love them. I don't know what it is about them but I love the pure power they exude. The thunder, how if its close enough you can feel it reverberate through you. The brilliant flashes of lightning as it splits a dark sky. The smell which accompanies it all. Spectacular."

He lifted his head and peered out of the screen. The only light aside from the fire was the lightning. He'd never enjoyed storms as she seemed to do but he wasn't afraid of them. However, sitting here with her and listening to her describe how she saw them, he began to see it from her point of view.

"Ready to head to bed?" she asked.

"You want to sleep out here?"

"No. We'll keep the doors to the bedroom open and will still get the fresh air."

"Sounds good."

They headed for her bedroom—he loved how the porch led right to it. In fact, her entire house was amazing. In the bathroom, they got ready and eventually made it to the bed.

* * * *

When he woke the next morning, he swung out of bed and padded to the porch where he checked on the fire. It had gone out and the rain had stopped, but the air was heavy and thick with fog. He scratched his chest as he bent over to spread out the ashes, ensuring the fire had all been extinguished. Movement to his left had his head coming up as the fog parted, allowing a slender figure to step through.

His heart stopped before starting again. He didn't want to believe what he was seeing. Blinking, he tried to lose the vision but nothing worked. The figure stopped right outside the screen and stared at him with large brown eyes.

"Hello, Levi."

The voice was as gentle as a soft night breeze in Georgia when it carried the smell of magnolias upon it. And as she had when she'd been alive, she smelled like the flower as well. He swallowed hard, looked back toward the bedroom where he'd left Ta-Mara sleeping, then faced the person he'd never believed he'd see again.

"Calliope?"

Chapter Eleven

Ta-Mara rolled over in bed only to be met by cool sheets instead of a warm, hard body. Opening her eyes, she saw he wasn't in bed. She sat up and glanced around. Who knew where he was. Out of bed, she took care of her morning needs then dressed after her shower. Back by her bed, she noticed the fog outside as she made up the blankets. Thick. Almost eerie.

"Levi?" she called as she made her way through the living room with a quick peek in the kitchen only to continue up stairs to the room she'd given him when he'd first arrived.

No response came. His room was empty and clean, as he tended to leave it. The past few nights he'd been sleeping with her anyway so the only time he was here was for a change of clothing. Either way, he wasn't there now.

A stab of disappointment flooded her but she chased it away. There were plenty of places he could be, just because he wasn't there when she woke wasn't any reason for her to get all psycho and crazy-weirded out.

Regardless of her pep talk, she checked the other rooms upstairs as well as the porch off one of the bedrooms, telling herself it was because she was worried he might be passed out somewhere. Nothing.

Not like she had to go anywhere, for this was her second day off. The phone rang and she hurried down to pick it up.

"Hello?"

"Hey, girl. You got a minute?" Heather.

"Of course, what's up?"

"No, I mean a face-to-face talk, not over the phone."

"Sure. Want to meet somewhere?"

"Can you come to Shane's?"

Shane's was their local coffee bar, which many of them preferred to support as opposed to one of the huge national chains. Glancing at her watch, Ta-Mara nodded only to realize her friend couldn't see her. "On my way. I'll be there in about fifteen."

"Thanks, Ta-Mara."

She replaced the phone on the base and grabbed a piece of paper and pen before jotting down a note to Levi and leaving it on the kitchen counter right beside her Keurig, well aware how much he enjoyed making coffee. Swiping her keys and purse, she was on her way out to her SUV and headed to meet Heather.

True to her word, she pulled into Shane's fifteen minutes later. The fog was still thick and it felt like pea soup—heavy and almost suffocating. She pushed through the door and grinned at the scents that hit her nose.

"Morning, Shane!" she called out as the proprietor waved to her.

"Looking good, Ta-Mara!" he hollered back. "Usual?"

"Please, and a piece of that coffee cake."

"You got it."

She wove through the tables to one at the back, which could be considered their usual spot, and took a seat. Heather wasn't there yet. When a woman named Michelle brought her coffee and cake, Heather still hadn't arrived and Ta-Mara didn't like that. She wasn't a woman who ran behind. If she were meeting Jasmine or Rachel, she'd expect it, but Heather despised being late.

Five minutes later, Ta-Mara was digging for her cell phone. "I'm here." She looked up at the words and saw Heather moving through the tables, a stressed look on her face. Getting up, she embraced her friend before they both sat down.

"Are you okay, hon?"

Heather looked ragged and about to fall apart. She shook her head and took a bite of Ta-Mara's food. "Sorry, I'm just...so blippin' hungry."

Leaning back in her chair, Ta-Mara said, "What's going on, Heather?" She took her coffee and sipped it, all the while keeping her attention on her friend.

She rolled her lower lip in her mouth for a moment. "You know the guy I've been seeing?"

Ta-Mara blinked. "Um, no. Who's this guy you've been seeing? Why haven't we met him?"

Heather ducked her head. "I thought I told you about him."

"I would remember if any of us had said we were dating someone."

"You are."

Ta-Mara shook her head. "No, I'm not."

"You're not dating Levi?"

Just the mention of his name sent pulses of heat through her, had her core throbbing and craving his touch. "Nope. He's just staying at the house."

"Booty call?"

This was the Heather she recalled, not the pale, worried one. "Enough about me," she steered the conversation back to where it rightfully should be—on her friend, Heather, and off Ta-Mara's relationship status. "This is about you and this mysterious man you're dating."

"You've met him."

Leaning forward, she rested her elbows on the tabletop, brow furrowed in concentration. "I've met him? Sweetie, you need to be a bit more specific than that. I meet quite a few people daily and since *no one* said they were dating you, it's not sticking in my head."

"A few days ago at the bookstore. He was in there."

She pursed her lips. "Sweetie, I *really* need more than that to go on. What'd he look like and why the hell are you being so secretive?"

The hair on the back of her neck stood up and she knew someone was behind her. Turning her head, Ta-Mara saw a tall man, almost as tall as Levi, standing there. He was a good-looking man, fit. Cajun country—that was the first thing she thought while staring at him. He wore jeans and a T-shirt and had a beat-up ball cap on his head. Cowboy boots stuck out from the bottom of his jeans. Shaggy blond hair poked out from beneath the cap and she was taken in by the green of his eyes as the man looked them both over.

"Hope I'm not too early," he said in a slow, unhurried way typical of the locals. Cajun all right, his accent flowed seamlessly and made her smile—many people she knew couldn't stand it, but personally, she loved it.

"Hi, Matthew," Heather said.

Ta-Mara watched as he walked to Heather's side, tipped her face up and gave her a kiss that could have melted an ice cap. Then he settled beside her and turned his green eyes on her again.

"You must be Ta-Mara," he said, reaching a hand out over the table. "I was in your store the other day with my friend."

Accepting his hand, she shook it while nodding. "I recall." She sliced her gaze over to where her friend sipped on her drink. "Nice to meet you, Matthew."

"And you, Heather's told me a great deal about you."

Well, Ta-Mara couldn't say the same but she smiled at him anyway. "How did you two meet?"

"At a club," Heather said.

Ta-Mara smiled at her friend, unsure exactly why she wasn't acting like her normal self. "And what do you do, Matthew?"

"I'm a fisherman." He shoved a toothpick in his mouth and leaned back in his chair.

At his declaration, she saw Heather tense slightly. It dawned on her then Heather might be worried how she'd take what the man did for a living. Personally, she had no problems but she understood Heather's concern. For all her heart, Jasmine was a woman who prided herself on appearances. Men needed to have a large bank account for her, and Jasmine could be very vocal about her disapproval.

"You know what I do, so that's not a surprise." She smiled and winked at Heather.

Matthew rose to get himself a drink after checking if he could get either of them a refill—they both declined—and she watched him walk off, a natural swagger drawing her eye.

"Wow, Heather. He's…hot. Nicely done, sweetie."

"I'm sorry I didn't tell you about him but you know how Jasmine is... I was just worried."

"You know I don't give a damn what a man does so long as he treats you right. But I've known you long enough, Heather, what the hell is bothering you? The truth, now. I know it's more than me meeting that hot-ass man you're dating."

"I'm pregnant."

The words were so soft that for a second, Ta-Mara thought she might have been imagining them. The panicked look on Heather's face told her otherwise. Leaning forward, she took her friend's hand. "What did you say?" She kept her gaze out for Matthew's return.

"I'm pregnant."

"Matthew's, right?"

Heather nodded almost imperceptibly.

"Have you told him?"

This time it was a negative shake.

"Sweetie, you need to tell him."

"I can't."

"Why not?"

"I'm scared he'll leave me. I haven't even told my parents. In fact, you're the only other person who knows aside from the doctor. And to get that confirmed, I had to go out of town and visit a clinic, just so the rumors wouldn't be started and my father wouldn't find out. I know from being a doctor at the hospital how quickly your business can get spread around when you don't want it to."

Ta-Mara understood that need. Heather's father was a serious man who, similar to Jasmine, was extremely concerned about appearances. She caught enough flak from the man for not being model-skinny or fit like her other siblings. To not only be bringing home a boyfriend who wasn't even corporate but also what the man would determine 'backwoods' as well as being pregnant by him... Ta-Mara could understand her hesitation.

"What are you going to do?"

Tears welled up in Heather's eyes. "I don't know."

Matthew retrieved his drink and began heading back toward them.

"Wipe your eyes, here he comes." One final squeeze then she released Heather's hand. "We'll figure something out but I still think you need to tell him."

The man turned back to the counter.

"We could always be like *Three Men and a Baby* just with two women and a baby. You're always welcome at my house." The offer was immediate and took no thought at all to reach her decision. There was none to make—Heather was her friend, and she would always be there for her.

"Thank you, Ta-Mara."

"What are you two ladies talking about and looking so serious?"

"Jasmine's birthday party. She makes it so difficult to throw her one," Ta-Mara lied easily as Matthew sat back down. "You will be bringing Matthew, right, Heather?"

"If he wants to attend."

"Who doesn't love a good party? Drinks, food, music. We'd love to have you there, if you can make it."

He gave her a slow grin, one that only increased his handsomeness. "I'll have to check dates with Heather here and see if I can."

"Wonderful." She gave a pointed look to her friend, who gave a small smile in response.

"Hey, y'all!" Another feminine voice broke amongst them as Rachel dropped an arm around her shoulders. "What's going on and why wasn't I invited to the party? Are we planning Jasmine's… Oh…oh my, hello there. I'm Rachel, and you are?"

"Matthew. Heather's boyfriend."

Rachel looked at her and mouthed "Oh my God, he's fuckin' hot!" before turning her attention back to the lone man at the table. "Heather, where have you been hiding him?"

Their friend sat down and soon they were actually planning the party and Matthew didn't seem to mind being the only man at the table. His attention didn't waver from Heather, and that to Ta-Mara was very telling. A wonderful sign. She waved to Shane for a refill and leaned forward as they went back over the plan to get Jasmine out to her house so they could throw the cranky bitch a party.

* * * *

"You're dead," Levi said, even as he stood and made his way to the door of the porch. "I saw your body."

Calliope tracked his movement, her gaze remaining focused on him. She glided up the steps and he struggled with the urge to pull her into his arms and sink into her softness and scent.

"Yes, I am. I see the desire to touch me in your eyes, Levi. That cannot be. We can no longer touch."

"Why?" he croaked. "Why are you here?"

"You're not letting me go, Levi. I'm here until you allow me to go."

He shook his head in fierce denial. "Let you go? You were taken from me, Calliope."

"Yes," she said, the patient smile he admired so much about her curving up her lips. "And you were taken here to have a second chance at love. This Ta-Mara LeBreaux seems to be the one for you."

His heart torn, he didn't know what to say. He dug his short nails into the flesh of his palms to keep from reaching for the woman who stood before him in a simple dress of pure white.

"How am I supposed to do that?" Christ, he hated how his voice strained. "How am I supposed to let you go, Calliope? You were ripped from my arms, taken from me before we even had a chance to begin."

She stepped closer, the scent of magnolias winding around him like a warm blanket. "Let go of your anger. Of your hate."

"Never," he swore. "I saw, Calliope... I saw what they did to you. They told me with great glee in explicit detail."

"This anger will eat you alive, my love."

He gave into the urge and reached out for her. Fluidly she stepped back out of his reach and he dropped his arm back to his side in frustration. One more touch—was that so much to ask for?

"Let me go, Levi. Please, I want to go home."

She faded right before his eyes and he called out, "No! Don't go. Don't leave me again, Calliope."

It was too late, she'd gone. Like a whisper in the night. Same as when she'd been taken from him and killed. One minute there, the next, gone.

"Let me go." Her voice was so faint he almost didn't hear it and yet at the same time, he heard it louder than anything else.

He closed his eyes, sinking to his knees and bowed his head. The slamming of a door had him lifting his head. No fog surrounded him—in fact, the sun had skated across the sky and had begun its afternoon descent.

Levi felt disoriented and confused. He sat on the steps leading to the backyard. Where had all his time gone?

"Levi? You here?" Ta-Mara called out to him.

It took him a few tries to get the words out. "Back steps."

Moments later she appeared, her brown eyes sparkling at him. "Hey. You have a good day? Sorry I was gone so long, didn't expect to get so caught up in the plans for Jasmine's party. Plus I met Heather's new boyfriend, so that took a bit more time. He's a great guy, fishes for a living. Kind of the quiet sort, like you. I think you'd like him."

She crouched beside him and handed him a beer. "Looks like you could use one." Tilting her head to the side, she studied him. "Are you sure you're okay?"

What was he going to say? *No, I lost a few hours this morning when my dead woman came to visit me. I don't even remember getting dressed, much less anything other than Calliope.*

"Yes," he lied smoothly. "I'm fine."

Ta-Mara looked delicious. She wore a maxi dress tie-dyed in all the colors of one of those old time soda shoppes she'd shown him. Light and crinkly, it flowed around her and made him think all kinds of naughty things when he watched her in it.

"Okay. Are you hungry? I could eat, like, a pizza myself. All I've had today was a piece of coffee cake and way too much coffee. But, at least the plans are finalized and we're ready to tackle this thing."

He listened to her ramble on about her day and the anxiety within him began to slow. She had that effect on him, calming. To his soul anyway—to his libido it was the opposite. He drank some beer and watched her as she recounted more about her day with Heather and Rachel. The way her throat moved when she swallowed, the dimple in her left cheek when she smiled. The endless joy in her laughter and of course the way the sun shone off her skin and hair.

"I'm sorry, listen to me carrying on about what I did. What did you do today?"

He didn't mind, in fact he loved listening to her talk. "Little bit of this and that. Not much. Sat outside and just rested."

"I'm glad." She pushed to her feet and he smiled over the fact she no longer wore shoes and her turquoise nail polish glittered in the sunlight. "I'm going to start something to eat. My stomach has been growling the entire way home and I really don't need to be drinking without some food to counteract the alcohol." She squeezed his shoulder and walked away, leaving him alone with his thoughts and beer.

Dropping his head to his hands, he groaned. What was going on? Her book. None of this had happened until he'd touched that book of hers. Perhaps all he needed to do was take another look at it. A closer one, this time.

He stood and walked inside the screened porch. Music filtered through the living room to him and he knew she would be in the kitchen dancing and singing along as she fixed whatever it was she was making. Suddenly being with her and the joy she put into everything she did became more important than looking at the book. He traversed the porch, living room and ambled into the kitchen.

She'd not changed and he stared at the flare of her hips covered by the colorful cotton as she moved them to the beat of the music. He recognized the artist. Trey

Songz. He placed his bottle on the counter and went up behind her, gripping her hips and moving with her.

Ta-Mara spun in his hold so they faced one another. She looped one arm around his neck, fingers sinking into the hair at the nape of his neck, while her other hand settled upon his chest. As did her face.

He held her close and allowed the slow motion they had convey words he didn't know how to verbalize. He loved holding her like this, so close, so intimate. So perfect.

"What can I do to help?" he asked in her ear as the music kicked up its beat yet they continued their slow dance.

"Mmm. I'm good right here." She burrowed closer.

"Me too, but if you're hungry…"

Her sigh was loud and exaggerated, bringing a smile to his face. "How true. If you can cut up the fruit for the salad, that would be great."

He tipped her head back and kissed her. A gentle kiss. An exploratory kiss. At least that was how it should have been. And it was…right until she released that sexy little mewl from the back of her throat.

Levi gathered her tight to him, growling low as he angled his mouth to kiss her better. He couldn't get enough. He wanted more. Even as he deepened the kiss, he began tugging up her dress to grant him access to the smooth, supple flesh beneath.

She didn't fight him. In fact, she helped. He just needed to not think about what had happened earlier in the day. And if he were going to lose himself in something, truly he couldn't think of anything better of losing himself in Ta-Mara.

He groaned in pleasure as he located her skin. Without breaking the kiss, he lifted her to the countertop. She widened her legs, allowing him to rub against her. Tugging on her panties until they snapped, he sank two fingers deep inside her.

"Ohh," she moaned, thrusting her hips forward, bringing him in even further.

Leaving her succulent mouth, he followed the neckline of her dress, laving the tops of her breasts before sucking one after another into his mouth. He grazed the nipples as he continued to thrust his fingers within her.

She dropped her head back as one hand sank deep into his hair, holding him closer. Her gasps and groans filled his ears as he unfastened his pants. Freeing himself, he sank within her heated depth in one smooth stroke.

"Oh yeah," she whispered. "Just like that."

He couldn't agree more.

Chapter Twelve

Ta-Mara folded the rest of the laundry she'd just taken out of the dryer and put it in the basket waiting by her feet. She was still sore from the most recent assignation with Levi in the kitchen before she'd actually got around to making something to eat. *Thank God I'm on the pill since we've done away with condoms.*

Jessie Mae had called and had needed some help with a broken window, so Levi had gone to take care of that and she'd begun her laundry. Well, she'd begun doing *their* laundry.

"Hell, he should just move into my bedroom."

"Who should just move into your bedroom?"

She turned with a squeal and glared at the person waiting there. He lounged against the doorway, arms crossed, sending her an evil grin.

"Trent!" She jumped the basket and dashed to his embrace. "Oh my God, it's so good to see you! When'd you get in? How long are you staying? Where are you staying? You know I have room here if you—"

"Damn, woman. Let a man get a kiss and a breath before you start on them so much."

He pressed a kiss to her cheek and she returned it. "I think my question should be answered first."

"Your question?"

"Yes. Who should just move into your bedroom?"

She flushed. *Damn it, no one was supposed to hear that.* Of course, what did she expect—she didn't lock her house so people could, and did, just walk in.

"You were eavesdropping, so I don't have to answer you."

He snorted. "That's what you think."

She rolled her eyes and hugged him again. "You're a horrible man."

"Perhaps. You have room for me to crash here?"

"Of course I do. You know I have plenty. How long are you here for?"

"A while. Have some things to take care of here. So, get me some food and tell me who you are thinking of moving into your bedroom. Is he here? Locked up somewhere?"

"You know I would never let you know where I keep my men locked up." She went to the basket and shoved it into his arms. "Carry this."

He took it to her room before they returned to the kitchen and sat at the counter where she shoved a plate full of ham, greens and macaroni and cheese before him. There was no talking as he shoved food into his mouth as if he'd not had anything edible for a long while.

"Hungry?" she asked when the plate was cleaned.

"You have no idea. I've missed your cookin'."

"More?"

"You know it. Any cornbread?"

She smirked and nodded as she fixed the second plate. "Of course. But had I known you were coming, I would have made a fresh batch of it up. Just for you. God, are they starving you up there?"

"Sometimes I think they are trying. Luckily I know I can always come back home to someone who loves me."

She slid the heated plate before him a second time. "Who loves you?"

"You do."

"Are you sure?"

Trent glared at her before picking up his fork and shoveling more in. When the sound of a screen door slamming hit them, she sat up with a slight bit of apprehension.

"I'm back, Ta-Mara."

Trent paused with the forkful halfway to his mouth. "Is this who should be moving into your bedroom?"

Shit. This could end up being ugly. "Be nice, Trent."

He batted his eyes at her. "I'm always nice."

"Right."

Levi strode into view and she saw him hesitate as he gazed over the two of them sitting so close to one another. She sent him a smile. "How's Jessie Mae doing?"

"She's okay, the window wasn't really broken, just stuck and she couldn't get it fixed, being stuck in the wheelchair and all."

"Thanks for going and taking care of that. This is Trent Babineaux. Trent, Levi Madison." It was as if the temperature had gone down in the room and there existed an edge of danger that hadn't been there before. She licked her lips, refusing to look away from the slight frown Levi sported, and added, "He's my cousin."

The man didn't relax his protective stance. In fact, neither of them did. She groaned and shook her head.

"Knock it off, you two. Please, I don't have the energy for all the posturing." She slipped from her seat and moved to Levi. Placing a hand on his chest, she waited for him to meet her gaze. "Cousin."

"My woman."

"What?" She wasn't following.

A sparkle returned to his gaze. "I thought we were playing word association. You say something and I say what first pops into my head."

She pushed up on her toes to kiss him. "Silly man." Glancing between them both she said, "I'm going up to fix a room for Trent. Y'all play nice now." With the hope there would be no bloodshed, she went up the stairs and got the room with the attached porch ready for her cousin, well aware how much he liked staying in that room when he came.

The men were talking about college when she returned. Levi had a mug of coffee before him and Trent drank a beer.

"So you never went to college?" Trent asked.

She paused at the fridge to hear his answer. "No, I was enlisted in the Army."

Grabbing her own drink, she went to lean against the counter. Trent frowned and swirled his beer before speaking again.

"You mean you signed up."

"No, I had no choice."

"There's always a choice," Trent argued.

She met Levi's gaze and he shook his head. "Not in my house with my father."

Thankfully, Trent accepted that answer. She didn't know how they would be explaining about where he came from and all of that. She pulled out the fixings for some fresh cornbread and got to making it while they carried on a conversation around her.

Trent was a familiar fixture in her house and she couldn't explain how grateful she was he and Levi got along. Her cousin was finishing up his last year of law school and she didn't get to see him as much as she used to, so his visits were always important to her.

Masculine laughter had her smiling as she slid the cornbread in the oven. Once it had gone in, she joined the men who'd migrated to the living room. They watched some shark show and she merely rolled her eyes and sat beside Levi, who immediately tucked her in close to his side. Ta-Mara saw the understanding look on her cousin's face.

A little while later she walked with Trent up to the room he'd be staying in while he was here. As expected, he grabbed her arm and held her gaze.

"You two seem serious."

She arched an eyebrow. "Is that a problem?"

"Only for the fact he doesn't look like a man who's ready to settle down. How long will he be around? And what will you do when he leaves?"

Questions she had no way of answering. So she shrugged. "I don't know, Trent. But I'm good with how things are right now. I'm not looking for forever and a big diamond ring."

Trent frowned. "Since when do you play fast and loose?"

She scowled right back at him. "I'm not doing that."

"Really? Have you told your parents about him? The family?"

"Well no, but—"

"Why are you hiding him then?" He crossed his arms over his chest. "You're playing that with him and I know you, Ta-Mara, you don't do casual. You get attached. I don't want you to get hurt because you're settling for what this man will give you."

Damn it, she hated that he was right. Refusing to admit it aloud to him, she shrugged. "I know what I'm doing, Trent."

"I hope so, honey. I don't buy it and I already think you're in love with this man." He took a deep breath. "I'm your cousin, not a parent, so I'll be in your corner."

She smiled at him, grateful for his support.

"However," he continued. "I have no problems beating the shit out of him, just on principle, because he hurt you."

"He hasn't hurt me."

"He will." Trent kissed her on the cheek and pushed her out the door. "'Night."

She paused right outside his room and leaned against the wall. *He will.* Two simple words that sounded ominous when they came from Trent in that situation. Ta-Mara took a deep breath and made her way back down to find Levi in the kitchen putting away the rest of the cornbread. He looked up when she entered and gave her a smile that made whatever she might go through in the future worth it.

"Your cousin is nice. He cares a great deal for you."

"He is and yes, he does." She moved to his side. "You didn't have to put that away."

Levi pinned her between him and the counter. Her nostrils flared and her slit grew wet as she recalled what had happened between them the last time she'd found herself in this position. At the memory, a little moan slid free. Levi arched an eyebrow at her a sexy grin titling up one corner of his mouth.

"You, Ta-Mara, are one hell of a woman." He lowered his face so his lips brushed along the edge of hers. "You know what I want to do with you right now?"

Words caught in her throat so she shook her head. His scent wafted around her. He brushed his hard body against her and she nearly whimpered at the feel of his stiffness along her hip.

"Would you like me to tell you?"

"Yes." That one word sounded more like a croak than anything.

Levi didn't seem to notice or care. He told her. Then showed her.

* * * *

Levi watched Ta-Mara as she stood on stage and sang with Heather. Jasmine and Rachel sat with him, talking and scanning the crowd for men they would consider hooking up with. Honestly, this time had become very confusing for him.

It wasn't that he didn't agree with women having rights, but he still didn't understand why they would deliberately go out looking for a man to sleep with just for the night. He sipped his drink and kept his gaze riveted upon the woman he spent each night in bed with.

Tonight she'd dressed in a black denim skirt sporting a leather belt, which was buckled in the back. She wore a gold tank top with a black fleur-de-lis emblazoned on the front. It flattered her and showed off her figure. He had no problems watching and listening to her. She had this...this *thing* about her, he couldn't describe it.

When she and Heather finished and left to an enthusiastic applause, Jasmine and Rachel got up, downed their drinks and sauntered up to the stage for their next turn. He leaned in for a kiss when Ta-Mara sat back beside him.

"Sounded wonderful."

She grinned. "Thanks."

"Can I get y'all more drinks?" Levi asked.

"Just Coke for Heather, and I'll take the same," she said, before Heather could speak.

He wasn't used to Heather not drinking alcohol but kept his questions to himself. It wasn't his business.

"Any more thought on whether or not Matthew will be coming to the party?" Ta-Mara asked.

"He wants to. I told him the day and time but he's not sure he'll be back from fishing by then."

"Okay, tell him he can stop by anytime. It's not like the doors will close." She looked at Levi and filled him in. "Matthew is Heather's new boyfriend."

"Congratulations."

Heather's grin was a bit strained but he didn't dwell on it. Ta-Mara glanced up to the stage and scooted closer. She was between the two of them. "All right. Let's make sure we have all this ready because I know that woman is getting suspicious. You're bringing her out to my house for drinks before we head out. We'll have a small thing with just us so we can get the urge to celebrate out of our system before we could possibly embarrass her in public."

Heather laughed. "Oh, that would be so much fun to do though. Wouldn't you love to take her somewhere and have the staff come out with a piece of cake with a candle and sing happy birthday to her?"

The idea had her chuckling as well. Just to see the look on Jasmine's face... She'd be pissed but it might just be worth it.

"We should do that—not on her birthday though, just on some other day."

"Oh, she would kill us."

"With pleasure she would. But I'd go out with a smile on my face."

Levi listened to the women banter back and forth as they put together the final plans for the party. He was looking forward to it. He'd met a good number of Ta-Mara's friends but now he'd get to meet those he'd not.

After loading up the drunken duo, Rachel and Jasmine, followed by Heather as well as Ta-Mara, Levi climbed behind the wheel to drive the women. When it was just him and Ta-Mara, he headed for home.

That gave him pause. He had begun to think of her house as an oasis. Not just a place he was staying, but an actual home for him. Slanting his gaze to her as he drove, he wondered if she thought the same.

He'd been trying to focus on something other than the odd meeting he'd had with Calliope yesterday. He was still unable to reconcile the time he'd lost during that day. None of it made sense — her comments, why he'd seen her. And honestly, it was tearing him apart inside.

He'd love to talk about it with Ta-Mara. She had, after all, accepted the fact he'd traveled to her from the past. Perhaps talking to her about seeing a ghost wouldn't be so far-fetched. However, would she want to discuss the woman he'd loved so long ago and with such passion?

He wouldn't want to talk about another man like that with her. He blew out an exasperated breath and slowed to turn into her drive. "Wake up, Ta-Mara," he said, pulling beneath the *porte-cochère*.

She moaned and sat up. "God, it's a good thing you can drive now or I'd be in the back of some taxi that someone probably had thrown up in."

He hurried around to open the door for her. "Come on. I'm sure Heather would have driven you home. She didn't drink."

"She can't. She's pregnant." She clapped a hand over her mouth. "Don't tell. I am not supposed to tell anyone, so be surprised when she tells you."

He nodded. "Right. I won't mention it." He led her up the steps, her movement slow and wobbly.

"Good. She'd be disappointed in me if she learned I blabbed."

Laughing softly, he guided her through the house to her bedroom where it took him three tries to get her to brush her teeth. He didn't mind undressing her, however—peeling back those tempting clothes was a highlight of his night. She put up an argument when he tried to get her to put on a nightshirt.

"No," she pouted. "Don' wanna wear it."

"Your cousin is here, what if you walk out there naked?"

"Which cousin?" she asked sitting up, tempting him with her firm breasts. "I have so damned many of them."

"Trent."

"He's okay. He won't look. I'm not his type, even if we weren't related. He's batting for the other side." She patted his cheek. "You may want to wear boxers." Laughing at something only she understood, she flopped back. "It's hot, I don't want to wear anything." Her eyes closed and he knew she had passed out again.

After shutting the bedroom door, he undressed and slid into bed beside her, gathering her against him. She didn't stir and he willed his cock back under control. He might be horny as hell but he had no intention of taking advantage of her in this condition.

She wiggled her ass against his groin and he groaned. This was going to be a long night.

* * * *

He woke alone and sat up instantly. Had she gone strolling out nude into the living room? Yes she had the right to do it but sue him, he felt more than a bit protective of her and her body. Cousin or not.

Climbing out he went to the bathroom where he found a note taped to the mirror over the double sink.

Went to Jessie Mae's, back by nine.

He took care of his morning ablutions then padded back to the bedroom where he found himself standing before the book, which had yet to make it back to the store. For a moment, he just stared at it. *Unbreakable Bonds.*

Reaching out for it, he paused when Trent's voice shattered into his little world.

"Ta-Mara! You down here?"

Pulling on some pants, he then went to the door and opened it. Trent had his hand poised to knock. His brown gaze scanned him from head to foot.

"Sorry, man. I'm looking for Ta-Mara."

"She went to Jessie Mae's, said she would be back by nine."

"Okay. I'm off for my run. You can join me if you wish."

Levi held up a hand. "No thanks. Not a runner."

"Suit yourself."

Trent headed off wearing nothing more than running shorts, socks and shoes. Levi didn't get the concept of running for fun. Not something he had plans on doing. Instead, he went to the kitchen, brewed himself a cup of dark roast and added the creamer and sugar before heading out to the porch and enjoying the morning.

Ta-Mara returned shortly before nine.

"Hey, Ta-Mara," he called out from where he was rinsing out his mug in the sink.

She grunted in return. He followed her into the bedroom and saw her sitting on the edge.

"You okay?" he asked.

"I drank too damn much." She flopped back. "At least Reggie is opening the store so I don't have to go in until noon. My God, I feel like death warmed over."

He sat beside her and rubbed her temples. Her full lips parted to release a groan of pleasure. "So sleep. I'll wake you later."

"Where's Trent?"

"He said he was going running."

"That's right, he enjoys torture. I need a shower."

He ignored the visceral reaction her simple statement gave him. "Up you get," he said, assisting her.

Leaving her alone in the shower was one of the hardest things he'd done in a long time. He pivoted on his heels and walked out despite all that luscious temptation he saw behind the glass door.

He readjusted his hard cock and continued back on his way to the kitchen where he brewed himself another coffee. Something, anything to keep his hands busy so he wouldn't think about the woman standing under all that hot water, soaping up her body, touching parts he wanted to touch. Slick skin, wet skin. Her touch. Her scent.

"Damn it," he growled, rubbing his aching shaft.

Cup in hand, he strode outside to her shed and got to work building the arbor she'd asked him to build for the party. Physical exertion. That was all he needed.

Fucking her into exhaustion could, and would, be considered physical exertion. He shook his head, refusing to give into the devil riding his shoulder, hard. Time to work off this erection or it would drive him crazy.

* * * *

Ta-Mara rubbed the towel down her legs as the heat lamp above her helped to dry her. She could feel some wet strands on the back of her neck but for the most part, she'd kept her hair dry. The pounding in her head had receded a tiny bit. Not enough for her to be pleased but enough that she no longer wanted to kneel before the porcelain god. Which in her case was a blessing.

After hanging up her towel, she made her way from the bath to her large walk-in closet then searched for something to wear into work today. She picked up her shirt and found some shorts then went to grab some lingerie—choosing a peach lace bra and matching lace trim Cheeky panties from Victoria's Secret.

It didn't take her long to apply her lotion and draw on her shorts. She loved these shorts—cut off blue jeans that rode low on her hips. She didn't trim off the frayed edges either. Tugging her shirt on over her head, she turned a three-sixty in the mirror and checked out her appearance. Her black shirt had a burnout pattern all over it, and on the back there were silver seraphic wings. One of her favorites as well.

She brushed her hair and left it down then headed out of her room. After making a cup of coffee, she took the filled mug with her as she followed the sound of hammering out to the back. Levi worked by her shed on the arbor.

Even though it was relatively early in the day, he'd already stripped off his shirt. His jeans didn't hide anything from her hungry imagination. He wore a tool belt that hung low. She licked her lips. "Damn," she muttered watching him sweat as he cut, sawed and measured.

"Hey." She went down the steps and approached.

Levi looked up and grinned at her. "Feel better?"

"A bit. Coffee's helping for sure." She gestured with her mug. "How's it coming?"

"Good. I'll be done by the time you are finished with work. If Trent is around, I'll have him help me move it to where you want it."

Levi had seen her looking at an arbor in a catalog and said he could build it for her. She'd wanted one for a while now to put before entering her garden area. So she'd jumped on his offer.

"Wonderful."

He put down the measuring tape. "Are you sure you're okay?"

"Missed you in the shower," she said with a grin.

"You needed one without me interrupting."

"I like those interruptions. I'm going to get some work done in my office, yell if you need me."

He gave her a nod then turned his attention back to his job. She stood watching him for a bit longer before she turned and went back into the house. In her den, she powered up her computer then answered emails as she drank her coffee and willed her hangover away.

The willing didn't work, but at least she finished cleaning out her inbox. A lot of her friends—okay, most—were hooked on this having their smart phones, while she had no desire to get one. She didn't need the Internet at her fingertips twenty-four hours a day. She liked getting away and being unreachable. They might think her crazy but hey, she also lived somewhere she didn't have to lock her doors at night either, and if that was being crazy, she was proud to wear the title.

When the time came to leave for work, she brewed another cup and filled her travel mug. She went back out to say good-bye to Levi. Damn if the man didn't look better than when she'd seen him before.

"You sure you'll be fine?"

He brushed a kiss over her lips. "I'm good. I'll see you when you get home."

Raking her gaze over him once more, she sighed. Oh, the things they could do if she didn't have to work. "See you then."

She waved at him as she headed back inside. Trent showed up as she opened her car door.

"Long run?" she asked him as he stretched out.

"It was. You heading for work?"

"Yes. Levi is in the back building my arbor. I'll be back in time for dinner. There's plenty of food in the fridge, so y'all will be fine."

"I'll take care of him, cuz. Don't worry none."

"I don't need him taken care of, especially not with that tone, Trent. Y'all be nice."

His grin didn't exactly set her at ease. "Always."

"Yeah right," she muttered under her breath. Always, her ass. Trent was one of the most protective of her cousins. And she had a lot of them. Mostly male. She got in and went to work.

"Hey, Reggie!" she called out entering the store.

"Hi." He waved at her before returning his attention to the person he was currently helping.

She stored her things and smiled at some wanderers before slipping behind the counter and helping a woman who walked up. A while later, it was just the two of them.

"How are you doing, hon?" he asked.

"Good. You're coming to Jasmine's party right?"

"You actually got her to agree to one?"

"Not hardly. I'm lying to her to get her there. Telling her we're meeting at my house for drinks before we go out, so we can give her our gifts. We did it last year so she's not suspicious. But the party is at the house. Last year we let it go but this year, it's not happening."

"Sure, I'd love to come. Can I bring anything?"

"Nope, not a thing. It's all planned, just show up and be prepared to have fun."

"Karaoke?"

"Of course. Wouldn't be a party without that." She laughed, well aware of how much Reggie enjoyed his karaoke.

"Sounds great. Remind me the day of."

"Will do. Everyone's parking down at Jessie Mae's and coming through the woods so she doesn't see the cars."

"You're sneaky."

"Have to be with her." She shook her head in mock disgust. "If she would just let us celebrate her birthday, it wouldn't be such a big production."

"I think she secretly enjoys the attention."

After reaching for a stack of books, she began cleaning off the stickers. "I'm sure she does but...she's Jasmine."

"Very true. All right, I'm out. Have a wonderful rest of the day. We got in three more boxes, they're in the back. No rush on them. You look like you could use an easy day."

"Bite me," she snipped, knowing he spoke of her hangover. Damn man, he knew how she looked when she had one.

He snapped his teeth at her. "Time and place, baby."

"Get out of here." She rolled her eyes.

"You know if I wasn't leaving and the owner, I may just take offense at that."

She ignored him, focusing on the book before her. His laughter trailed him out of the door and she grunted as she worked on. The day seemed to pass in a blink. Amazingly enough, her hangover had disappeared by the time she had to leave for the night. She closed up quickly and made the night deposit before heading home.

The setting sun blazed upon the house when she pulled up and when she entered, she heard a mix of feminine and masculine laughter. Levi walked in as she left her bedroom, a plate in his hand.

"Company?" she asked.

His smile melted her heart. He kissed her and nodded. "Jessie Mae and Susie are here. Trent went and got her and we called Susie to come here after work."

Ta-Mara went to the fridge and filled a glass of tea, adding a lemon slice as Levi grabbed a few more beers after putting the plate in the sink. She followed him out there, a smile of her own filling her face as she saw her friends in the backyard. Trent was manning the grill, and there was laughter all around.

Chapter Thirteen

"Hey, come on in." Ta-Mara hugged Jasmine and Rachel as they entered her house. "Where's Heather?"

"Not sure, she just said she would be coming later." Jasmine glanced around as if expecting something to jump out at her.

"Wow, you are really suspicious, Jasmine. Maybe they're all hiding under my bed with their cars."

"A girl can't be too cautious."

"Whatever. Let's get a drink and see if Heather shows up before we finish. Maybe her boyfriend is dropping her off."

"Ohh, yeah, he's fine as hell. You've not met him yet, have you, Jasmine?" Rachel asked.

"Nope. I've heard about him but I haven't met him yet." She opened a bottle of wine. "Speaking of hot ass men, where's your man, Ta-Mara?"

"My man?"

Both her friends looked at her as if she had lost her ever-loving mind. "Yes, you know that hottie with the amazing blue eyes and a body which doesn't quit." Jasmine flipped her hair over her shoulder.

"Oh, Levi."

Jasmine glared at her. "You have someone else lying around?"

Wine poured, she lifted the glass to her lips. "Not that I'm aware of. But to answer your question, Trent is here and they went out. Didn't want to get in the way of our soirée." She lifted her glass. "Happy birthday, Jasmine."

The women clinked glasses and sipped the wine. As Rachel and Jasmine talked, Ta-Mara called Heather.

"Hello?"

"You on your way, Heather?"

"Just pulling in the drive now. Sorry I'm late. I was...sick."

"Okay," she said so the others didn't ask about the sickness. "We'll see you in a few." She snapped the phone shut. "She's just coming up the drive now."

Sure enough, soon Heather joined them and had a glass of wine before her—which Ta-Mara switched out with non-alcoholic wine the moment she could. Heather flashed her a grateful smile.

"Let me get your present, Jasmine," she said, heading to the living room where it sat on the coffee table.

The other women put theirs up on the counter as well. They rarely sat in the living room, the kitchen their favorite hangout spot. Topping off her wine, Ta-Mara said, "Open them."

"Mine first," Heather said.

Jasmine tore into it and opened the small box. "Oh, Heather, they're gorgeous."

She'd gotten her two ear wraps. Jasmine had a thorn tattoo around her hips, and these depicted bramble thorns. It swept up the ear, weeping tears of blood-red crystal, and had been handcrafted out of pewter.

"Thank you."

Rachel's gift was a gift certificate for a tattoo at the place where Jasmine had gone for her first one. She'd been talking about acquiring another one. Then it was Ta-Mara's turn.

The painting she'd gotten Jasmine was a lithograph of Sleeping Beauty, her favorite Disney film. The prince cut through the thorns upon his mighty steed and you could see the dragon in the background and Aurora lying upon her bed awaiting the kiss that would wake her.

"Y'all are the best," Jasmine said hugging each of them.

"Good. Remember that," Ta-Mara advised her.

Blue eyes narrowed. "Why?" Her voice laden with suspicion.

Seconds later when everyone burst in shouting "Happy Birthday!" she knew Jasmine understood. The look her friend gave promised retaliation. Blowing her a kiss, she retreated to Levi's side and slipped her arm around him.

When the doorbell rang later, she waded through the people and opened it. Matthew stood there, thumbs hooked in his belt loops.

"Hi, Matthew. Glad you could make it."

He tipped his hat slightly. "Thank you."

"Come on in, Heather's around here somewhere." She led him through the house to the backyard where the party was in full swing. Trent was singing karaoke, his deep baritone easily recognizable to her. "There are drinks and food, help yourself and make yourself at home.

On the top steps of the porch, she saw Levi lift his head and pin her with his gaze. The anger that flashed across his expression followed by the sense of danger, shocked her. Then she realized his attention remained on the man beside her. Levi stalked toward them, menace in each stride.

"Levi, this is Matthew. Heather's boyfriend."

He didn't respond, just appeared as if he wanted to tear the man from apart. This couldn't possibly be good.

Levi clenched his fist, striving to not rip the man limb from limb. He couldn't believe that Matthew Kline was Heather's boyfriend. That this monster who had ruined his life was himself dating a woman of color.

"Nice to meet you, Levi." Matthew held out his hand.

Levi stared at it fist clenched aching to knock it away. *"Let go of your anger. Of your hate."* Calliope's words echoed in his head. Levi breathed out then shook the offered hand.

"Matthew." He nodded. It was all he could manage as he tried to stop his instinctive reaction to hurt him.

Matthew stared at him then his face clouded. He inclined his head then turned to Ta-Mara. "I'll go find Heather."

He glanced at Levi once more then left. Ta-Mara moved closer to Levi and glared.

"What is your problem?"

"Nothing."

"Don't give me *nothing*." Ta-Mara poked at his arm. "You were rude to him. He's doesn't need it right now because of what he will have to deal with."

"What do you mean?" Levi glanced at Matthew. He was with Heather and smiling at her. His eyes narrowed as he recognized the expression on Matthew's face. He cared for Heather. It was shocking to equate him with someone who could be that way with anyone.

"Heather is nervous about introducing him to Jasmine."

"Why?"

"She's a snob and when she finds out he's a fisherman, she'll definitely act like it."

"Why does what he does have to do with anything?"

"Exactly. It shouldn't, but to Jasmine it does." Ta-Mara crossed her arms over her chest. "We'll see what happens and if he can stand up to her sharp tongue."

"Why are you all friends with her if she is that way?"

"Just because she is a snob doesn't mean she doesn't care about us. She's a friend." Ta-Mara frowned. "But I want to know why you are acting like an ass around him."

"Nothing." Levi rubbed his hand along the back of his neck. "I'll fix it."

He wasn't sure if he would, but he said it to appease her.

"Try fishing. Since you watch all those fishing shows, maybe you can bond over fish." Ta-Mara glared at him. "Be nice. Maybe take Trent along. He doesn't think you like him."

"What?" Levi didn't know either way how he felt about Trent.

"Make nice, Levi." Ta-Mara left.

Levi sighed, knowing from her snippy tone she was upset with him. He glanced at Matthew then looked around for Trent. If he had to try to make nice, Levi needed some fortification first. He went to get a beer then took a long drag before he went to approach Matthew. He came from behind the couple. *I have to stop thinking of him as the bastard who killed Calliope and tried to kill me. He's a different man, we both are.* He paused when he spotted Jasmine coming toward the couple. Levi waited to go to them, close enough to overhear.

"Heather, you've been keeping secrets. Introduce me to your friend," Jasmine said in the same flirtatious way she talked to him.

Levi winced in sympathy.

"This is Matthew. Matthew, this is Jasmine, my friend," Heather said nervously.

Levi had no idea why she cared so much what Jasmine thought.

"Hiya, Matthew." She shook his hand and held it too long. "Heather hasn't told me a thing about you. So fill me in, all about you. Who are you to her, and where has she been hiding you?"

"I'm her boyfriend." Matthew placed his hand on Heather's waist. "Nice to meet you, Jasmine. I've heard a lot about you."

Levi held back a snicker hearing the emphasis on the last part.

"I'm at a disadvantage then." Jasmine smiled.

"I'm a fisherman so you needn't bother wasting your time with me." Matthew shrugged. "I'm not someone who you'd find anything in common with."

"Matthew!" Heather watched him wide-eyed.

"What? You didn't think I knew who she was. Not at first, but a buddy of mine had a date with her once. When she found out what he did, she was out of there so fast." Matthew smiled broadly. "You're Heather's friend and we'll be cordial to each other, but not bond, and I'm good with that. Just be warned, I don't want to hear anything negative about her. Got it?" His tone was firm.

Jasmine blinked then swallowed. "Yes."

Matthew bent and kissed Heather on the cheek. "I'm gonna get a beer. You want anything?"

"A juice, and how the hell you did that." Heather gestured to Jasmine. "She's stunned and mute now. I've never seen her like that."

"It's a gift." Matthew grinned then went to get their drinks.

Levi knew he should walk away but he was curious, so he stayed to hear.

"Heather." Jasmine blew out a breath. "Where did you find Mr. U—?"

"If you are about to say something negative, remember what Matthew said."

"He said not about you. It was about him." Jasmine crossed her arms over her chest, looking toward where Matthew went. "He's—"

"My boyfriend." Heather lifted a hand in warning. "And you can't say anything about him. I won't allow you to in my presence. I was so nervous about your meeting him and caring what you thought. I was stupid." Heather shook her head. "I love you, Jasmine, but take the snobbery out your ass and make him feel welcome."

Jasmine's choked then laughed. "Oh God, girl, when you tell me off, you do it well." She put her arm over her shoulder. "Fine, I won't comment when you come hang with us smelling like fish."

"Jasmine."

"Okay, okay." She sighed. "Damn, first Ta-Mara finds tall, luscious and intense and now you get tall, sexy, broody and speaks his mind. You lucky heifers."

"Maybe if you didn't act like such a diva, you would find someone too."

"Now what fun would that be." Jasmine fanned herself. "All these fine men in here and I'm old. I'm gonna get you all for this party."

"Be grateful." Ta-Mara came up to the women.

"And say thank you," Rachel, who had come with her, said.

"Thanks." Jasmine smiled softly. "Love you guys."

"We know," the three women said together.

They all laughed. Levi turned and made his way to the other side of the yard. He walked toward Matthew and knew he had seen him from the way—his stance became rigid. Levi stood by him and drank his beer. Matthew sipped from his, not saying anything. Familiar laughter caught Levi's attention and he stared at Ta-Mara as she lifted her head back, teasing her friends. A warm feeling filled him and Levi he knew because of her he had to try.

"So you're a fisherman?"

"Yep." Matthew didn't say anything further.

"Come on. I'm trying." Levi glared at him.

"That's trying?" Matthew looked at him in disbelief.

"Yes," he said icily.

"Then you need loads of practice." Matthew lifted an eyebrow. "You shoulda started with 'I'm an asshole who didn't know you but acted like an idiot'."

"I... Can we just talk about fish? I like fishing," he said.

"Okay." Matthew studied him. "Is this where I'm supposed to ask you to come fishing with me? What I do isn't for leisure, it's work."

"I know that but you have to like it, right?"

"No, you don't. I happen to love what I do." Matthew lifted his bottle. "So if you ever want to come fishing, you can come with me and the guy who I work with. It's my boat, but he pays some of the expenses we have and we share the profits of what we make."

"Is his name John? Was he in the bookstore with you?"

"Yes. I forgot that you were there."

Levi didn't know if he would be comfortable with not just one but both of them on a boat. *You're thinking of the past. This is the present and you need to give them a chance.*

"Fishing would be good." Levi looked for Trent. "Can I bring Ta-Mara's cousin?"

"Sure. The more the merrier. We'll go for fun instead of when I'm working. I'll let you know when I have some time." Matthew put out his hand. "So, do over."

Levi shook his hand and hoped it was indeed a do over and Matthew was as he seemed. "Doing fishing as a job, how difficult is it to get started?"

"You looking for a job?"

"Maybe." Each time Ta-Mara paid for something, Levi didn't like he didn't have any money to contribute his share.

"It is back-breaking work. Some do it and hate it, which pisses them off every day. You should find something you love. At least that's what I think." Matthew shrugged. "That being said, I can take you out one time with me and John when we're working, and you can see if it is something you want to do."

"Thanks." Levi thought of what he had seen on televisions and imagined doing that every day.

He had no idea if he would like it or not. They went and joined the women. Levi stood beside Ta-Mara and listened absently as the others conversed.

"Levi."

He brought his attention back to the group. "Yes?" he answered Jasmine, who had called him.

"Ta-Mara was telling us you made the arbor"—Jasmine waved toward it—"from a picture she saw in a catalog. It's beautiful and I checked it out earlier. Very well put together. Seems like you are good with your hands." Jasmine smiled.

Levi was surprised to find she wasn't acting flirtatiously as she usually did. Jasmine looked at Ta-Mara and winked. Levi wondered what that was about—he made a mental note to ask her later.

"Yes I did."

"That's good." Jasmine bit her lip then said, "Maybe if you have time, you could build me a back deck on my house? I've been wanting one but can't find someone I think would do a good job. I'll pay you for your work. Give you a down payment for the work then the rest when you complete it."

"Let me know what you are looking for and I'll do it." Levi immediately was excited—he loved working with his hands. "There is no need to pay me."

"Yes, there is. You're going to be doing an extensive project for me." Jasmine waved her hand. "I insist."

"I—"

"He'll do it." Ta-Mara touched his arm, squeezing it. "And will accept payment."

"Okay." Levi wasn't sure what was going on but he went along with it.

"Good. I'll show you some pictures of decks I like and we can figure out what features of each we will need and come up with something."

"Sound good," Levi said.

"You're a carpenter?" Matthew asked. "Why aren't you doing that as a job?"

Levi had no idea. He'd never thought of building things and fixing stuff as a possibility of supporting himself.

"You want a job?" Ta-Mara looked at him.

"We'll talk about it later," Levi said.

Ta-Mara didn't push and focused back on the people around them. They parted ways as she went to check on her guests. Levi walked around the party and when people complimented him on the work he'd done for Ta-Mara, as well as Jessie Mae, he didn't know what to say. People asking if he would be willing to do some work for him, fixing stuff or making things, baffled him. He took their information and said he'd be in touch. By the time the party wrapped up, people were slightly drunk and very happy. As they took their leave, he stood by Ta-Mara's side and saw them off.

"Thanks for making my birthday so fabulous." Jasmine hugged Ta-Mara.

"Anything for you." She kissed her cheek then held her before she could step back. "You're still a sexy woman, Jasmine. Like fine wine, you get better with age."

"So damn corny." Jasmine chuckled. "But I love you, girl. Call me, Levi, so we can get started on that deck."

"Okay." He watched as she left.

Ta-Mara closed the door then hummed as she headed to the kitchen. Levi followed.

"Did you put Jasmine up to asking her to build her a deck?"

She stopped and looked at him. "What? No."

"Then why did she ask?"

"Because she looked at the arbor you built for me and was impressed. I mentioned that you did it then she asked questions." She pursed her lips. "One thing you should know about Jasmine—she doesn't blow smoke up your butt. If she didn't think you have talent, she wouldn't have asked you to do the deck for her. Even if I had asked her to, which I didn't. So take the props she gave you and do it. And the payment for it. I know it bugs you that you don't have any money of your own. Now here is a chance for you to get some of your own. Give her a fair price, then go from there."

"I didn't know you realized I was bothered by that."

"You grimace every time I pay for something." She smiled. "So I sort of figured it out."

"Okay." Levi hesitated then. "Others have asked me to build things for them and do odd jobs."

"Really? That's great. There you go. You can have your own little business. Word of mouth travels fast and you'll be making your own funds." She bit her lips then made a clicking sound with her teeth. "We're gonna have to get you set up with a bank account, that way you can deposit money you make. We can do that now."

He'd heard of a bank account. "I won't need that."

"Yes, you will." Ta-Mara grabbed his arm. "Let's go figure out what's reasonable prices for building a deck then look into bank accounts."

"Ta-Mara, I'm not sure about this."

"From what Matthew said, seems like you discussed getting a job with him. Which surprised me, since you didn't seem all that keen on him."

"I went to make nice and it came up." He hugged her. "We're going fishing and taking Trent. Although I think it is the other way around. Your cousin doesn't care about me too much."

"He just doesn't know you well enough." Ta-Mara paused. "Wait, maybe he can help you with the deck."

"Isn't he studying to be a lawyer?" Levi frowned. "Does he even know anything about building things?"

"He spent his summers working on construction sites. So yeah he does, and he could be a help getting you good prices on materials. He can ask some of his construction buddies." Ta-Mara bounced on her heels. "That would be great. You all can get to know each other over building shit. All manly and stuff."

"It seems important to you that we like each other."

"It is."

"Okay then I'll try." Levi hugged her. "For you."

He would do that for her. Like he had talked to Matthew earlier because of her. Levi stared, realizing he would do a lot for her.

"Then do something else for me?" She shifted on her feet.

"What?" He cupped her cheek.

"Move into my bedroom." She bit her lip then said, "It's stupid for you to have your stuff in your room and me in mine, when we sleep mostly together. I want it to be all the time."

"That would be my pleasure." Satisfaction filled Levi at her asking.

It was a step in the right direction. Maybe Ta-Mara was lowering the walls she had in place.

"Yes." She blew out a breath. "Good. Now let's go plan your first of many jobs, get you a bank account then moved into my bedroom."

Levi went with her as she took him to do all she said she would. Of all of them, he especially couldn't wait to be sleeping by her side every night. He would make sure he didn't do anything to mess what they had up.

You need to tell her about Calliope. Levi stopped, not sure how to go about that. He'd called her by the name of a woman he loved. He didn't know how Ta-Mara would react to learning about her.

"Are you okay?" She rubbed her hands up and down his arms.

"Yes." Levi put it away for now.

There was no rush for him to reveal stuff from his past. They had time.

Chapter Fourteen

Levi sat back and wiped the back of his hand across his forehead. He glanced down at the foundation of the deck. Jasmine had decided she wanted it slightly raised, so there were a few steps up. Levi had been surprised at how informed she was on what she wanted. After getting an idea of her preference, he'd ended up using the different decks she had pictured and drawing something up for her. That had impressed her as well as Ta-Mara. Levi smiled as he thought of the woman who was his.

In the last few weeks, they had gotten even closer and he loved it. He'd also gotten to know Jasmine more over the last two weeks, when they'd spent time together getting materials then later with him working on the deck. She wasn't all that bad. A little brash and abrasive at times but she was a good person.

"Stop slacking and daydreaming about my friend," Jasmine said behind him.

Levi turned and he chuckled. "Caught me."

She laughed and looked at what he was working on then back at him. "I can't believe how this is coming together so quickly."

"Yes." Levi smoothed his hand on the wood. "It took us longer to get it figured out what you wanted."

"I know." She chuckled ruefully. "But you got it for me. Oh, here."

Levi rose and went to her, taking the paper she held out. He glanced at it and his eyes widened as he saw his name on the check she handed him.

"We agreed you'd wait until I was done to pay me anything."

"Nope, you said that. I didn't agree. What I said the first time is what I meant. Here is a partial payment for your work. The rest, I will pay when you've finished." Jasmine slid her hands into her pockets. "I've been bragging about you doing this deck for me. I showed the drawing to some people I know, so you'll probably be getting more calls to do work for people."

Levi was surprised. Since Ta-Mara's party, he'd been busy doing work. His checking and saving accounts now had some money in them. It was such a good feeling to have funds of his own.

"Don't look so shocked." Jasmine squeezed his arm. "You're a hard worker and very good at what you do, so that will make people want to hire you."

"Thanks." He hugged her.

Jasmine chuckled then returned it, patting his back. "Don't make Ta-Mara kick my ass by getting too touchy feely."

"Like I'm worried about you," Ta-Mara said close by.

Levi looked at her, not having heard her arrive. "Ta-Mara?"

"The big bad boss you are working for decided to give you freedom for the day." Ta-Mara lifted on her toes and kissed him on the cheek. "I have someplace I want to take you."

"Okay." He glanced at Jasmine.

"Why do you think I came outside?" Jasmine waved. "It was to distract you so she could surprise you. Now go."

He put the check she had given him in his pocket then went to put away his tools. The women talked as he did and Levi stopped to call to Trent. Trent had been a help and Levi would miss him when he left to go back to law school in a few days. He took out his ear buds and Levi told him to knock off early. Trent nodded and rose. Levi returned to Ta-Mara.

"Hey, Trent," she called.

"Hey, cuz." Trent hugged her then left.

They followed him. By the time, they reached the front of Jasmine's house, he had driven away.

"Jasmine told me she gave you a check."

"Yes, I need to get to the bank to deposit it," Levi said.

"Not needed. Let me show you the wonders of electronic deposit." Ta-Mara wiggled her fingers. "Lemme have the check."

He gave it to her then watched as she took out her cell. She went to the website of the bank they both used.

"Sign in," Ta-Mara said.

Then Ta-Mara held up her phone and snapped a picture. Soon she showed him the screen and Levi frowned, seeing the picture of the check. She pressed a few buttons then showed him the completed transaction.

"That's it. Your funds are there and availability will be in about a day or so."

"Are you sure?" Levi couldn't wrap his mind around that his money would be there. Then again, despite all he had seen, there was a lot he was still learning.

"Yep." She smiled and gave him back the check. "You can frame that as your first pay check you ever received. I don't use the mobile deposit because I prefer to go to the bank, but I figured I'd show it to you so you know it is an option."

"Thanks, but I think I like going in person better." Although he knew technology was supposedly good, he was still leery of it.

"Okay. But you have the opportunity to do either." Ta-Mara gestured to her Mariner. "You drive. I'll direct you."

"Where are we going?" He opened the passenger side door for her and after she was in, he went to the driver's side then got in and started the car.

"It's a surprise." She leaned back against the seat.

"I've liked your surprises so far, so that's good." He backed out of Jasmine's drive then turned onto the main road.

They chatted and in between, she gave him directions. Levi didn't recognize where they were. They had explored a lot of and he was getting to know the area. He pulled into the gates she pointed to and he grinned.

"We're going riding," he said, having seen the sign on the entrance they'd come in.

"You're going riding." She shook her head. "As I mentioned, I'm not much of a rider."

"You have to come with me," he protested.

"This is for you."

Levi parked and got out before meeting her at the hood of the vehicle. Ta-Mara led him to the stables.

"Ta-Mara." The man who came to them was tall as Levi was and reminded him of the pictures he'd seen of Vikings. He had the hair, eyes, coloring and build.

He hugged Ta-Mara and Levi's eyes narrowed. He stifled a growl. Although he'd got used to Ta-Mara being so outgoing, it still made him want to stake his claim when she was touched by another man. She turned to him, holding out her hand. Smug, Levi slid his hand into hers as she brought him to her side.

"Levi, this is Malcolm McGarrett, he's the owner of the MM Stables. Mal, this is Levi."

"Nice to meet you." Malcolm held out his hand.

Levi shook it. "You too."

Now that he wasn't touching Ta-Mara, Levi actually meant it.

"Ta-Mara told me you know about horses." Malcolm crossed his arms over his chest. "Before anyone gets on my horses, they have to show me they know what they are doing or I have to teach them. So show me what you have."

"Mal!"

"It's okay, Ta-Mara." He kissed her cheek, watching Malcolm deliberately. "I would do the same to anyone who wanted to be on my horses." He straightened then gestured. "Show me your horses."

Malcolm led them inside. Levi inhaled, loving the scent. Immediately the animals started putting their heads outside their stalls. He released Ta-Mara and went to each. He greeted them and spoke softly to them. He lost himself in being around horses again. At the last stall, Levi's heart clenched as he saw the animal there. It was beautiful and regal, reminding him of his favorite one. He stroked the nose, memories filling him of riding across the fields, excited at the feel of the horse beneath him. The escape it offered was one he appreciated. He turned and was surprised to see only Ta-Mara.

"Malcolm said take your pick." Ta-Mara smiled. "The gear is in the room over there. Don't know what he saw when you spoke with his horses, but it impressed him enough to trust you."

"You're coming with me." Levi held her hand. "We can ride double so you don't have to feel afraid."

"I—"

"Do it for me," he urged.

Ta-Mara stared at him then nodded. Happy, he went to get the gear. Soon he had the horse ready and led it outside. Ta-Mara was waiting a little way from the stables. He got into the saddle then rode over to her. Levi paused before her and leaned over, holding out his hand. She accepted it without hesitation and he lifted her onto the horse behind him.

"Just hold on to me."

"Okay." Ta-Mara slid her hands around his waist and pressed herself against his back.

He touched her hand then, taking the reins and got them on their way. Levi followed a path and as they rode, he felt a sense of peace in his bones. With Ta-Mara at his back and the world laid out before him, Levi knew life was going to be good. He lifted one of her hands and kissed her fingertips. Levi kept along the path then stopped. He turned, shifting Ta-Mara to his lap and held her. The sun started to set and, glancing down into her face bathed by the light, Levi couldn't believe how lucky he was to be here with her.

"So beautiful." She touched his cheek.

"That's you." He turned his head and kissed the palm of her hand. "Inside and out." He gazed at her then kissed her.

Ta-Mara's breathy sigh made him tighten his hold. Yes, he was indeed blessed to be here with her.

* * * *

Levi wiped off the railing then went down to the yard where he stood back and took in the deck he'd built. A sense of pride filled him at seeing what he had accomplished. Building the deck for Jasmine made him certain this was what he wanted to do as a job. Two weeks of working daily and the job was completed. Levi went and packed his tools then headed outside to wait for Ta-Mara. He glanced at the clouds overhead and remembered the news had said it would rain.

He sat on the front step and observed the neighborhood. The eclectic mix of people still amazed him when he saw them walking together. Yes, he knew there was still some who hated people because of their color, if it was different to their own, but it wasn't as widespread as it had been during the time he was from. The familiar vehicle came down the road and he stood, going to the sidewalk to meet Ta-Mara.

He got in. "Hey." Levi leaned over and kissed her gently.

"Hey, there." Ta-Mara grinned widely and she placed her hand on his thigh.

Even through the cloth, Levi felt her touch as if it was on his skin. "How was your day?"

"Same as usual." She put her hands on the steering wheel and set off toward home. "Selling books to people and reading when it wasn't busy. Love being able to do that."

"Loving what you do is a good thing." That reminded Levi. "Matthew called me and I'm going fishing with him this weekend."

"Great." Ta-Mara made a turn. "Too bad Trent left already. He would have liked it."

"Yeah. I miss your cousin."

"No need to sound so surprised." Ta-Mara chuckled. "I knew your working together would let you get to know him better. And he you."

"We did." Levi was surprised her cousin wasn't quite like what he'd thought.

Working with Trent, Levi had learned a lot more about him. Trent had shared about himself and given Levi some insights into Ta-Mara and her family. The man had actually turned out to become a good friend.

"Why have I never met the rest of your family?" Levi absently noticed it had started to rain.

He'd heard her talk to them on phone but not seen any of them in person, although he knew they lived in town. At the time he'd wondered about that, but he'd figured they were busy. As time had passed, that didn't seem as likely. After being around Trent, he'd further been made aware that her family was close-knit. That only made it stranger to him they hadn't been around, even once. His only conclusion was that Ta-Mara was keeping them hidden from him, or him away from them. Either one didn't sit well with him.

"Just been busy, I guess." Ta-Mara clenched the steering wheel.

"It's not because you have been avoiding them?" Levi paused. "Or because you don't want them to see me?"

"Levi." She stopped then continued, "I have been avoiding them, and yes, I didn't want them to see. At first because I didn't know how to explain you. Then when we got you all set up and you got more used to this time, I didn't want to have them influence what we have."

"Influence? How would they do that?" Levi watched her.

"By asking questions and being nosy." She turned into her drive. "I didn't want to share you. That's the main reason."

"But we see your friends and others."

"Yes." She parked then shut off the car before facing him. "But it's not the same as if I share you with family. They would want to get to know you more and I'm not ready for that yet. Want your time to be just with me. Yes we see friends, but it's limited. I'm selfish and want you to myself for a little longer."

"Okay." He touched her cheek. "I like you being possessive of me."

Her explanation eased his concern — at least for now. He could understand her need for it to be just the two of them, since he too felt the same when they were with other and he couldn't wait to get her alone.

"Good. Because I can more than do that. Be possessive and keep you to myself." Ta-Mara looked out of the windshield. "Figures it would rain when I thought the weather man was lying. Humph, half the time he gets the opposite of what happens with the weather. But not today. I didn't bring an umbrella. Let's make a run for it."

"Wait for me to get your door." Levi got out. He closed the door, ran around to her side of the vehicle and opened her door.

Ta-Mara got out, smiling. He closed the door then held her hand, running with her.

Suddenly Ta-Mara jerked on his hand. "Wait."

Levi stopped. "Ta-Mara, we need to get out of the rain."

"Why?" She pulled her hand away. "Enjoy it. I love storms."

Ta-Mara moved away from him and she looked up and spun, laughing joyously. Levi smiled hearing the sound. Lightning flashed and Ta-Mara spun again then met his gaze. Levi's breath caught at her beauty. Backlit by nature's majesty, she was stunning. The storm raged around them but all he saw was her. This woman who had gotten under his skin from their first meeting. Ta-Mara kept him on his toes and challenged him to strive for more. She'd helped him take that step to start his carpentry business when he'd doubted if he should. She had been in his corner from the time she'd found him and had never wavered.

Ta-Mara pushed her hair back from her face then swayed in the rain. She moved slowly and sensuously and Levi was captivated. Ta-Mara kicked up her heels and danced around the area, her giggles echoing. She came to him and when she was close, Levi pulled her to him. She wrinkled her nose and, unable to resist, he kissed it. Levi placed his hands on her waist and danced with her in the rain. Ta-Mara smirked and waltzed with him. He kept moving and her eyes closed as she let him lead her. The trust of her in that moment humbled him. Levi twirled her away from him then brought her back into his frame.

"Yes, Levi." She chuckled, her hands pressed against his chest. "That's the sprit. Enjoy the storm with me."

He did it again and her hearty guffaw made him *want*.

"I'm enjoying being with you." Levi placed his hand on the side of her face. "I love you, Ta-Mara."

She stiffened then her eyes widened. "Levi—"

"I do." Levi didn't know for sure when it happened but he did love Ta-Mara. Loved her with all his being.

"I…" She bit her lip then blurted out, "Love you too. But, Levi, we don't know what will happen."

He already knew they didn't but he didn't care. Ta-Mara loved him and that was all he needed to hear. He was home, and Levi would do everything in his power to not let her go.

"You never know what happens when it comes to life. Nothing is promised to anyone." He hugged her. "We love each other and for now, that's all that matters." Levi kissed her gently. "I promise to take care of your heart, Ta-Mara LeBreaux."

"And I yours, Levi Madison." She placed her hand over his heart. "I trust you, Levi."

"Ditto." He chuckled as he used the slang. He was blending in and each new thing he learned, she shared it with him.

Levi kissed her, holding her and they continued to dance in the rain. Ta-Mara sank against him, fitting him perfectly. Just as she had brought him into her life, Levi was still surprised and pleased how well they fit. He raised his head and stared into the eyes of the woman he loved. At her sultry smile, he hardened. Levi pulled her tighter against him. With her breathy gasp as she felt his erection, he wanted to be horizontal, vertical or any way he could have her.

"I need you, Ta-Mara." He shifted his hold then lifted her into his arms.

Ta-Mara wrapped her legs around him and whispered against his lips, "Take me to our bed."

He kissed her first. Deep and sure, affirming that she was his. Ta-Mara gave as good as she got and Levi's knees went weak. He pulled away from their kiss and held her ass as he carried her toward the house. Ta-Mara tightened her legs around his waist, rubbing on him. He hurried up the steps then paused for her to open the door. Shortly he stood by their bed then stripped her down, as well as himself, before he laid her on the sheets. He lay on her, smoothing her wet hair away from her face. Ta-Mara pulled his head down and kissed him deeply. She widened her legs and he settled between them. Levi stared into her eyes as he stroked into her. Ta-Mara's gaze darkened and she arched, moaning.

He thrust, enjoying the way her eyes changed with each motion he made. Levi shuddered as she clenched around him.

"Ta-Mara," he said softly, "I love you."

At his words, Ta-Mara's heart again filled with joy. She hadn't expected him to say it and had never thought they would have a chance. Levi was on borrowed time since they had no idea when or if he would be taken back to his era. Yet that didn't stop the hope that swelled when he said those three little words. Levi loved her and Ta-Mara loved him. He was hers and she his. Anything else, they would have to figure out.

"Mine." She rocked her hips under him.

Levi plunged again and she gasped. He knew her so well, knowing just what she liked in and out of bed. She gripped his shoulders, moving with him as he took her. Ta-Mara held him, loving the delicious tightening in her pussy. She groaned, countering his rhythm and he intensified her pleasure. Levi gripped her thigh and pulled it higher on his hip, changing the angle of his thrusts. She moaned at each slide of him, in and out.

"*Levi*." She stiffened as she came.

Ta-Mara grabbed his ass, holding him. He thrust once more then grunted as he joined her in release. Levi collapsed on her and Ta-Mara enjoyed his weight. She rubbed her hand up and down his sweat slick back then kissed his shoulder. Levi turned his head, kissing her before he rolled off of her. He came back to her and covered her with his body, gathering her close.

Ta-Mara yawned. "I have to dry my hair or it will be a mess."

"Stay here." Levi levered off the bed.

She watched his bare ass as he padded into the adjoining bathroom. When he disappeared from view, she was disappointed to lose the sexy sight. In moments, he was back and had the hair dryer and big tooth comb. Levi came to her side of the bed and plugged it in.

"Up," he demanded

Ta-Mara sat up and reached for the items. Levi held them away then made a turnaround gesture. Ta-Mara did as he bid. He started the dryer and pulled the comb through her hair. She sighed at the firm pull. She'd have to wash it tomorrow but for now, she let Levi take care of her. He dried her hair and when he'd finished, he pressed his lips to her bare shoulder before he put the dryer away and came back to bed. Ta-Mara lay against him and he placed his hand on her ass. Levi kissed her before he yawned then settled down to sleep. Ta-Mara watched him before she too followed him into slumber.

* * * *

She stared up at Levi, heart pounding as he positioned himself over her. He put his leg between hers and opened her for his taking. Clenching her pussy, she waited for him, aching for his touch as she did every time they were together or apart. She gripped his forearms, which were braced over her, and he pushed into her. The fullness as he slid home made her arch. And that was where he was – home. Moaning, she stared into the eyes of the man she loved.

"Levi." She moaned as he moved inside her, setting off sensations she had become so used to.

He was her home and she knew she was his. They had declared themselves and all that was stopping them from taking that step to become man and wife was the law. The law that made them hide so they could be with each other. The fear that made them unable to acknowledge each other in public. Except here, in private, they let their emotions free. Let their bodies meld to show their love for each other.

"Calliope." His gaze was intense. "No one will take you from me."

She believed him. This man, despite everything, wanted her. Her. She would not let anyone dictate to her that this was wrong and make her stop seeing him. She would fight for him and love him forever. Levi Jefferson Davis Madison was her man, the other half of her soul, and there was nothing she would not do for him.

Calliope stared off to her right. "Will you be willing to sacrifice your pride and all else for him?"

Ta-Mara sat up, gasping. She shivered as she thought of what she had just experienced. She'd felt each motion of Levi as he took Calliope. Lived in her thoughts, knowing the fierceness of her convictions to have Levi. When the woman had spoken, Ta-Mara could swear she was speaking directly to her. "But that is impossible," she whispered.

"Ta-Mara." Levi's sleep-roughened voice sounded from beside her. He put his hand on her back. "Are you okay?"

She flinched at his touch then forced herself to turn and smile at him. "I'm fine. Go back to sleep. I just need to get some water." She rose.

"I'll get it for you," he offered.

"No." She inhaled, clearing her throat. "I'll do it. Sleep."

She couldn't look at him. Ta-Mara grabbed her robe from over the chair then shrugged into it before heading for the door. Space. She needed some space from him. Being a voyeur during what he and Calliope had shared had been arousing yet painful. He'd loved someone else as deeply as he loved her. Ta-Mara was raw from that, and she needed to get herself together so he didn't know anything was wrong.

"Are you sure you're okay?" Levi called.

"Yes." She closed her eyes. *Except your woman from your time came to stake her claim.*

Saying that was not an option. One, it sounded crazy. Two, she didn't even know how to articulate what had happened. Three, it sounded like she was wacko. Yeah, she counted losing her sanity twice. She opened her eyes and went out of the room. Besides, she'd not even told Levi she'd known of him before she'd met him. Ta-Mara thought of the book on her dresser. She hadn't read it since Levi had arrived and still had no clue how it had ended up in her bedroom. After the incident when she'd touched it, Ta-Mara hadn't gone near it again. Levi had never asked about it. She leaned against the wall, just out of view of the door. If Calliope was invading her dreams and she hadn't even touched the book, Ta-Mara was definitely not moving it from her dresser. She slid down, sinking to her knees.

"God, I'm losing my mind," she whispered. "What is happening to me?"

Chapter Fifteen

Ta-Mara pushed her hair back from her face and breathed deeply. Shakily, she rose and went to get something to drink. In the kitchen, she grabbed a bottle of water then slammed the fridge closed before she turned and braced herself against the kitchen island. She held the cold water bottle against the side of her face and slid it down.

"Are you sure you're okay?"

Ta-Mara jumped and glanced toward the doorway. She hadn't heard Levi approach. He was leaning against the doorframe, staring at her with concern in his gaze. Warmth filled her and she went to him. He opened his arms as she neared and gratefully she stepped into his embrace. She sank against him and inhaled his scent. It calmed her.

"I'm good now."

Levi rubbed his hands up and down her spine then kissed the top of her forehead. "Come back to bed."

She let him lead her to the bedroom. *Please don't let me have any more dreams.*

In moments, Levi had them settled in bed and Ta-Mara tried to relax but sleep eluded her. She stared off into the night outside the windows. Suddenly a ghostly face appeared and Ta-Mara sat up, gasping as she stared. The woman stared back at her and Ta-Mara blinked. It was still there. Looking at the spitting image of herself, Ta-Mara tried to calm her racing heart. She figured she was making the ghost of Calliope into her own image. Ta-Mara didn't even try to figure out why she was doing that. The see-through woman smiled then looked beyond her to Levi. A sad expression filtered across her face then she returned her attention to Ta-Mara. The vision blew on the window and a foggy, freaky mist appeared. With a finger, the ghost started to write. Ta-Mara stared wide-eyed as she read what it said.

Wise up, Ta-Mara, and get you head out of your ass before you lose him.

She frowned then rolled her eyes. "Really, you're from the great beyond or some shit and you decide to send me a smart-ass message. I would think you would have a better use for your time."

The specter with her face glared at Ta-Mara then floated backward and lifted its middle finger.

"Now you're giving me the bird. Real mature." Ta-Mara crossed her arms over her chest.

The image gestured behind Ta-Mara. Ta-Mara glanced at Levi who still slept, oblivious to anything going on, then to the mirror.

"I'm not going to let him go." Ta-Mara paused then added, "I know his heart in the past belonged to another but he is mine now." *At least as long as he is here with me. Please don't take him away from me.*

Ta-Mara didn't say that fear out loud. In her thoughts was bad enough. The ghost smiled then faded.

Ta-Mara rubbed her fingers along the bridge of her nose as she whispered, "Yeah, I'm really losing it. First, I get a man from the past coming to me, I fall in love with him and don't want to be without him. Now I'm having dreams about another woman's life. Then to top it all off, I'm seeing a ghost of said woman. And damn if she doesn't look like me too. There is just so much a psychiatrist would have to say about that." She chuckled wryly. "Pull it together, Ta-Mara. Come back to sanity. All of this is a dream." Looking at Levi, she amended, "God, I hope it isn't a dream because it would hurt me if he wasn't real."

Ta-Mara lay beside him and put her hand on his chest. The rise and fall as he breathed steadily made her believe the reality of him being here. She snuggled against him and Levi pulled her close, not waking. Even when he was asleep she felt cherished and protected. She listened to him breathe and finally went to sleep.

* * * *

Ta-Mara yawned as she shuffled around the store. Thankfully they were not so busy today. She paused and stared off into space. As they had all day, her thoughts turned to last night and all that happened. She still couldn't explain the dream that had felt so real or the ghostly visitor. When she'd woken, this morning she'd still been feeling a little weirded out about it. But just a little, since with all that had been going on lately in her life, and Levi appearing as he had, and her knowing he was from the past, she wasn't really that shocked that more shit was happening. At least last night she hadn't dreamed again.

Don't let it happen again. Don't let me dream about her again. Ta-Mara repeated what had become her mantra since she'd woken this morning.

The sound of the bell ringing as the door opened made her turn and head back toward the front. Entering the area, she was surprised to see Matthew and his fishing partner John. She smiled in welcome and went to them but Ta-Mara noticed that John had a sneer on his lips and a nasty look on his face. In the next moment, it was gone and he was the same jovial man who had come in before with Matthew. She shook it off as she imagined it.

"Hey, Matthew and John, nice to see you again." Ta-Mara stopped before them.

"Ta-Mara." Matthew's greeting was warm.

John nodded curtly but didn't say anything. Uneasy, Ta-Mara glanced at John and she couldn't put her finger on it, but he seemed different. The first time he had come to the store he had seemed friendly enough, but now she wasn't so sure. Cautiously, she glanced at him then focused on Matthew.

"What can I do for you?" Ta-Mara slid her hands into the pockets of her blue sundress.

"I've been telling John about your great collection of military books you have." Matthew grinned. "I saw some really good ones the other day and we were talking about it so we came here to browse."

"Feel free." Ta-Mara gestured. "Do you need me to sh—?"

"Nah. I know where it is." Matthew touched her shoulder. "You go back to work, we can help ourselves."

Ta-Mara nodded and they went down the aisle. John glanced back at her and Ta-Mara tried to still her unease. When they disappeared from view, she went to the counter and straightened up. Soon the men returned to the front with their books. As she checked them out, Ta-Mara answered their questions and she felt silly, as John was his charming self.

"Have a great day." She waved as the men departed.

With them gone, she sat on the high stool and drummed her fingers on the countertop. She checked the time and seeing it was only an hour until she usually closed, she decided to leave early. Quickly she completed the shop closing and headed out. Moments later in her vehicle, Ta-Mara tapped her finger on the steering wheel as she drove. She'd make it home before Levi for a change. She smiled at the thought then considered how she could greet him when he arrived. Ta-Mara licked her lips, thinking of what she wanted to do. Meet him naked and get their night off to an invigorating start. She hummed along with *We Got Hood Love* by Mary J Blige on the radio as she went. Deliberately she kept her mind blank and didn't let any of her worries intrude. She kept up her humming and tapping through a few songs.

When she pulled up into her driveway, she turned off the engine mid-song and got out. Shaking her hips, she went up the drive singing the last song that had been playing under her breath softly. She went up the steps quickly then, bypassing the door, she went to the back, planning to relax on the swing for a little while before putting her plan in action—to be ready, willing and waiting for Levi to return. As she turned the corner of the wrap-around porch, Ta-Mara inhaled, enjoying the familiar scent of her gardens and home. She went toward the swing but stopped when she spotted the man sprawled on the porch on one of the seats she kept by the back door for just such a thing. Levi was asleep and Ta-Mara went closer, studying him. In sleep, he was still sexy as hell and she loved him with all her heart.

She stopped standing over him, gazing at him. Levi smiled and opened his eyes.

"Hey."

"So you were playing possum." Ta-Mara smiled.

"I heard when you came around the side of the house." Levi put his hand on her ankle. He rubbed his finger along her skin.

Ta-Mara shivered and heat pooled in her belly. Levi's slow smile made her know he was aware of what he did to her. He slid his hand up the back of her lower leg then down. She bit her lip.

"Ta-Mara," he said in that husky voice she so loved.

Levi put his other hand on the front of his jeans. He rubbed along the bulge growing there. Then with his one hand, unbuttoned and zipped his pants. Ta-Mara stared at the bare skin he revealed.

"Get naked," Levi said softly.

She didn't need any further urging. She took off her sundress then pushed down her panties. Levi groaned, sitting up as he stopped touching her. He reached for her and Ta-Mara stepped over his legs then lowered herself onto him. They kissed urgently and she moaned as she felt his strong thighs between hers. Levi slid his hand down between them and sank his fingers into her wetness. Ta-Mara whimpered as he touched her just how she liked it—deep and firm. She rocked onto his fingers, widening her legs to give him deeper access. He didn't disappoint as he delved into her, making her arch her back and shake at each motion. The sensation of pleasure raced through her and she wanted him inside her.

With that intent in mind, she lifted up slightly then held his cock in her hand. Levi stroked her clit then pulled back. He held her hips as she sank onto his erection. She gasped and he groaned as she took him in. Shuddering, Ta-Mara closed her eyes briefly, enjoying the feel of him within her. She braced her hands on his chest then went up and down, setting a fast pace. Levi clenched and unclenched his hands on her hips as he let her take the lead.

"Levi."

She stared into his face, loving each and every line there. She tightened around him and the muscles in Levi's neck went rigid as he arched under her. Ta-Mara did it again and the power of having him at her mercy filled her. Ta-Mara dug her nails into his chest and his hiss pleased her more.

"Mine," she said firmly.

Levi stared at her and nodded sharply. Ta-Mara rolled her shoulders and continued to move on him. Each push of his cock inside her set off tremors of need and warmth in her belly, spreading throughout her body. She went faster, wanting the release that awaited her. Levi licked the side of her neck then nibbled on her pulse. She trembled and goosebumps came over her skin. Levi rubbed his hands gently along her back and she pressed into the touch. She rotated her hips then moaned as she came.

"Ta-Mara." Levi grunted as he, too, found his release.

His eyes glazed and his harsh breath tingled along her skin. Ta-Mara cupped his face and kissed him. Levi opened for her and met her tongue with his own. He lay back and Ta-Mara stretched out over him. She rubbed her toes up and down his legs. Slowly she pulled back from their kiss and stared into his warm gaze.

"Love you, Ta-Mara," Levi said softly kissing her nose.

"I love you too." Ta-Mara wrinkled her nose.

Levi chuckled and held her close. She rested her head against his chest, listening to his heartbeat.

"So are you going to feed me?" Levi asked.

"Why am I the one who needs to feed you?" Ta-Mara snuggled in.

Levi cupped her ass. "It's your turn to cook."

Ta-Mara couldn't dispute that. Since she'd taught him to cook, they'd started splitting the duties in the kitchen. Actually now that she thought about it, they shared so many things — the household chores, grocery shopping and since Levi was making his own money, the bills for the house. She and Levi had melded their lives together. Ta-Mara sighed in contentment then got up. At the loss of him inside her, she wanted him there again. She reminded herself she would have him soon.

"Let's get you fed." Ta-Mara held out her hand.

Levi rose and accepted her hand, lifting it to kiss the knuckles. He led her inside and Ta-Mara smiled.

I don't have anything to worry about. I have a man who loves me and we're happy.

They parted ways inside to get dressed again then came back into the kitchen. Ta-Mara couldn't believe she was worried about some silly dream or ghost. She went to the fridge and pulled open the door. Reaching for the vegetable she wanted to cut up, Ta-Mara started to hum.

The knife felt familiar in her hand and she gripped it, cutting the carrot. She stopped, setting it on the counter before she wiped her forehead.

"Get back to work." The harsh voice of the man she dreaded ever being alone with reached her.

Forcing herself not to stiffen, she grabbed the knife then started to cut vegetables again. All the while, she could feel him staring at her and even though she couldn't see him, she knew in his gaze there would be lust. It made her skin crawl yet she could not do anything about it for fear of Levi.

Levi, I have to bear this for him. Soon we will be free of this place. Of this man who although he hates my very color wants me in his bed.

"Calliope," the man said with longing in his voice.

She kept her head down and continued cutting, willing him to leave. He came closer and her skin crawled at his nearness. Suddenly he grabbed her chin and forced her to look at him. Calliope gasped as she looked into the eyes of a demon and wished he was in hell instead of here in her presence. She clenched her hand on the knife, wanting to plunge it into his chest.

"Ta-Mara, what is for dinner?"

Ta-Mara jerked, shaking. *John — the demon is John.* Lifting a hand, she pushed back her hair from her face, breathing deeply. She pushed it away to think on later and forced a smile on her face. She couldn't let Levi know anything was wrong.

Ta-Mara turned to him and said, "Some grilled chicken and stir-fry."

"Yummy. I love your stir-fry." Levi came closer. "What can I do to help?"

She gave him something to do that would buy her some time. Even when it was her turn, she knew he would have offered to help. She did the same when it was his time, for they enjoyed cooking together.

Ta-Mara grabbed the vegetables then set them on her board. Then she retrieved a knife and got to work. In moments, she was in the rhythm of preparing the food.

What the hell is going on? How does John fit in with Calliope and Levi? Ta-Mara stilled as she recalled the story of men chasing them and wondered if John had been one of them. *Even if he was, that is past. John isn't like that now.* Ta-Mara recalled the brief look on John's face earlier in the store.

No, she would not think like that. She would not make assumptions on someone. Ta-Mara blew out a breath. She had bigger things to be worried about. The dream she thought she'd had wasn't a dream after all. *A flashback. I had a flashback to someone else's life. No, Calliope's life. Fuck, I don't need this. I have my own shit to deal with. I don't need someone else's too.*

"Ta-Mara, the chicken is ready." Levi brought her attention to him.

"Good." She kept cutting.

Levi touched her waist. She jumped then relaxed.

"Are you sure you're okay?" Levi asked.

She glanced at him and forced a smile. "Yeah. I'm fine."

Levi frowned and Ta-Mara hoped he wouldn't push. When he didn't, she breathed a sigh of relief.

I'll deal with this. I can't let him know I'm reliving what Calliope went through. He doesn't know I even know things about them.

Her decision made, Ta-Mara took up the vegetables and went to the stove.

* * * *

Glancing inside Roberta's Reads, Levi looked on as Ta-Mara helped a customer near the window. He frowned at the lines of strain and the tiredness on her face that was plain to see. Something was wrong, yet each time he asked, she said she was okay. Ta-Mara was hiding something from him and he had no idea how to get her to open up.

"Lurking around, I see," a familiar male voice said.

"What is your problem with me?" Levi turned to face the owner of the store.

Reggie crossed his arms over his chest. "Ta-Mara is too good for you."

"Yep." Levi stared at him, waiting for what else he would say.

Reggie narrowed his eyes then scowled. "She should be with someone who appreciates her."

"Like you."

"Blunt. I like that. So let me be blunt too." Reggie rubbed his hand over his head. "I'm not good enough for her either, but I'm a better bet than some yokel like you who came out of nowhere."

Levi wondered what Reggie would think if he knew really where Levi had come from. He smiled at the thought.

"This isn't funny. Ta-Mara deserves to be happy."

"And with me she is." Levi stared at Reggie. "Look I know you've known Ta-Mara a long time. Do you really think she would be with someone who she didn't think was right for her? Someone she chose to be with."

"Namely she didn't choose me and had an opportunity to if she wanted to." Reggie glared at him. "I know that. But there is something fishy about you, Levi, and I can't put my finger on what it is."

"You dislike me so you are looking for an excuse to find something wrong with me." Levi shrugged. "Frankly, I don't give a fuck. So we can just keep it civil for Ta-Mara's sake."

"Okay," Reggie said grudgingly.

The tapping on the glass made them glance toward the store. Ta-Mara stood there, her eyes narrowed, looking between them.

"Shit, I know that look. Ta-Mara is about to make someone's life hell." Reggie slapped Levi on the shoulder "What did you do to piss her off?"

Ta-Mara came to the door and opened it. She waited until the customer had walked past her and left before saying. "I need to speak to you, Reggie."

"I'm not the one whose life will be hell," Levi said cheerfully.

Reggie groaned and sighed. He went to Ta-Mara then passed her, going into the store. Ta-Mara glanced at Levi and a warm smile curled her lips.

"Are you coming in or staying outside?"

He went to her and she stood on tiptoe and kissed him briefly.

"Give me a sec and I'll be right with you." She patted his hand. "I need to have a quick chat with Reggie."

"See if he can give you the rest of the day off. I have a surprise for you." Levi squeezed her hand gently.

"No worries. He'll give it to me." Ta-Mara sounded certain.

She left and went down the aisle to the office. Levi leaned on the counter and waited for her. Although he didn't hear what was being said he knew, just as Reggie did, the look she'd had on her face. He had no idea what Reggie had done to make Ta-Mara mad but

Levi was glad it wasn't him. An angry Ta-Mara was sexy as hell but he didn't like being on her bad side.

Soon Ta-Mara came from between the shelves and had her purse. Levi smiled seeing it. Looked like she had gotten the day off.

"Let's go." Ta-Mara stopped before him.

"Don't you want to know where we're going?" Levi straightened and went to her.

He slid his hand behind her back and led her to the front door.

"I'm with you and I trust you, so no matter where we go, I'm good."

The faith she placed in him humbled him. Levi paused before the door and kissed her. This woman had all of him and he would never do anything to hurt or disappoint her.

Now I just need to find the right time to tell her about Calliope.

Chapter Sixteen

"Okay, I'm going to retract that I'm good with wherever we go." Ta-Mara turned to him and frowned.

Levi chuckled and went to her. "Come on, you rode with me last time. Now it's time to teach you to ride. There is no need to be afraid."

"I'm not afraid." Ta-Mara nibbled on her lip. "I just have a healthy respect for horses. I know they can hurt me badly if they choose too. So we have an understanding. I give them their space and they give me mine."

"If you really don't want to go, we can do something else." Levi rubbed his hand along her back.

He wanted this to be something fun they could do together, not a traumatic experience. Ta-Mara glanced at him then the look he knew so well came over her. She put her head back, squared her shoulders then jutted her chin out. Levi smiled as she went into stubborn Ta-Mara mode. He was proud of her for being willing to learn.

"Okay, let's do this." Ta-Mara blew out a breath.

"Okay, first let's get you comfortable with the horse. Think of it as learning about each other." He led her to the horse.

* * * *

"I still can't believe that I've come to look forward to horseback riding," Ta-Mara said.

Levi glanced at her and noticed she looked easier in the saddle today. Since that first day he'd taught her to ride, she'd surprised him at how well she took to it. As she'd slowly gotten over her fear, she'd become better and better. A little over two weeks of practicing daily and she was well on her way to being an excellent horsewoman. It reminded him of Calliope and how he'd taught her. Immediately guilt at the thought of another woman filled him. He'd didn't want to compare them — they were two different women in two different times. He loved them both and knew they were not the same people. Levi vowed silently to not compare them again.

"I enjoy riding with you." He smiled at her.

The time they had spent each day with him teaching her then they going riding had become a great end to his days. After, they went home, cooked then ate before going to bed.

"Me too." Ta-Mara chuckled. "I was afraid of the horses but you helped me overcome that. Thanks. I'm glad I could share this with you. I know you missed your horses and being here…well, it relaxes you. I love seeing that."

"You being here makes it even so much better."

"I want to teach you to ride too." Ta-Mara smiled mysteriously.

"Why does that sound ominous?" Levi frowned. "What do you mean teach me to ride?"

"You'll know soon enough. It will be surprise, like your bringing me here was." Ta-Mara took the lead. "But for now let's ride."

He followed her, watching her move. Her hair lifted in the wind as she rode. Her laughter flowed back as he went to join her. The joy of it filled him with warmth and he couldn't wait to get her home.

Ta-Mara glanced back at Levi and she was happy that she had gone along with learning to ride. It was something they shared that was familiar to Levi. Yes he was getting comfortable in her time, but there were still had moments where she'd see a faraway look on his face. She couldn't imagine being in his shoes — displaced from your time and in a new one, learning how much the world had changed.

She'd started thinking about that more and more as she had dreams, flashbacks or whatever the hell it was she had when she saw Calliope. The dreams still continued and she still had no idea when it would happen.

The feel of the horse beneath her made her feel free. The sense of freedom was precious to her and she loved Levi for giving her this gift. Glancing at the man who had her heart and soul, she smiled. He was such an imposing figure on horseback. The commanding presence he portrayed, in her opinion, became even more pronounced.

"Calliope, are you okay?"

"Ta-Mara, are you okay?" Levi called.

She focused on him and from the concern on his face he'd been calling her. Ta-Mara bit her lip. That his calling her had overlapped at the exact same moment in flashback was eerie. As usual she pushed it away and didn't let him see anything was wrong. She'd gotten very good at hiding it.

"Sorry, just thinking." Ta-Mara forced a chuckle. "Riding helps me clear my mind."

"It does." Levi stopped. "Let's head back."

She nodded and they went. Absently—as she did every time she experienced something Calliope did—she tried to make sense of why she was seeing it. And again she had no clue why or what was going on.

Haunted by a woman who loves the same man I do. Maybe it's her celestial way of warning me to stay away from her man. Ta-Mara chuckled at being so fanciful.

There was no such thing. It was just her subconscious taking the things she'd read in the book and making them seem real.

But there are things you are seeing that are not in the book. How do you explain that? She couldn't but Ta-Mara dismissed it. She was just filling in the gaps of the story based on what she assumed happened. At that thought she felt better. *Yeah I can deal with that.*

* * * *

Ta-Mara rubbed along the bridge of her nose. With the increase of the flashbacks, dreams or hauntings she was out of sorts. Hell, she had no clue what to call it—she was at a loss of what to do. Whatever it was led to sleepless nights, which made her days at work even longer. She put her hand over her mouth, stifling a yawn. The bell over the door made her straighten and smile for the customer. A sliver of unease filled her as she saw John—this time he was alone. Since she'd had the flash of Calliope concerning him, she hadn't see him.

John stared at her but didn't say anything as he went down the aisle for the books on war he'd looked at last time. She rubbed her hands up and down her arms.

You have no reason to be nervous around him. It's just your imagination. With that thought in mind, Ta-Mara turned her attention to the inventory she was putting into the computer. She got lost in cataloguing the books before she put them on the shelf.

"I'll take this." John's gruff voice made her jerk.

Ta-Mara tried not to show she was caught unaware. "Sure."

She took the book and when he didn't release it, she glanced at him curiously. John let the book go when their gazes met. She couldn't read what was in his expression but she took the book and rang it out. They were silent as he paid, then she bagged his purchase before handing it over. He accepted it then left without looking back. Ta-Mara watched through the window as he went down the sidewalk then out of view. She blew out a breath and shook her head. Getting paranoid over something imaginary was not her way.

"You're losing it, Ta-Mara." She rolled her eyes.

She went back to work. Soon the silence made her itchy. To dispel it, Ta-Mara turned on the radio and started to groove as she worked. She let the worries and everything that was bothering her go as she let the rhythm take her.

* * * *

Later in the day as she was gardening, she played music again to keep the feeling going. The soil felt great between her fingers. She dug her hands in and calmness flowed over her. Picking up the bulb, she set it in the ground then scooped the soil onto it, covering it. She sat back on her heels and glanced down the line of what she'd already planted, imagining how they would look next year when they really took root. Her thoughts drifted to Levi in the garden with her next year as the flowers grew, then they would plant new ones.

"Looks good."

She jumped, startled, then glanced at Levi. He came around the side of the house to her. Ta-Mara went to rise but he gestured for her to stay. He squatted beside her and kissed her gently. She opened and they dueled tongues lazily then he pulled back.

"Thanks. How was your day?" She smoothed her hand along his arms.

"Good." Levi moved beside her and picked up a plant. "Let me help you."

"Sure." Ta-Mara accepted the plant before placing it in the hole, after which Levi covered the roots. "Did you figure out what was wrong? Why the deck wasn't working as it should?"

"Yes. The planks were not the right dimensions that I ordered." Levi placed another plant. "I'm redoing the drawing and making it based on what I have."

"Okay. Is the client good with that?" Ta-Mara planted it.

"Yes. Since they are the ones who insisted on ordering everything and gave the wrong dimensions, they are going to pay me extra for a new design." Levi shrugged. "It will still be done in the time they wanted it for."

"That's good then." Ta-Mara dusted her hands then said, "Finally completed. It does look stellar." She grinned.

"We're a good partnership." Levi hugged her.

She pressed against him. "So what do you want to do tonight?"

"Just chill."

"Sounds like a great plan." Ta-Mara rose and held out her hand. "Tonight we chill then tomorrow I'm gonna take you for a ride."

"Why wait until tomorrow? We can do that tonight." Levi grinned.

Ta-Mara laughed and winked. Levi stood then they strolled toward the house. They continued discussing their days and relaxed. Ta-Mara stopped a moment and appreciated just being with him.

* * * *

"Come on, slow poke," Ta-Mara told Levi. "Get on. I promise it won't bite you."

Levi sighed. "When you said you would teach me to ride, I wondered what it could be, but this I would have never thought of."

"I could say that I'd taken you for a ride like last night if you do this, but that's a given." Ta-Mara snickered. "Now come on, I'll teach you to ride."

"I get there are many modes of transportation in this time but I still don't think less than four wheels is safe." Levi eyed her narrowly.

"The bicycle is safe." Ta-Mara bit back a smile. He wasn't afraid to ride a horse but give him a bike and he balked. "Think about it as another type of horse. Let's first let you get to know it." She smirked. "Hey, you can even name it."

"I'm not going to name the bicycle." Levi frowned. "You should just take this back to who you got it from."

"It's yours, Levi. I got it for you." Ta-Mara held the bike. "Surprise."

"You got it for me?" He looked surprised.

"Yep." Ta-Mara held out her hand. "I enjoy bike riding and thought that would be something we can do together — similar to horseback riding."

"Okay." Levi blew out a breath then rolled his shoulders. "I'm gonna do this. Let's ride this bike."

"Yeah, sweetie. Make it yours." Ta-Mara held it.

Levi straddled the bike then she started walking him through what to do. As Levi took to it as he did everything else, Ta-Mara smiled. She was so proud of him. She let him go and he rode around the yard with a big grin on his face.

Levi came to stop in front of her and smiled. "Why are you standing there? Go get your bike and let's go riding."

Ta-Mara did as he stated. Soon she returned and got on her bike. Levi set off and she pedaled behind him. They biked down her drive then to the street. It was just like the times she'd taught him to drive, cook and so many other things. Ta-Mara crossed her arms over her chest. They both had taught each other so much and she couldn't wait to see what else he showed her.

* * * *

Ta-Mara propped her hand on her chin and watched Levi repair the tire. After that first day, they had added biking to their activities — rotating between that and horseback riding. He completed his task then rose. Ta-Mara stood and dusted off her pants.

"What time are we supposed to meet the others?" Levi asked.

"Six-thirty." Ta-Mara glanced at her watch. "If we leave now, we'll just make it. There was an idea of us having dinner together afterward. Although she isn't coming for the ride, Jasmine will join us if we do."

"Sounds good." Levi got on his bike.

She did the same and they headed off. They chatted as the rode and stopped to pick up Heather, who joined them on her own bike before heading and getting Rachel and Matthew. It was the first time they all had gotten together for a while, with all of them being so busy. As they rode, Ta-Mara listened as Matthew and Levi talked.

"So are you up to me finally taking you fishing next week?" Matthew asked.

"Sure." Levi's brow furrowed. "Do I need to wear something particular to go fishing?"

"Clothing." Matthew grinned. "Nakedness scares the fish and would scare me too to see you that way."

Levi chuckled. Ta-Mara enjoyed the way the men interacted. Since the barbecue, Levi had become more comfortable with Matthew. She wasn't sure all had been said but she was glad they seemed on their way to building a friendship.

"You look happy," Rachel said to her left.

Heather spoke from her right, "And content. I'd say very sexually satisfied."

The two women chuckled. Ta-Mara glanced between them and laughed.

"Nosy women." Ta-Mara briefly looked at Levi then back at them. "I'm happy and all what you said."

"You look a little tired. Tell Levi I said he should let you get more rest," Heather teased.

Although it was said that way, Ta-Mara saw her concern. She kept her face so it didn't reveal anything. Hell, she didn't even know how to explain what was happening with her. Experiencing things as Calliope was a bit much to share with them. Yes they knew about Levi and had accepted that, but how could she possibly explain that she was experiencing things about a woman who had died so long ago. She was living her life and didn't know if it was real or imagined. Even with them being understanding about Levi, she didn't think this would fly over well. She hadn't even mentioned it to Levi and still didn't know how to start with him or her friends.

"Ta-Mara," Rachel called.

"Hmmm...yeah?"

"Are you okay?" Rachel looked concerned.

"Yeah," she replied by rote.

They didn't ask anything further. Instead they chatted about what they had been up to. Absently Ta-Mara listened as Levi and Matthew continued making plans for their fishing trip.

* * * *

"I'm getting ready to go," Levi said.

Ta-Mara glanced up from her book she was reading. "Ha—"

The phone rang and since he was closest, Levi picked it up. "Hello... Hey, Matthew." He was silent for a while then said, "That's okay. If you need my help, let me know. We'll go out another time then. Okay, bye."

When he hung up he glanced at Ta-Mara then came over to sit beside her. She leaned forward looking at him.

"We're not going today. Matthew had to go out with John to check on their traps. They've been having some trouble with their lines disappearing."

"Okay." She frowned. "That's not good."

"Does he know what has been happening?"

"He didn't say much." Levi shrugged. "But he sounded stressed about it."

"I hope everything works out."

"Me too." Levi shook his head. "I feel bad about it. They depend on what they bring in to live on. I told him if he needs help to let me know."

"I heard." Ta-Mara moved closer. "That was good of you to say."

"Matthew is a good guy." Levi sounded surprised then. "But John I don't know so well."

Ta-Mara thought of the continuing images she had of John and Calliope. Then her own interactions with him. John didn't say much and she didn't know him either. He was more of a friend of a friend than a direct one.

"I don't either." Ta-Mara snuggled against Levi. "Maybe we should have a get together with everyone and invite him. We should get to know him since he is Matthew's business partner and friend."

"Maybe—"

The phone rang again and Levi rose and went to answer. "Hello... Yeah she's right here. It's for you, Ta-Mara."

She went over and accepted the phone. "Hello."

One of the neighbors who had been helping out at Jessie Mae's as her daughter worked said, "Ta-Mara, I'm sorry to bother you but I have an emergency. Can you come sit with Jessie Mae?"

"Sure. I'll be there in a few." She hung up then turned to Levi. "I'm heading over to Jessie Mae. I don't know when I'll be back."

"No problem." Levi came over and kissed her gently. "Tell Jessie Mae I said hi."

"I will." She hurried to grab her shoes and a few things before heading out.

She walked through the trees separating their properties and when she pushed the branch out of her way, Ta-Mara blinked. The landscape didn't look anything like she was used to. Suddenly a woman rushed across the area looking behind her.

"I need to get away from him."

At the words, Ta-Mara recognized Calliope. She looked at Ta-Mara then narrowed her eyes and came closer. Calliope stopped a few steps away from her then stared at her. Ta-Mara's eyes widened and she stumbled a step back and the area reverted back to how she recalled it.

"Oh my God." She lifted a shaking hand, placing it over her mouth. "Not a dream or flashback. I could swear she talked to me and saw me, but that's not possible."

She looked around and didn't see anything to explain what just happened. Ta-Mara bit her lip, hurrying on to get to Jessie-Mae's. *Another thing to add to a long line of weird.* She glanced back over her shoulder and when it was her usual path, she shrugged and decided to ignore it as a strange foible.

Chapter Seventeen

Ta-Mara sat back on her heels and stared off into space. She yawned, feeling the tiredness that had been her constant companion for the last few weeks. It was the sexual dreams Ta-Mara hated the most since she felt like an interloper to their love. Yes it was arousing, since she herself knew how it was to make love to Levi, but living it through Calliope's thoughts and to feel him do it to her was not something she wanted to experience. Through the weeks, she'd gained a deeper understanding of Calliope and Levi's relationship — the struggles they'd undergone to be together, their courage for standing up for their love during the time they'd lived. She'd gained even more respect for them as a couple and for Levi, who she knew so well. Ta-Mara had no idea why she had a front row seat to what had happened between Calliope and Levi. That was bugging her — even more so now because she'd not gone near the book.

She much preferred just having read it rather than feeling as if she lived it. Rubbing the back of her neck, Ta-Mara didn't know how much longer she could go on like this. Levi was looking at her, seeming more and more concerned. She couldn't form the words to tell him what was happening. Each time she thought of it, her throat closed up. Firm hands touched her shoulder and dug deep. Recognizing Levi's touch, Ta-Mara relaxed back into his ministrations. She lowered her head, giving him better access.

"Right there." Ta-Mara groaned.

"You're so tight." Levi pressed a kiss to the back of her neck then went back to massaging the knots in her shoulders. "You're not sleeping well. Tell me what is wrong, Ta-Mara."

She couldn't. Hell, she didn't even know how to say it. *Hey, Levi I'm dreaming of your dead lover. I know all about what you all did and what happened. How do I compare to her? Maybe I should let you call me by her name again.* At the last two thoughts, she felt bad. Not sleeping was making her wacky. Ta-Mara could only imagine what he would do or say. None of it would be good. He'd probably look at her as if she'd lost her mind and would want to take her to the hospital. She wouldn't blame him for doing so.

"I'm okay." Ta-Mara faced him. "Just a little worn down."

"You work too hard." Levi put his hand on her side. "You need to rest, Ta-Mara. You go to work all day then help so many people."

"They need it and I can do it." She shrugged "You should talk. Your business is taking off and you're hectic too."

"I know." Levi gave that smile she loved. The one that showed he was humbled by people wanting him to work for them. Levi didn't know that it was his talent that got people calling him however once he was there it was openness that made them hire him.

His honesty made them confident in their decision to have him there.

"I'm so proud of you." She kissed him.

Levi pulled her into his lap. "Are you done cleaning?"

"Maybe." She put her arms around his neck. "What did you have in mind?"

"A bath where we soak and I can take care of you." He kissed her hard. "Then maybe I'll let you have your way with me."

"Sounds just like what I need. How'd I get so lucky?"

"I'm the one who is lucky." He kissed her again.

Ta-Mara returned it. Levi was wrong—she was the one who was lucky to have him. She thought of the marks on his throat when he'd first arrived. He'd never said, but she thought they were from someone trying to hang him. Yes, she was lucky that he hadn't died and had instead come to this time to be with her. He was hers, and no matter what dreams she had, Ta-Mara wasn't about to give him up.

* * * *

"I'm heading out."

Ta-Mara glanced up from where she was stretched out on the couch. She felt so much more rested today. Last night after Levi had pampered her, there had thankfully been no dreams.

"Looking good." She smiled. "I like the hat."

"Thanks for getting it for me." Levi took it off, looking at it. "Are you sure it doesn't look strange? I don't understand why one would need a hat for fishing."

Levi was finally going fishing with Matthew. They had both had been so busy and although they'd made plans to go, either Levi or Matthew had ended up canceling.

"It's not for fishing, per se. It's for you to shade your face." Ta-Mara wiggled her fingers. "I don't want you to get sunburn."

Levi looked at her as if she was nuts. "Ta-Mara, much of the work I do is outside."

She knew that and his skin had become tanned because of it.

"Fine, you caught me." Ta-Mara pouted. "I just wanted to buy you something."

Since Levi had started working and making his own money, he hadn't wanted her getting him anything. He insisted she had already done too much. She'd agreed only if she was allowed to for special occasions.

"Ta-Mara —"

"It's your first fishing trip," she interjected. "So it's an occasion. As per our agreement, I can buy you something."

"Why do I think I'm going to regret agreeing to that stipulation?" Levi narrowed his eyes. "That you're going to find loopholes in it."

"Because you know me so well." Ta-Mara chuckled.

Levi came toward her. "When are your friends arriving?"

"Any minute now." She sat up, kissing him.

"Have fun." Levi straightened then headed for the door. "I'm heading to docks to meet Matthew and his partner John."

"Drive safe." Ta-Mara waved. "Say hi to Matthew for me."

Levi has started taking her vehicle more and more. He dropped her off at work in the morning then headed to whatever job he had then came back to pick her up.

"I will," he said then went out of view. She heard the sound of the door opening then Levi. "Hey, ladies."

Her friends replied then the sound of the door closing echoed in the house. Ta-Mara sat up and smiled as Heather, Jasmine and Rachel came in.

"Hey."

"Hi," they all echoed.

Ta-Mara looked at Heather and noticed she looked upset. "What's wrong, Heather?"

The other women glanced at Heather. She blinked then her lips wobbled and tears fell from her eyes. Ta-Mara rose, pulled Heather down beside her and rubbed her hand up and down her back. She looked over her head at Rachel and Jasmine. They didn't look like they knew what was going on.

"I told my family about Matthew and that I'm pregnant," Heather said in a rush.

Ta-Mara waited for her to continue, but when she didn't she urged, "And?"

"Dad pitched a fit and said I was lowering myself for Matthew. That I was a whore having a child outside of wedlock." Heather smiled tremulously. "But it's okay. Matthew loves me."

"He does." Rachel sat on the center table.

Jasmine sat beside her, taking Heather's hands in hers. "Hell, even if he flakes on you when you tell him, we'll be here. Raise the baby ourselves. The little one will have four mamas. We'll put the fear of God in anyone who tries to hurt him or her. Including your asshole dad."

"Matthew won't flake on me." Heather lifted her hand. "Before I even told him I was pregnant he asked me to marry him. I told him after I said yes. He was mad at first I hadn't told him right away, but thrilled he's going to be a dad."

"He asked you to marry him." Ta-Mara hugged her then held her out. "But wait, why did you dad say you were having a baby out of wedlock if you are engaged?"

"I didn't get a chance to tell him. He lost it when he heard what Matthew did. Said he wouldn't be able to support me, much less a baby. I don't need him supporting me. This is a fifty-fifty partnership. I'm a doctor in the hospital and he's a fisherman. We'll be a team."

"Yes, a team," Jasmine said. "He's a good man."

They all looked at her.

"What?" She scowled then grinned. "Anyone who stands up to me is good in my book."

They laughed.

"Let's celebrate. Champagne." Ta-Mara squeezed Heather. "Milk or juice for the expectant mother."

"I'm going to be a mom." Heather grinned.

She glowed, and Ta-Mara wondered how it would feel if she was getting married to Levi and pregnant with his child. She put her hand over her womb and sighed.

You all would make a lovely child together. Ta-Mara glanced up and went still.

The ghostly figure of Calliope stood before the window with a soft smile on her lips. She inclined her head and faded.

"Ta-Mara, are you okay?"

Heather's question drew her attention.

"Yeah. Let me get that champagne."

The others rose with her and they went toward the entry of the living room. Ta-Mara looked back and, not seeing anything, she wondered if she imagined Calliope. She was awake, so maybe she had. She dismissed it as being fanciful as she exited the living room.

* * * *

Levi exited the Mariner and pulled out his cell. He read the text Ta-Mara had sent. He was happy for Heather and Matthew—they were getting married and would be having a little one soon. He put away his cell and strode toward the docks. He checked the slips, looking for the number Matthew told him was his. Levi reached a corner and went to go around it but paused when he heard raised voices.

"I can't fucking believe you invited that man."

Levi didn't recognize the masculine voice.

"Who? Levi?" Matthew sounded confused. "I told you I did that a while ago. Why is it a problem now?"

"He's with that woman."

"Ta-Mara?" Matthew was even more baffled. "She's a nice woman, John. What's your problem with her?"

"She's black," John roared.

"So?"

"He's dating her and fucking her," John said.

"So what?" Matthew said softly.

"It's nasty. Not right. She's a n—"

"Don't say it."

"Why not? You can't possibly like the woman." John sounded disbelieving.

Levi waited to hear what Matthew would say.

"I not only like her. I love her like a sister because she is best friends with my woman. The woman who will be the mother of my children and my wife." Matthew lifted his voice. "And just to make sure it's clear… Heather's African American. And I love each and every inch of her."

The sound of flesh hitting flesh reached him. Levi went around the corner and he paused, watching as Matthew wiped his mouth then spat. Blood was leaking from the corner.

"I gave you that one," Matthew said softly. "Our partnership is over. I will send your shit to you. How did I never know you were a racist asshole?"

"I can't believe you're ending our partnership over a n—"

Matthew hit him, and John dropped to his knees. He was up and swinging at Matthew and the men exchanged blows, swearing at each other. Light reflected off a blade John pulled and Levi went to step in. He grabbed John's arm and the man turned on him with a snarl. The hate in his eyes made Levi flash back to another time. He felt the bullet ripping through him. Then saw this man standing over him before he strung him up. Levi roared and hit him. John reared up to stab him, and Levi blocked it. He hit him again and twisted his arm, disarming him. He flung the knife away then kicked John in the knee, going to the ground and beating him. Levi straddled him, hitting him repeatedly. Hard arms grabbed Levi, pulling at him. Levi resisted and kept hammering John.

"Levi." Matthew's voice broke through the fog clouding his brain. "Stop before you kill him. He deserves it but you'll go to jail. Think of Ta-Mara," he yelled in his ear.

Levi stilled, reason flooding back into him.

Matthew held him tight, and Levi said, "I'm okay. Let me go."

He did, but pulled him back from John, who was in a pile on the planks of the dock. Levi looked at the battered face and tried to feel regret but didn't.

"I'm going to call the police," Matthew said. "It was self-defense, since he came at me with a knife, then you. But we need to make sure to do this right so we don't both get arrested."

"Why would they take our word for it?" Levi faced Matthew.

"Thank God the dock owner installed cameras all over." Matthew pointed up. "Sound and video. It will cover our asses."

"Okay." He held out his hand to Matthew. He took it and they shook. "Thank you for defending Ta-Mara."

"No thanks needed, man. John was insulting my woman too. I never knew he was a racist. When you think you know people, you find you don't..." Matthew shook his head as he dialed.

Levi glanced up and he shuddered. The rage coursing through him brought everything back to him. He just wanted to go home to Ta-Mara but knew that wasn't possible yet. Soon he would.

* * * *

Levi stopped on the porch, looking up into the night. The day had slipped away from him as the cops came and questioned him and Matthew. They had taken John to the hospital. Neither he nor Matthew had called Ta-Mara or Heather, thinking it best to tell them in person. They had spent a few hours at the station as the police reviewed the tapes to confirm their accounts. John was being charged with assault instead of them. When they had left the station, they had gone for a drink and something to eat.

"Where have you been? I was getting worried." Ta-Mara spoke from inside the house.

Levi watched her through the screen door. "I missed you, Ta-Mara."

She came outside and grabbed his hand. "Levi, what's wrong?"

He explained what had happened. Ta-Mara's eyes were wide when he was finished.

"Oh God. It's a good thing we got you identification." She smiled. "See, I knew it would come in handy." She squeezed his hand. "Coming to Matthew's aid like that... It was good of you to do."

Levi knew it was time. "I didn't do it for him."

"What do you mean?"

"Matthew and John look exactly like the men who almost killed me before I came here."

Ta-Mara drew in a harsh breath. "L—"

"I need to tell you about my past." Levi held her hand tighter. "About Calliope. You might hate me for calling her by your name when you find out about us."

"Levi." Ta-Mara looked guilty then she disentangled her hand from his. "Wait here a second."

She turned and hurried into the house. Levi frowned, wondering why she would leave when he needed to talk to her. Ta-Mara came back into view in moments. She pushed open the screen with one hand and Levi immediately was drawn to the book she carried. Ta-Mara stopped before him and held it up so he saw the cover. The words *Unbreakable Bonds* seemed to glow. He reached for it but she held it away from him.

"This book is my favorite. I was reading it when you appeared at my job a few months ago." Ta-Mara lowered her head then lifted the book again and touched the cover. "It's the story of a man named Levi Madison and his love, Calliope."

Levi narrowed his eyes. Ta-Mara told him of the story in the book and Levi listened in disbelief as it detailed a lot about him and Calliope. Then how Ta-Mara had fallen in love with him in the book, thinking he was such a great man.

"The book isn't complete and left a lot out. I know that now." Ta-Mara raised her head. "I've been having dreams of Calliope, experiencing things like I'm in her shoes."

She told him about the dreams and Levi went rigid as his most intimate moments with Calliope were laid out by Ta-Mara.

"I should have told you before that I knew about you." Ta-Mara held out a hand to him. "I didn't know how."

Levi stepped back before she could touch him. "So let me get this straight. You know me from some book. So basically, you love this man from a page." He gestured to the book. "I'm not that man, Ta-Mara. You fell for some hero in a book. I'm just a man, Ta-Mara. I have faults and am not perfect." He turned away. "I thought you loved me but I see I'm wrong. I wish you luck in finding a man who can live up to the expectations you have built up from the man you read about."

"Levi—"

He ignored her call and went down the steps. He went into the woods and to the trail that led to Jessie Mae's, but he veered off and went to the water. He stood on the bank staring out at the moon.

"For God's sake, Levi," Calliope said behind him.

"Go away." Levi pivoted to face her then turned away.

"Between you and Ta-Mara being so stubborn, I'm not going anywhere." Calliope sighed. "Don't get all broody and withdraw, Levi. Ta-Mara loves you."

"She loves the myth of our love. Why did you let her see your memories?"

"I—"

"Don't deny it. Her dreams were you somehow messing with her. Why?" He glanced at her.

Calliope averted her gaze. "She needed to know everything about us. Not just things from a book."

"What we did during sex wasn't necessary for her to know."

"It was." She met his gaze glaring at him. "We were great together, Levi."

Levi clenched his fist. "If it was so great, then why did fate take you from me? Why did you die and I live to be transported here?"

"Levi, it is as it should be."

"Don't give me that." He turned on her. She was still dressed in white. He closed the distance to her. "You know something, Calliope, and you need to tell me."

"I don't know anything," she protested, backing up.

"I know you, Calliope, like I know my soul." Levi advanced. "You are lying. Tell me."

"Fine. I interfered, Levi," Calliope said, "I could not let you die. I made sure you would find the one woman who is yours."

"That was you," Levi said shakily.

"No."

Levi stared at her and it dawned on him what she was inferring. "Ta-Mara."

In a whisper, Calliope spoke, "Levi, you are a man whose love is pure. In a world divided by color, you never faltered. Despite everything put to you, you stayed true to your heart and never turned your back on your soul mate. For that, I tell you this—rest now, fear not, for you shall be returned to the arms of your love. Trust your heart, for it won't lead you astray."

He stepped back, recognizing the words. Memory flowed into him and in this time, no longer in pain, he realized it had been her voice.

"Why?" He shook his head. "No, it makes no sense. You're my soul mate."

"I was, for an all too brief moment." Calliope blinked, tears raining down her face. "Ours was a love that survived throughout time, Levi. My love for you made me know I had to let you go. I had to bring you to this time so you could find a woman who would be yours. You are meant to be with her now. She is your heart, soul and body. Bu—"

"You interfered." Levi pivoted. "I'm tired of women making decisions for me. Keeping things that are important from me."

"Le—"

"I don't want to hear it."

"L—"

"Didn't you say you needed me to let you go?" Levi slashed his hand. "I did. I let go of the anger, and you should be gone."

"You were always such a stubborn ass," Calliope said.

He turned, glaring, and she faded from view. Levi focused on the lake, crossing his arms. Pain ripped through him with the discovery of Ta-Mara not really loving him, but only caring about him because of some book she'd read. And now Calliope and her interfering... Levi sat on the ground, legs under him. He needed to figure out what he would do.

Chapter Eighteen

Ta-Mara staggered when he walked away. She went to the railing and gripped the post, staring after him as he went into the trees.

"Levi," she whispered.

She knew he would be angry but she'd never expected the hurt in his gaze. She had messed up so badly. Ta-Mara sat heavily on the porch. She held the book to her chest. *What the hell am I going to do?*

"Get off your ass and go after him."

Ta-Mara gaped at the ghost before her then started to laugh. "Perfect. First the man I love walks away from me, now I'm seeing things. Yes, I am going crazy."

"You're very sane." Calliope put her hands on her hips and tapped her foot. "Why are you still sitting there? Go after Levi."

"I'm not doing what some ghost tells me." Ta-Mara rolled her eyes. "God, I'm talking to a ghost."

"I'm not a ghost." Calliope paced back and forth before her. "I'm a spirit."

"Excuse me, oh Miss Spirit," Ta-Mara scoffed. "Ghost or spirit—it doesn't matter because you are not real."

Calliope narrowed her eyes then squatted by her and reached out. Ta-Mara scrambled back, gripping the book.

"Well if I'm not real, why are you afraid to let me touch you?" Calliope snickered. "Not afraid of a ghost, Ta-Mara?"

"Don't taunt me." She sat up and glared. "What the fuck is your problem? In my dreams, you were much nicer."

"I'm nice, but right now I'm pissed." Calliope set her hand on her knees, glaring at her. "After all, I did to get Levi to you. You go and fuck it up with that damn book. I wish now I never gave it to you."

"What?" She started at the cover then Calliope. "You gave me this?"

"I put it where you could find it." Calliope rubbed her fingers along the bridge of her nose then lowered it. "I wanted you to know him before you met him. Hell, I've been haunting you—get it, haunting you—a ghost reference. Never mind. I let you see what we had."

"Why would you want me to know him? He was the love of your life." Ta-Mara narrowed her eyes. "Hey, wait, you've been fucking with my dreams. I should deck you!"

"You can try." Calliope beckoned to her. "That is, if you are over your being afraid of me. As if I am frightening." She smiled widely.

"I want to know why you gave me this." She held up the book. "And why you would mess with my dreams."

Aliyah Burke and Taige Crenshaw

"I already told you why I gave you the book." Calliope pursed her lips then sighed. "My memories were to show you what we had. So you could see the man he was and the one he was with you. You are his and he yours."

"But you are his soul mate."

"He said the same thing." Calliope narrowed her eyes. "Now listen up close. For my time, Levi was my soul mate. But it was brief and I made a deal that he would get love again—that he would find someone else who was his soul mate. One he would have a long happy life with, and many kids. Levi will be a wonderful father. It has taken a long time for what I set in motion to be fulfilled. Now it is happening and I'm not going to let you muck it up. Go after him."

"He's hurt. I need to give him time," Ta-Mara said. *Myself some time, so I can figure out what to say to make it right.*

"Stop being a coward and go after him. To hell with time." Calliope shook her head. "If you give him time to brood, Levi will get stubborn and dig his heels in. He'll have himself convinced you did only love him because of the book."

"He wouldn't listen to me. I was trying to tell him that was not true." Ta-Mara rose.

"Don't tell me that. Tell him." Calliope stood in a fluid motion. "I swear, between you and Levi, I'm going to be stuck here forever."

"Why don't you just leave?"

"Because I want him to be happy," Calliope roared. "With you, the one who is the soul mate, that he will grow old with. That is, if you can get your shit together."

"You really have a potty mouth."

"Too much television." She smiled sheepishly.

"You watch TV?" Ta-Mara was surprised.

"What else do I have to do to pass the time?" Calliope made a shooing motion with her hands. "Stop stalling and go after Levi. Or maybe you don't want him? Maybe I made a mistake and you don't deserve to be with him. You're not worthy of his love."

"I love him and he is mine," she said forcefully and went to the steps.

"Wait. Don't take the book with you."

Ta-Mara set the book on the porch and ran down the steps, hurrying toward the trees. She had no idea where Levi was but she would find him. She went toward Jessie Mae's but then turned to the lake. Ta-Mara burst through the trees and when she saw Levi, she kept going. He stood facing her.

"I—"

"Shut the hell up." Ta-Mara stopped before him. "You listen to me. I might have liked you from the book but to say I loved you because of it is an insult. I will admit I did find the man in the book an honorable one who loved his woman enough to face anything for her." She pushed her finger in his chest. "You are that same man, Levi, but I now know you on a personal level. I learned about you from the book but fell for the man before me. The one who would build a ramp for a woman he didn't know. The one whose gentleness was so seductive. I love you and you love me. Deal with me knowing stuff about your past. That is past, but I'm your future. And I'm not letting your stubbornness get in the way of our happiness." She crossed her arms over her chest. "Don't you have anything to say?"

"You told me to shut the hell up." He smiled crookedly. "Just following what my love says."

"Good." She harrumphed.

"I love you, Ta-Mara."

Her heart skipped a beat as he said it. Relief filled her that he wasn't walking away again.

"Love you, Levi."

He held out his hand and she placed hers in it. He drew her to him and kissed her. Ta-Mara rested on him, opening for him, loving the kiss. Levi pulled back and rubbed his knuckle gently along her cheek. She turned into it.

"Let's go home."

She nodded and he led her toward home. Ta-Mara put her hand on his waist as they walked.

"You have a lot of baggage." She thought of Calliope. "You come with a ghost... Wait, excuse me, a spirit."

"Calliope interfering again." Levi chuckled. "She's always been one to be stubborn and try to make you come around to her way of thinking about things."

"She has a set of lungs on her." Ta-Mara looked up as they approached her house. "She wants you to be happy. She's a spirit matchmaker."

Levi laughed. "That totally fits her." He escorted her up the steps.

Ta-Mara noted the book was gone. She figured Calliope had taken it.

"Sit." Levi helped her then sat beside her, pulling her close. "Calliope shared with you what she remembered. You read whoever put it on paper's account of what happened, but I want to tell you what I recall. That is what I was trying to do earlier—share my past with you. You are my future but I want to tell you this. Will you listen?"

"Of course." Ta-Mara put her hand on his knee, palm up.

Levi put his hand on hers. "I have to start from when I first spotted Calliope. There she was, this sassy woman whose regal bearing made me want to know her. Sh…"

Ta-Mara leaned on his shoulder as he told her the story of his life.

* * * *

Ta-Mara propped her chin under her hand and stared at the clock. Time was moving so slowly. She and Levi had a date and she really wanted the day done so she could meet him. After Levi had shared his story about Calliope, they had gone in to bed. He'd held her all night and when they'd woken, Levi had made slow, sweet love to her. She shifted on her stool, getting wet just thinking of him taking her with that intense look on his face.

Come on, clock, move, so I can go to him. She was looking forward to hearing more about the life he'd led. Levi had started with his love story but over the last few weeks, he'd shared more and more about his past. Having a firsthand account of how it was during his time was interesting. The history books didn't have as much insight as hearing it from someone who'd lived it. Again checking the time, Ta-Mara figured Levi and Matthew would be returning from their fishing trip. After the last disastrous time when they'd got into the fight, the men had had to again find time to go. A thump made Ta-Mara jerk. She watched around, leery. The store was empty expect for her. She got up and headed toward where she'd heard the noise.

"Don't worry, it will be fine." Going around the corner, she stopped.

In the middle of the aisle, Ta-Mara stared at the book there. The yellowed pages and cover made her know which book it was.

"Calliope, why did you give me the book back?" she called.

She waited and when there was no answer, Ta-Mara picked it up. A chill raced through her and she almost left it there, but she didn't. Ta-Mara took it to the back, where she set it on the shelf next to the radio then went back to the front. Only moments had passed when Ta-Mara retook her previous seat, staring at the clock.

* * * *

Levi put a plate in front of Ta-Mara and bent to kiss the side of her neck. She lifted her hand, stroking along his cheek then turned, winking at him.

"No kissy face over fish," Matthew teased.

Levi chuckled and sat beside Ta-Mara. Heather leaned against Matthew, who was across from them. She lifted a fork and ate. After their success at fishing, Levi and Matthew had decided to cook some of their catch for the ladies. When he and Ta-Mara had gotten home, they had got to work fixing some sides. By the time Heather and Matthew had arrived with the clean, gutted and already seasoned fish, they'd just had to slip it the oven. While they'd waited for the fish to cook, they had talked, laughed and had fun. Levi knew he and Matthew were on their way to becoming friends.

Although Matthew looked like the man from his past, he'd shown he was nothing like him. Levi was amazed how in one time he was a racist murderer and in this one he was a good guy, getting ready to be a husband and a dad.

"How are the plans coming along for the wedding?" Ta-Mara took a bite of her fish and made a humming sound. "Good."

"It's going well." Heather smoothed her hand over her belly. "Just another two weeks and I'll be a wife."

"My wife." Matthew lifted her hand and kissed the back of it.

Heather smiled, nuzzling her nose to his. Levi glanced at Ta-Mara and the smile on her face was wistful. He wondered what it was about but her expression cleared and she went back to eating. She asked more about the wedding. They all talked about it then later, when Heather and Matthew had left, he followed Ta-Mara to bed. They got ready then soon slid between the cool sheets. He held her and, listening to her breath, Levi moved his hand over her stomach. A shaft of longing filled him. He wanted her to have his child. Have a little one with her eyes and smile. Levi closed his eyes, imagining her with their child. Pleasure filled him at the thought.

* * * *

Levi stopped outside the bookstore window. He looked in and smiled. Ta-Mara was bopping around behind the counter and from the way her lips were moving, he figured she was singing. All day he hadn't been able to get her out of his mind. He'd felt compelled to leave his current job and come see her. He opened the door and went in. The bell over it tinkled and Ta-Mara glanced at him. She smiled and hurried in his direction. Levi opened his arms and hugged her when she was close. He swayed with her and she laughed delightedly.

"What are you doing here?"

"Came to see you." Levi winked. "Maybe have a quickie I've heard so much about?"

"I'd love to but" —Ta-Mara pouted —"I can't. I have a shipment of books coming in. The driver should be here any minute. I was actually going to text you and tell you I would be home late. I need to check and make sure everything is there. Get it on the shelves."

"I can help you out."

"I don't want to take you away from your project you are on," Ta-Mara protested.

"I'm ahead so I have time," Levi said. "I want to spend the time with you."

"Okay." She held his hands and walked backward, leading him. "I'll show you what to do and we can have fun together. Just like old times. Those first few weeks when you first came here."

"Yes." He went with her.

She chatted as she showed him. Levi worked by her side and when she bumped hips with him, Levi chuckled and did it to her. They moved around each other like a well-oiled machine. Customers came and went and many greeted him, saying they had thought he'd moved on since they hadn't seen him at the store anymore. Levi hadn't realized that he'd made such an impression on people.

"Sure, I'll show you the military books, Mr. Carlson." Levi led the elderly gentleman to the section.

He showed him what they had as he usually did. Mr. Carlson took a seat in the chair Levi had placed there for him months earlier. He was pleased to see it was still there. When he'd been here working before and had conversations with Mr. Carlson, Levi had noticed he had tired but had stubbornly kept talking. To save him his pride, Levi had put in the chair. Levi leaned against a bookcase, settling in for a nice chat about the military with him.

"So, young man, have you been watching the news?"

"I have." Levi found it a hoot that Mr. Carlson called him 'young man' when technically, Levi was born way before him.

"Don't just stand there." The man waved his hand imperviously. "Tell me what you think. Before you do, make sure you come by at this day of the week at this time. I will be here." The man glared at him. "You will be too."

"Yes, sir," Levi replied.

"Good." He gestured. "Go ahead and tell me what you think."

Levi did just that. He and Mr. Carlson had a lively discussion. He noticed Ta-Mara peeked in the aisle to check on them, smiling each time she did.

Much later, when Levi escorted the man out, he said, "See you next week."

"See you then."

Levi held open the door for him. He went through and Levi watched after him. Mr. Carlson's wife came out of the hairdressers and they hugged. He'd met Mr. Carlson's wife a few times and had heard the story of how they met, how long they had been together, and all about their lives. Levi watched them and another type of longing filled him. He glanced at the store and noticed it was empty. Levi flipped the lock then walked to the display that Ta-Mara was straightening. She glanced at him curiously.

"You had a good visit with Mr. Carlson?"

"Yes."

"He asked about you every week when he came in."

"I promised him I will be here next week." Levi smiled. "I'll make sure to make time for that."

"Good."

He took her hands then, looking into her eyes, he went down to one knee. Ta-Mara's expressive eyes widened.

"I don't have a ring to give you yet. But in my heart I know I need to ask you now." Levi took a breath. "Will you marry me, Ta-Mara?"

"Yes, Levi. Yes." Tears filled her eyes. "I'll marry you."

Levi rose and hugged her fiercely. "Thank you, Ta-Mara. Thank you for trusting me with your heart."

"And me with yours." Ta-Mara put her hand on his chest.

Levi lifted her, swinging her around. Ta-Mara kissed him and he held her, slowly setting her on her feet. A pounding on the door had them breaking apart.

"Did you lock the door?" Ta-Mara asked.

"Yes, I didn't want us to be disturbed."

"I'll tell them we are closing earlier." Ta-Mara went toward the door.

"I'll go get your things." Levi went to the register.

As he passed her, Levi touched her back. Ta-Mara pushed into his touch and blew him a kiss. He continued on his way. At the counter, he stopped and stared at the book with *Unbreakable Bonds* on the cover. The words glowed and Levi reached out to touch it.

"No! Don't touch the book." Ta-Mara screamed.

There was a whooshing sound in his ears and he stumbled as dizziness overcame him. Levi dropped to his knees and moaned, holding his head. He gasped as pain swamped him. Touching his side, Levi lifted his hand and looked at his fingers in disbelief. The blood was bright in the moonlight. Immediately he realized it was dark, and he lifted his head. Confused, he stared at the canopy of trees over him. Levi shifted and the feel of his clothing gave him pause. He gazed down at himself and the Confederate clothing made his breath catch. His hearing came back with a pop and Levi heard the wind rising and the rain falling on him.

"There is nowhere for you to run, Levi. We will find you." A deep, drawling voice rose above the storm, carrying through the trees.

Chills ran down his spine and Levi glanced into the darkness. *No, this can't be happening again.*

Chapter Nineteen

Fear gripped him as he realized he had returned to the time when he'd lost Calliope — that dreadful night. The night they'd hanged him. The noose choking him was vivid in his mind. He touched his neck and shook, knowing what was coming. Levi inhaled deeply and the scents of the forest filled him. Disbelief raced through him at being back in the eighteen hundreds.

Memories of the last few months appeared and Levi shook as he saw the beautiful honey-skinned woman who had taken her into his home. That first glimpse of Ta-Mara and her fear of him, yet being willing to help. Her taking him home and making him feel at home. The shopping trip and their first kiss. He touched his lips and imagined never tasting her again. Never feeling the press of her satiny skin against his. In his mind, he saw her on the stage singing karaoke with her friends, then with him before singing to him. The moments they spent together flashed through his mind like a movie just beyond his reach.

"It was real," Levi whispered.

It had been and he'd lived it with her, and he'd thought he would be there forever. He'd gotten comfortable, not believing that fate would be so cruel to part them—yet here he was. On the breeze, he heard her pain as she screamed his name. Lifting his head, Levi saw the wavering image and his heart clenched as Ta-Mara held him and he disappeared. He didn't know how he was seeing what had happened. It ripped him up as she wept for him, sounding so lost. He lifted a shaking hand to the image and it vanished, taking that last bit of her from him.

He'd been brought into her life. The woman who had loved him despite the possibility of him being taken from her. Levi relived those last moments. He'd asked her to marry him and she'd said yes. Her eyes had sparkled with tears and joy he had put there. He'd envisioned a long life with her with the children they would have and raise together. Levi wanted happiness with the woman he loved. It had been so close but yet so far, across centuries. Time he had no way of knowing how to overcome.

"Ta-Mara," he said.

Her name echoed on the wind, resounding back at him. Mocking him with what he could not have. He prayed Ta-Mara wouldn't mourn him. Levi wanted her to have someone to love even if it could not be him.

Knowing his life wasn't going to be spared again, he put his head down and wept—for the past he had left and been returned to and for the future. The fleeting love he'd had not once but twice, and had lost. With two different women who had done only one thing— love him. Spikes of pain made him want to curl up and just let them take him. The sound of baying came even closer. Levi raised his head and stiffened his spine. Yes, he would die this night but he would not do so on his knees. It was not in him to give up. He would not do so now. Levi painfully got to his feet and he swayed there, weak from the blood loss and empty from the space where his heart had been. Ta-Mara had his heart now. Shouts echoed through the trees and Levi ran.

Ta-Mara, please forgive me for leaving you. Levi hoped she would find what he'd left her. Hopefully it would give her some small comfort.

As branches ripped at his clothing, he gasped, his breathing labored. The pain roared through him and he didn't know how he was still moving. How he still lived when he was dead already inside. The bitter taste of tears wet his lips and he swallowed thickly. Fate had again taken from him. Hate swirled and Levi cursed fate to the heavens. He was powerless to do anything about it. That, above all, enraged him.

Levi stopped and howled into the night. "Ta-Mara."

* * * *

"Sorry we're closed," Ta-Mara said to the customer through the closed door.

My man just proposed and I need to take him home and thank him properly. She smiled widely, not about to say that.

The patron nodded and walked away. A chill encompassed her body and her knees went weak. Ta-Mara lifted her hand to her head and gripped the door with the other one. Nausea made her almost gag. *Turn around.* Urgency filled her and she did. As if through fog, Ta-Mara stared at Levi at the counter. Automatically, she smiled. He'd asked her to marry him and she'd said yes. He reached out and Ta-Mara looked where his hand was heading, recognizing the yellowed pages. Ta-Mara frowned, wondering how the book had come to be there. She recalled specifically putting it in the back by the radio. Ta-Mara opened her mouth but couldn't even speak to curse Calliope for putting it there.

She took a step to him, her legs feeling like mush. His finger hovered above the book a millisecond then he touched it. The power over her voice and limbs came back to her in a rush.

"No! Don't touch the book," Ta-Mara screamed, running.

She didn't know why she didn't want him to. Levi stumbled then shook his head, holding it. His legs folded under him and she reached him, sliding under him and catching him as he fell. Her heart raced and Ta-Mara didn't know what was wrong. She pushed his hair away from his face. He had to be okay. Levi hadn't said anything about feeling sick. Ta-Mara gasped as his body wavered, blinking out then coming to form again.

"Levi." Her shaky lost voice echoed in the store.

He flickered again then faded out of her arms. Shocked, she rose up on her knees. Ta-Mara couldn't believe he was gone. He'd just disappeared and she could do nothing about it. All the scenarios she had thought of for months about him leaving — she realized in that moment she had been saying he might be taken but she'd never actually believed it. She pressed her hand over her heart, shivering, so cold. It was bone-deep and Ta-Mara rubbed her hands up and down her arms. There was nothing to combat this and she didn't think she would survive it. His face in all the times they had been together flashed through her mind and her shaking got worse as she relived being with him. And now to him leaving.

"Levi!" she roared, rocking, holding herself and closing her eyes.

"You put aside your pride and went after him," Calliope said in front of her.

Ta-Mara opened her eyes and glared at the spirit. "You have him. Go to eternity with him and leave me the fuck alone."

"Fuck you, Ta-Mara!" Calliope screamed. "I don't have him. His soul will be lost and never to be again."

"What?"

"When Levi dies, this time it will be forever. His soul will be gone and you will never have the chance to ever meet him in another life." Calliope hugged herself. "I brought him here to make sure that didn't happen, so he would be able to meet his soul mate from this point forward. Their paths would cross in many lives. But if he dies in the eighteen hundreds, that will never be. We will never be able to love him — to be loved by him." Calliope put her hand on her belly. "Never bear his children or grow old and die together when it is time then be reborn and search for each other again and again for all eternity. Our souls are kismet and I will not lose him." Calliope wiped at the tears on her cheeks. "You have done pride. Now what will you be willing to sacrifice above all else for him?"

"What? But you said he wasn't your soul mate."

"Look beyond your eyes and in your soul!" Calliope yelled.

Ta-Mara stared at her and she gasped as realization filled her. "You are my soul."

"Yes. Oh, God yes." Calliope reached for her.

"Why all the subterfuge?"

"I have no idea." Calliope shrugged. "I can only speculate that you created me as the manifestation of your past life so I could remind you to find him. The book was the guide. It's the beacon that brought his body and soul here intact. You are the reincarnation of Calliope from the eighteen hundreds."

"Then how did Levi see you?" Ta-Mara struggled to understand.

"His own version of me." Calliope moved her hand closer. "You know what needs to be done."

"If I do this, I won't need you anymore," Ta-Mara said.

"No." Calliope smiled gently. "I will always be part of you, inside of you."

"How do I tell Levi that I am you in this time?"

"There is no need to." Calliope closed her eyes then opened them. They were glassy with tears. "His soul recognized yours. He knew you were his as you knew he was yours, but you need to go through the journey you did to come to this point. There are strands of fate all around and this is yours and his."

Ta-Mara sensed every word she spoke was true. She reached for the book and placed her hand against Calliope. A charge of power flooded her and Calliope laughed, joy filling her. She flowed toward Ta-Mara and settled inside her. The sense of being whole made Ta-Mara shake and shut her eyes tightly.

"My love for Levi is strong. I am willing to give my life in this time for him if you will let him live. I will find you, my love, in the next time we are reborn," Ta-Mara said it out loud, needing to let it be heard to the heavens.

She brought the book to her chest then kept her other hand out and waited. She repeated the words over and over, silently reaching out. Inside her, she sought his soul with her own, willing them to connect. Ta-Mara jerked as pain rushed through her then ebbed. Suddenly her hand was gripped with callused fingers. Ta-Mara held on but was afraid to open her eyes and hope. The touch was faint then it got firmer. The scent of man and rain filled her senses.

"Ta-Mara." His gravelly voice came from before her.

Ta-Mara shook her head. She couldn't look at him. It would be cruel to her and him, since she'd given herself for him.

You have made a sacrifice above all else. Live with your soul mate and be happy, Ta-Mara. Tell Levi that fate might not go as he wants but it always, in the end, does as is destined.

She didn't recognize the voice. Ta-Mara opened her eyes and stared into the blue eyes that from the very beginning had made her heart race. It did the same this time and she lost her breath. Levi had come back to her and she was with him.

Oh God, if this is not real, don't let me ever find out.

"You brought me back to you." Levi shook. "I thought I was lost. That I would never see you again."

"Levi," she whispered unable to say anything else.

He brought her into his arms, holding her tight. The book was pressed tightly between them. Ta-Mara knew now it was just that, a book. She snuggled into him and inhaled, loving the scent that made up her man—Levi Madison.

* * * *

"I have something for you." Levi spoke beside her.

Ta-Mara lifted her head from where it rested on his shoulder. They had left the bookstore earlier and come home. They had kept each other close as they'd cooked, eaten then relaxed in the living room.

Levi sat up and she moved over to give him space. He reached for the book but hesitated.

"Go ahead, it's fine now." Ta-Mara rubbed her hand up and down his back. She'd told him the book was safe and what fate had said. Ta-Mara wasn't sure if that was who it had been, but that was what she was calling that voice. The one that had let her know her life with him would go on.

"I touched the book before to put something in it for you." Levi stared at it. "It didn't do anything to me except feel hot to my touch." He picked it up. "Not hot anymore." He flipped it open, pulled out something then set the book down and turned to Ta-Mara.

He held the item by the chain over his index finger. Ta-Mara gasped at the light from the windows reflected off the pendant—a gold book inlaid with diamonds. Etched on cover was infinity symbol, along with their initials. Levi scooted over and he opened the clasp. She held her hair as he put it on. Ta-Mara touched it and stared at him.

"I got it for you if I was sent back to my time. I wanted you to know I would always be with you." Levi held her hands. "Now I will be with you and have no fear of being taken again."

Ta-Mara had told him that much about what happened. She gripped his hand and stared into his eyes.

"Levi. There is more that I need to tell you."

"What?"

"There is a reason you were brought specifically to this time. To me." Ta-Mara cupped his cheek. "Calliope brought y—"

"I know she interfered."

"No she did, but it was because she knew if your soul died in the eighteen hundreds, it would never have another chance to find its soul mate." Ta-Mara tightened her hold on him. "In the eighteen hundreds, I was Calliope and I wanted to find you again, so I made it possible. Brought you here so you could find me and then we could live happily ever after. From now until we die. Then we will be again reincarnated and find ourselves together again."

"So you are partially my Calliope from the past in the woman I love today?" Levi's eyes crinkled. "How did I get so lucky? You save me then and today."

"You had an angel looking after you." Ta-Mara laughed. "I guess I've always been helpful, even in the eighteen hundreds."

"A woman who knew she had one chance at love" — Levi pulled her closer, draping her legs over his thighs—"to have her soul mate and she took it. Made time shift to bring him to her so she could have a life that would be happy."

"Yes." She stroked her hand down his cheek. "Now I want you to meet my family. I didn't want you to before because if you were taken back to your time I knew they would love and miss you as much as I did. Knew that they would ask about you when you were gone. And it would hurt to have to answer questions of where you were. I thought if I limited the people you interacted with, that I knew it would be easier when I lost you." She shook her head. "But I was deluding myself. I didn't believe you would be taken from me. Didn't know it would hurt so much."

"For me too." Levi stared at her. "I was so angry that I was losing you."

"Then I interfered again." She laughed. "I am quite the helpful person."

"I, for one, am grateful you did so. Then and now." Levi hugged her. "And I will be from now until infinity." He touched the necklace. "This is apt for me to give you then."

"Yes." She covered his hand with hers. "I will pass it down to our children. Like we will pass down the book. Tell them stories of a love that crossed all barriers of time."

"Yes, we will. I want to get started on our first child now."

"Yes." She leaned forward and kissed him. Levi lifted her and Ta-Mara moaned as she rose over him. His knuckles rubbed against her as he worked off his slacks. Then his strong fingers touched her. Levi rubbed her clit then he pulled aside her underwear. Ta-Mara whimpered as he pushed into her. The bare feel of him inside her set off a wave of need. She dampened and moved against him. Levi stroked into her and she kept her hand around his neck, staring into his eyes.

* * * *

Later Ta-Mara rolled out of bed and sat on the side, staring at Levi. He was sprawled on his back, snoring softly. She rose and stretched before she retrieved her robe, putting it on. She left the room, going down the hall. In the living room, the moonlight bathed the book that had started all of this. She grabbed a pen then sat cross-legged at the center table. Ta-Mara opened the book and flipped to the last page. She read the last few lines then started to write. Ta-Mara lost herself in the words.

"What are you doing?" Levi said softly, touching her.

She jumped, startled, having not heard him. She looked up from the book. He sat by her side.

"Finishing the story." Ta-Mara went back to writing. "Making sure it is known you didn't die but traveled through time to find your soul mate."

"No one would believe us if we told them what happened."

"They don't need to." She flipped the page then went on documenting the moments of what had happened. "We will know. When the book is passed from this generation to the next and through time. The others with our reincarnated souls will know. They will sense the truth behind what happened. Know—"

"Our bond is unbreakable," he whispered.

"Exactly."

Levi was right. It had started in the eighteen hundreds with a woman name Calliope whose love was so strong she'd made sure the soul of the man didn't die, never to be reborn. Instead, she'd brought the man of that time to the present and in path of his soul mate. Ta-Mara was grateful for her past life— Calliope. They had gone through so much to get to this point. Ta-Mara didn't have knowledge of any of her past lives, but between eighteen hundreds and present day, there had been many lives—she felt sorry for those who hadn't found their soul mate. She also was glad that from this point, and far in the future, her soul would seek Levi's and find his. Like the title of the book, their connection was indeed an unbreakable bond.

About the Authors

Aliyah Burke

Aliyah Burke is an avid reader and is never far from pen and paper (or the computer).She is married to a career military man. They are owned by three Borzoi, and a DSH cat. She spends her days sharing time between work, writing, and dog training.

Taige Crenshaw

Taige Crenshaw has been enthralled with the written word from the time she picked up her first book. It wasn't long before she started to make up her own tales of romance.

Her novels are set in the modern day between people who know what they want and how to get it. Taige also sets her stories in the future with vast universes between beautiful, strange and unique beings with lots of spice and sensuality added to her work.

Always hard at work creating new and exciting places Taige can be found curled up with a hot novel with exciting characters when she is not creating her own. Join her in the fun and frolic, with interesting people and far reaches of the world in her novels.

Both authors love to hear from readers. You can find their contact information, website details and author profile page at http://www.totallybound.com.

Totally Bound Publishing